The DANCE

Books by Dan Walsh

The Unfinished Gift

The Homecoming

The Deepest Waters

Remembering Christmas

The Discovery

The Reunion

THE RESTORATION SERIES • 1

The DANCE

A NOVEL

DAN WALSH
AND GARY SMALLEY

Revell
a division of Baker Publishing Group
Grand Rapids, Michigan

Published by Revell
a division of Baker Publishing Group
P.O. Box 6287, Grand Rapids, MI 49516-6287
www.revellbooks.com

Printed in the United States of America

Library of Congress Cataloging-in-Publication Data is on file at the Library of Congress, Washington, DC.

ISBN 978-0-8007-2148-0

13 14 15 16 17 18 19   7 6 5 4 3 2 1

To Gary, whose first book rescued my
marriage thirty years ago.

Dan Walsh

To all of my ten grandchildren,
because each one is growing closer to God.

Gary Smalley

My dear brothers and sisters, take note of this: Everyone should be quick to listen, slow to speak and slow to become angry, because human anger does not produce the righteousness that God desires.

—James 1:19–20

Many waters cannot quench love; rivers cannot sweep it away.

—Song of Solomon 8:7

1

Marilyn Anderson drove her car into the charming downtown section of River Oaks, Florida, holding her cell phone three inches out from her face. She hated talking on the phone with Jim when he was upset. She'd been dreading this day for months. And this call. Things like this should be said in person; she knew that. But she also knew that would never happen. She'd never muster up the nerve.

Sitting there at a stoplight, she looked at the phone. Jim was inside it. Him and his angry little voice.

"Please, Marilyn," Jim said. "I'm just getting back from a horrible lunch. Another tenant is canceling their lease. You have no idea the pressure I'm under right now. Can't this wait till later?"

Marilyn sighed. She wanted to yell back her reply but didn't dare. "No, it can't wait," she said.

"Well, it's going to have to. We'll talk about this when I get home. Love you, bye." He hung up.

Love you, bye? Did he really just say that?

The light turned green. Marilyn gently applied pressure to the gas pedal. *I have to do this. There's no other way.* Tears flowed down her face, but she refused to turn the car around. To silence the guilt that had been hammering her all day, she blurted out, "God, I know you understand me. Even if no one else does, I know you do."

Jim Anderson's workday ended like so many others, right at 5:00 p.m. His daily routine had unfolded according to his precise intentions. He locked the doors of his office suite for the day and tried to suppress dark thoughts about his cash flow situation.

It had slowed to a trickle from where it was a few years ago. His company—Anderson Development, Inc.—was located on the outskirts of the quaint downtown area of River Oaks, Florida, an idyllic planned community built along the St. Johns River, not far from Sanford. You wouldn't find this admission in any real estate brochure, but River Oaks had clearly been modeled after similar planned communities like Celebration near Disney World or the lovely town of Seaside in the Florida panhandle.

A few years after moving to River Oaks in the midnineties, Jim had started his own commercial real estate company. Business had boomed, and for years the money poured in. Right up until the bottom fell out of the market. Several businesses that leased properties from Jim had gone belly-up, and now another one was about to bite the dust. It was all he could do now to keep his nose above water.

For Jim, the name of the game was looking prosperous and successful while he scrambled to find new tenants to close the gaps. But no one wanted to get on board a sinking ship.

He drove his Audi A8 along River Oaks's tree-lined streets. It was hard not to look the part living in a place like this. Marilyn had fallen in love with it from the start. Every home was an architectural masterpiece. Most were built in old Southern tradition or, like the Andersons' house, with a decidedly Victorian flair. Large two-story homes with wraparound front porches, big windows, lots of ornamental trim. And, of course, every lot was professionally landscaped. Even the smallest homes were priced out of the reach of all but the upper middle class.

Jim arrived at Elderberry Lane, then turned down the one-lane service road running behind his house. All the homes had freestanding garages in back. Who wanted to see garage doors or grimy trash cans at the end of driveways? From the front, the homes looked pristine, immaculate, the epitome of neighborhood bliss.

After Jim clicked a button inside his car, the first of three garage doors lifted. Jim pulled his Audi into its spot and was instantly annoyed at the sight of his son Doug's little red Mazda. *Look at it. It's filthy . . . still filthy.* He'd been after his son to get that thing washed for a week. He grabbed his briefcase and suit jacket and shut the car door.

What had Marilyn fixed for dinner?

He walked through the utility room, surprised to find a laundry basket full of his clothes sitting on a counter beside the washer. Stopping to inspect, he lifted one of the shirts. By the wrinkles, he could tell it had been sitting there for hours. What was Marilyn thinking, leaving his clothes in the basket like that?

As he left the utility room and headed for the main house, he noticed his breakfast dishes still sitting on the glass table on the veranda by the pool. It was mid-July, but that morning had been unseasonably cool, so he'd asked Marilyn to set breakfast out there. He'd invited her to join him, of course, but she was busy doing . . . something.

Why were the dishes still there? She knew better.

He opened the glass patio door off the great room. "Marilyn?" he yelled. No answer. He noticed something else. Or, the absence of something. There were no dinner smells, no activity in the kitchen at all. As he walked inside, it was obvious dinner had not even been started. *What the heck?*

"Marilyn," he yelled again, loud enough to be heard in the center rooms of the house. She must be in one of the bedrooms. He walked through the tiled hallways toward their master bedroom suite, the only bedroom downstairs. "Marilyn?"

Again, no answer.

The bed was made, sort of. The fancy pillows were on the floor, not stylishly arranged as they should be. He walked into the bathroom suite. She wasn't there. He hurried out to the stairway, called her name again as he ascended. In all three upstairs bedrooms, there was no sign of her. No indication that anyone had even been up here today. That wasn't unusual.

Of their three children, only Doug lived at home, and he stayed in the little apartment above the garage. Their daughter, Michele, lived in her dorm at college. And Tom, their oldest, was married with two children. He and Jean lived in Lake Mary, about twenty-five minutes away.

Jim came down the stairs, certain now something was wrong. Pulling out his phone, he checked to see if he had any messages. He did not. The only call from her was that quick chat right after lunch, when he couldn't talk. But that was hours ago. He called Marilyn's number, waited for her to pick up. It rang a few times, then he waited through her voice mail message. "Hey, where are you? I'm home, and you're not here. Dinner's not even started. What's going on? Call me as soon as you hear this."

Jim remembered the message center on a short wall beside

the refrigerator. He looked; something was written on the yellow pad. He hurried over, but it was only a note from Doug.

Jason picked me up around 3. Eating dinner at his place. Be home by 9.

Jason, Jim thought. He couldn't stand that kid. Jason was into hip-hop, wore big baggy pants he had to hold up with one hand, his boxer shorts always sticking out for the world to see. Jim reread Doug's note. So, Doug left the house at three; that meant Marilyn hadn't been home then or he'd have told her instead of writing the note. Where was she? Maybe something had happened with one of Tom's kids, and she'd had to leave in a hurry. He quickly dialed Tom's home phone number.

"Hello?"

"Hi, Jean. Is Marilyn there? She wasn't home when I got here. Are you okay, are the kids okay?"

"Everyone here is fine."

"Any chance Tom might know where she is?"

"I doubt it, he just called me. He's stuck in traffic on I-4."

"I can't figure out where she is."

"She's probably fine. Maybe she just stepped out to get something she needed for dinner."

"Dinner's not even started."

"Hmm. I don't know what to say. I'll ask Tom when he gets home. Call us when you find out so we don't worry."

"I will."

He hung up and called Michele. By this time, she'd be done with her classes for the day. She was a senior doing a summer semester at Southeastern University, a small college in Lakeland. Of course, he didn't get her. He never got Michele when he called, always her voice mail. "Hey, Michele, it's Dad. I'm looking for Mom. Got home from work and there's no sign of her here at the house. I'm getting worried something might've happened to her. It's not like her to leave without telling me where she's going. Give me a call as soon as you get this."

After hanging up, he made another pass through the house, this time looking for any signs of foul play. As he cleared each room, his heart beat faster. Something must have happened. Had she been abducted? Had there been a home invasion? It seemed unlikely; crime was almost unheard of in River Oaks. Other than the house being a little messier than usual, there were no signs of a break-in. None of the high-ticket items appeared to be missing.

But where was she?

The garage. It just dawned on him, he hadn't seen her car there when he'd pulled in. He ran out to the garage to confirm it.

Marilyn's car was gone.

Had she been in an accident? He hurried back to the message board by the fridge, where they kept a list of important numbers. He was just about to call the local emergency room when his cell phone rang. It was Michele. "Thanks for calling," he said. "I'm getting a little frantic here. Your mom is missing. I think something may have happened to—"

"Dad, calm down," she said in a gentle tone. "I'm sorry I'm the one that has to tell you."

Jim's heart sank. He collapsed on a bar stool and braced himself for bad news. "Tell me what?"

"Mom isn't missing, Dad. She's left you."

2

What do you mean, she's left me?" Jim said.

"I think you know what it means, Dad."

"You mean like . . . for good? Like she's ending our marriage?"

"I don't know if it's for good. My guess is it's going to depend partly on what you do from here."

"What *I* do from here?" he repeated. "Michele, this is crazy. How long have you known about this?" Jim started pacing back and forth across the kitchen floor.

"You mean how long have I known she's been unhappy, or how long have I known she was planning to leave?"

"Don't play games with me, young lady."

"I'm not playing games, Dad. I know this is serious."

"Darn right it's serious. Where does your mother get off pulling a stunt like this?"

"It's not a stunt."

"You know what I mean."

Michele didn't reply. Jim walked over and opened the fridge, pulled out a glass pitcher of iced tea. "When did she tell you she was going to do this?"

"Last week some time. I think it was Thursday."

He poured himself a glass and sat back on the bar stool by the granite counter. "You don't think that was something you should have called me about?"

"No, I don't. Look, I don't want to get stuck in the middle of this thing between you two, but if I have to be on somebody's side, I think you know whose side it's going to be."

Anger flared inside him, but he had to keep his cool. He needed more information. Michele and her mother had spent a lot of time together lately planning Michele's wedding, and they'd always been close, but he never imagined they'd gang up on him like this. "So who is it?"

"What?"

"Who is your mother seeing? There must be someone."

"Don't be ridiculous. She's not seeing anyone else."

"Do you know that for sure, Michele? Maybe she wouldn't tell you something like that. It's the only thing that makes any sense." He thought he heard her laugh on the other end. "What?"

"You can't think of any other reason why she'd leave you, Dad? Nothing comes to mind, nothing at all?"

"What are you talking about? No, I can't. She's got a gorgeous house, a nice car to drive. A huge closet full of clothes. Money's a little tighter than usual these days, but we're doing okay. We hardly ever argue."

"Uh-huh . . . When was the last time you took her out?"

"What?"

"Took Mom out on a date. You know, even something simple like dinner and a movie."

"I don't know."

"Right. When was the last time you took her for a walk, asked her questions, really listened to her? Even simple questions like how she was doing?"

"What are you talking about? You're saying she left me because I don't take her out on walks?"

Michele sighed audibly. "Look, Dad, I'm not going to be the mediator here. Your problems are way over my head. I love you, but . . . I'm just going to say it. I don't have a hard time understanding why Mom walked out. Okay?"

Jim slid the bar stool away from the counter and stood. "She can't just walk out. We're both believers, for heaven's sake! She doesn't have biblical grounds for divorce."

"Stop yelling at me, Dad."

"I'm not yelling."

"Yeah, you are. And if you don't calm down, I'm going to hang up."

"Listen, Michele, I don't know where you get off talking to me like this. Who do you think is paying your way through college? Who's paying for that dorm room and your food tab?"

"That's great, Dad. Real helpful."

"Well, I don't know. How did I become the bad guy here all of a sudden?"

"It didn't just happen all of a sudden."

"What's that supposed to mean?"

"I'm talking about your problems with Mom."

Jim was sure that's not what she meant, but he let it drop. "Do you know where she is?"

"I do, but I also know she doesn't want to see you. Not now. If you go over there, it'll make things worse. I'm serious."

"Where is she?" He said the words as calmly as he could.

"Look, I've got to go. She told me she wrote you a note, maybe it's in there. I'd rather you just read that. I think it's on your dresser." She paused. "Really, Dad, I've got to go."

"Michele, wait."

"I love you. I do." She hung up.

Jim walked into the living room and looked at the stone fireplace. It was all he could do not to throw his phone across the room. Instead, he took a deep breath and put it back in his pocket. He headed back to their bedroom in search of that note, reeling from the absurdity of his conversation with Michele.

How could Marilyn do this? You don't just leave someone, not like this. Not after twenty-seven years of marriage. He'd given her everything a woman could want. A great house, a solid family, stability. He'd kept himself in great shape. He'd never been unfaithful to her. Not that he didn't have opportunities; a number of women had come on to him over the years. But he never went there. Not once.

She better not have gone there, he thought. But he couldn't think of anything else that made sense. On the way to his dresser, he walked past their large walk-in closet. Curiosity got the better of him, so he stopped to see if Marilyn's clothes were gone. What he saw surprised him. Her clothes seemed to all be there, hanging where they'd always been. Dresses, blouses, sweaters. A teakwood rack full of shoes. Had she taken anything with her?

He walked across the room to his dresser. The note wasn't sitting on top. He started opening the drawers, found it sitting on a stack of folded socks. He lifted it out and carried it to an upholstered chair in the corner, next to a long window that opened to the pool area. His first name was written across the front of a plain beige envelope.

He sat down and opened it.

Jim,

I'm sure this has come as a shock to you. That it has is only one more thing to add to my list of reasons for leav-

ing. You don't love me, I'm sure of that now. I think I've known it for years. You don't care about me or the things I care about. You don't even bother to try. You probably have no idea how many times in recent months I've tried to talk to you about how unhappy I am, how unhappy I've been. It goes right over your head.

I've dropped hint after hint, clue after clue. None of it gets past that hard shell of yours. There's only room for one person in your life. Here's another clue . . . it's not me.

It all became clear to me last month at Margaret's daughter's wedding. I don't want to get into all the reasons why here, but let's just say by the time that wedding reception was over, I knew in my heart . . . I had to leave. If I'm ever going to find any measure of happiness in my life, before I'm too old to actually enjoy it, I have to go. Since that moment, I've just been biding my time, trying to work up the courage.

I also had to get some practical details together for this separation to work. And notice, I used the word "separation" here on purpose. At the moment, I'm not planning on divorcing you. I have no plans of "taking you to the cleaners" or ruining your precious financial life. In fact, I'm not making any long term plans at all. I just need some time away.

I need you to respect that. In fact, the <u>worst</u> thing you could do right now is to come after me and start pestering me to come home. I NEED this time away. I can honestly say, if you don't respect my desire to have this time, it may be the one thing that would cause me to make this separation permanent.

I mean that . . . sincerely. Let me have this time. Don't

call me, don't come to where I'm living. It's not far away (somewhere in River Oaks). I've taken just a small amount from our savings account. Just enough to get me set up for a few weeks. But I plan to be earning my own keep after that. I've gotten a job doing something you would never let me do, or even discuss.

I've asked Michele to be available for any necessary communication. Don't be mad at her or make her feel guilty about any of this. She hasn't done a thing to try to talk me into or out of this decision. By the way, I haven't talked to Tom or Jean or Doug about this. Or anyone in the church. I'll leave that to you (and I plan to be going to another church too).

I'm sorry for the hurt and anger I'm sure you already feel inside. But it can't begin to compare to the mountain of hurt you've been piling up in my heart for more years than I can count.

Believe it or not, I do still love you and will be praying for God to somehow work this situation together for good (although at the moment, I can't see how such a thing could be possible).

Marilyn

Jim let the pages fall in his lap. His face was hot with rage. He looked out the window then pulled out his phone. A moment later he was on the internet, logging into their bank account. He clicked on the drop-down menu to check the balance in their savings account.

He wondered, just how much did Marilyn consider a "small amount"?

3

Marilyn Anderson was a woman unloved.

Sure, she had provision and stability. She felt protected for the most part. And as best she knew, there had always been faithfulness between them. But was that enough? Didn't she have a right to feel loved? Could anyone say they were truly happy on any level that really mattered in a relationship without love?

She looked around the room. It was small, maybe twelve-by-twelve. What was that, less than 150 square feet? Marilyn smiled. Her Victorian dream house on Elderberry Lane was just over 3,000 square feet. She was lying on a double bed. At home, she and Jim shared a king-sized bed. Big enough to ensure they would never touch each other once through the night.

The space separating their hearts was infinitely wider than that.

She sat up and glanced around the room. None of the furniture was hers. All made of white painted pressboard, probably in China or some other Asian country. But the room was cute, nicely decorated in its own way. The walls a pleasing shade of green, with white trim around the windows and doors. Pink flowers bloomed in a white vase on the dresser, cream-colored carpeting on the floor. It was cozy, but nothing she'd have ever thought to do in her home.

Her home, she thought. Had it ever really been her home? If so, was it still? It hadn't felt like a home for over ten years, not since the kids were younger. She had come to realize that what Jesus said was true. The words ran quietly through her mind: *Man's life does not consist in the abundance of his possessions.* She had a house full of them, two floors' worth. Four bedrooms (five, considering the garage apartment), three-and-a-half baths. Living room, great room, formal dining room, and a dinette area almost as big. A kitchen large enough for a small restaurant. Jim's home office that occupied the rounded corner room, a loft upstairs.

Every single room was filled with a collection of expensive furnishings, floor coverings, window treatments, and artwork. No decorating detail or accessory was too small. Guests would marvel when she took them on tours. She used to enjoy the jealousy it provoked, as if it were some kind of reward. It had taken her years to get every room just the way she wanted it. And then, she would sit in those rooms until the next church gathering or social event, feeling so lonely and empty inside, as if the house had been left to the ages, vacant and abandoned.

And in a way, it had been. Houses without love could never be homes.

Houses didn't love you back, no matter how big they were. Fine hardwood furniture, antique oriental rugs, and top-of-the-line appliances couldn't create or sustain joy. Marilyn felt more free and at peace here in this little apartment bedroom than she'd felt at Elderberry Lane in years. She looked around the room again. Nothing in this bedroom loved her either. But nothing here reminded her of the gaping void she'd felt inside for so long.

It was clear to her now. In Jim's world, life was all about goals, roles, reputation, and compartments. Marilyn's compartment had shrunk to where it would fit in a box under this little double bed.

She heard a knock at the door.

"Marilyn, dinner's ready. Heated up a Lean Cuisine for you. Sesame chicken. They really aren't too bad." It was her new "landlord," Charlotte Rymes, talking through the door in her strong Boston accent.

"Be right out, thanks, Charlotte." Lean Cuisine? she thought. But you know what? She didn't have to cook, and there'd probably be almost nothing to clean up.

She got out of bed, feeling light as a feather. Her future was totally uncertain, but she didn't care. She was about to eat some prefabbed sesame chicken, tomorrow she'd start her new job at Odds-n-Ends, and she was living with a boisterous single woman who was as sweet and kind as she could be. The thick cloud of heaviness and oppression Marilyn had felt constantly at Elderberry Lane was gone.

"Have a seat, Marilyn. I'll bring it right out." Charlotte had just changed out of her scrubs. She was a nurse at the River Oaks Urgent Care Center a few blocks away on Oakwood Lane, one of the main roads that ran through town. "Sometimes these things are wicked hot when they come out of the microwave. They'll burn your mouth worse than pizza, so watch it."

Marilyn sat down.

"Sesame chicken's my favorite, but I've found four or five others that are pretty good."

"Smells delicious."

Charlotte set trays of food on two plates, one on each side of a small dinette table. "You like iced tea? I make it with lemon, but I didn't add any sugar. I've got sugar and Splenda packets there in the bowl. Figured that way we can each make our glass as sweet as we want."

"Iced tea would be great. How'd your day go?"

"'Bout the same as usual." She sat down. "No big surprises. A few cuts that needed stitches, some moms bringing their kids in, swearing they need antibiotics. The usual. Okay if I say the blessing?"

"Sure." After Charlotte prayed, Marilyn took a few cautious bites. She had met Charlotte a few weeks ago while shopping at Odds-n-Ends, the little retail gift shop on Main Street. She'd overheard her talking to the cashier; apparently they both attended a church that had begun to meet in the local high school. Charlotte mentioned she was looking for a tenant to help her share the rent in her apartment. All the shops in the downtown area had apartments on the floor above, with cute balconies that overlooked the street. The view was actually quite nice; the whole downtown area was adorable, like an extension of Main Street at Disney World.

After swallowing a few bites, Charlotte said, "Are you doing okay, hon? How's your heart doing? Today was the big day, wasn't it?"

Marilyn nodded and continued to chew.

"How'd he take it? You know, your hubby?"

"I don't know yet," she said. "I wrote him a note."

"Smart," she said. "No sense having a big confrontation. I'm guessing he's not much of a listener anyway."

"That's why I wrote a note," Marilyn said. "That and I'm a total chicken."

Charlotte smiled, took another bite. Still chewing, she said, "Well, listen, you tell me as much or as little as you want. We're about the same age, you and me. I got divorced over fifteen years ago, but I still remember how it felt. You wanna talk, I'm here. You just want a friend who knows when to shut up, I can be that too."

"Well, I'm not thinking divorce at the moment."

"No? Sorry, I just assumed."

"I suppose it could come to that."

"Just needing a little time and space then?"

"That's a good way to put it." Marilyn ate another forkful of sesame chicken. It was actually quite good. After swallowing, she said, "I really appreciate you taking me in on a month-to-month basis. I'm sure you'd rather have a longer commitment. But I'm just not sure where things—"

"Don't worry about it, take as long as you need. A month, two, three. I don't wanna rush you. You got enough to worry about with what you're going through."

"Thanks, Charlotte, that's very kind of you."

"How your kids handling this? They're older, right?"

She nodded. "My youngest will be a senior in high school when school starts again. My oldest is married with two kids. Both boys. I haven't told them yet, just my daughter Michele. She's goes to a college in Lakeland. She's getting married at the end of September."

"September? Won't she be in school?"

"She wanted the wedding to be on the exact date Allan proposed a year ago."

"Is this . . . this thing you're going through gonna mess things up? I never planned a wedding before, but I watched my friend up north almost go nuts planning one."

"I hope not. Michele says we'll be fine. But clearly, I didn't pick the best time to—"

"Honey, there's never a good time for something like this."

Marilyn sighed. "Guess that's true."

"Well, don't worry. Let's talk about something else. You looking forward to your new job? Starts tomorrow, right?"

"Yes, I am. I haven't worked—well, outside the house—in forever. So I'm a little nervous."

"A stay at home mom," Charlotte said. "Not too many of you left on the planet these days. I never got the chance. My ex left me with nothing, so I worked while my boy Eddie was growing up. He turned out all right, though."

"Does he live here?"

"No, he's still back home. Finishing up school at Boston College. He's planning on coming down here in December when he graduates. That's one of the reasons I'm not too concerned about you signing a long-term lease."

"December, that's when my Michele graduates."

"That'll make for a nice Christmas."

A sinking feeling came over Marilyn. Christmas. What would her life be like by then? Where would she be living? What would—no! She couldn't think about such things now; it would only lead to trouble. "I'm really proud of Michele," Marilyn said. "And I love Allan, the guy she's marrying. He's a really nice guy."

Marilyn's cell phone rang. She could barely hear it coming from the bedroom. She looked at her watch. Jim would definitely be home now. She hoped it wasn't him. "Excuse me, sounds like someone's texting me." She got up from the table and headed for the bedroom.

She lifted her phone out of her purse, almost dreading to look at the screen.

But she did, then sighed in relief. It was from Michele.

Just two words.

He knows.

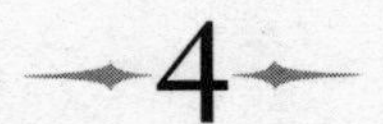

Before it got too late, Marilyn wanted to call Michele and hear a little more about her phone call with Jim, but she couldn't call yet because Michele's fiancé, Allan, had taken her out for dinner and a movie. So she decided to unpack while she waited. It didn't take long; she'd only brought her casual clothes with her and a few nice outfits to wear at her new job at the store. Besides, if she needed anything, she could always sneak back into the house. Jim never came home during the day.

To freshen up, she washed her face in the bathroom sink. The apartment had two bathrooms, which was nice. Through the mirror, she looked down at the little bathtub and smiled, remembering her decision to soak in her big garden tub that afternoon. It was a silly thing to do, but so relaxing. She'd just sat there, listening to soothing music, smelling the pleasant aroma of her bath lotion and bubbles. It was likely the last chance to enjoy her bathroom suite for a long time.

She dried her face and walked out into the living area. Charlotte was already on the sofa, sipping her coffee. As she poured herself a cup, Marilyn wondered if Jim had told their son Doug yet about her leaving, or if he'd called Tom and Jean. She put her cup on a coaster on the coffee table then sat on the opposite end of the sofa.

"You don't really need to use the coaster," Charlotte said. "Can't hurt that old table. I just bought them 'cause I thought they were cute, all the little palm trees." She took another sip. "So do you feel like talking? I don't wanna force you into anything. I've got some shows recorded on the DVR we could watch."

"I don't mind talking a little while." She could tell, even by the end of dinner, that Charlotte was easy to be with.

"So how 'bout we start with . . . what would you say is the number one reason you're doing this, you know, leaving your husband? Oh my, listen to me . . . is that too personal?"

Marilyn laughed. It was way too personal, but she had told Charlotte it was okay if they talked, and Charlotte didn't seem like one to beat around the bush. "No, that's all right. I guess if I'm going to live here awhile, you need to know a little of what I'm going through."

"Just as much as you feel comfortable saying, hon."

"The number one reason I left?" Marilyn thought back to the moment she had finally had enough and knew she had to leave. "I guess if I had to boil it down to one thing, I'd have to say . . . it's because my husband would never dance with me."

"What?" Charlotte almost coughed up her coffee. She set the cup down, picked up a napkin, and wiped her mouth. "Did you say . . . he wouldn't dance?"

Marilyn nodded. "I know that must sound strange."

"A little," Charlotte said, smiling. "Maybe a tad."

"He wouldn't even dance at our own wedding twenty-seven years ago. It was so humiliating. I was standing out there on the dance floor, waiting, the music playing. Everyone was pushing and prodding him, his friends and family. But he just said, 'No. I don't dance. She knows that.'"

"That's terrible," Charlotte said.

"Finally, thirty seconds before the song was over, his best man dragged him out of his chair. Then he just stood there like he was in agony, holding my hands, barely moving, until the song ended. Then he went right back to his chair."

"I'm sorry, that is pretty sad."

"Do you know how many wedding receptions we've been to over the last twenty-seven years? I've sat through every single one, watched couple after couple get up and dance. Even men who danced horribly and knew they did would at least get up and try to slow dance with their wives. But not Jim." She took a sip of coffee. "The only time I've ever danced at a wedding was a few years ago, at my son Tom's. You know, the mother and groom dance."

"Hope I get to dance that one with Eddie someday. He's seeing a girl now, but I don't think it's too serious." She paused. "So what triggered this? Is it because you've been planning your daughter's wedding?"

Marilyn shook her head. "It was a friend's wedding at church recently. Well, I guess she's a friend. We've never once had a conversation like this, and I've known her for years. As a matter of fact, I was going to ask you if it would be okay if I started going to your church. I really don't want to go back to my old one anymore."

"Sure, we'll go together this Sunday. I'll introduce you to some folks. They're a real friendly bunch." Charlotte took another sip of coffee. "You know, I'd like something sweet to eat with this. I've got shortbread cookies. Would you like a couple?"

"Sure."

Charlotte walked out to the kitchen, opened a cabinet. "So, you're not really leaving your husband because he won't dance. It's kind of like a metaphor, right? Dancing is just . . . the thing."

"I suppose," she said, sighing. "He doesn't love me. Well, maybe he does in a way. If you forced him to admit it, I suppose he might say he does. But he never tells me. We never talk about anything meaningful. We never go out, not on dates anyway, just the two of us. He drags me off to these dinner parties sometimes, or makes me host them at our house, for his business. But even then, no matter how nice I try to look or how much time I spend getting ready, he never notices. Doesn't say a word. Unless I make us late, then he talks."

Charlotte walked back, set two cookies down on a napkin beside her coffee cup. "You poor thing."

Marilyn was surprised; she had said all that and didn't break down. Maybe she'd cried herself out one too many times at home.

"You know, it's funny in a way," Charlotte said. "I haven't had a man love me for years, but I'm not that sad about it. I get sad every now and then, like when I watch romantic movies, but not in a day-to-day sort of way. I guess it hurts a whole lot worse when you've got someone sitting right beside you who is supposed to love you but doesn't."

That made sense to Marilyn, but it didn't help her mood. She took a bite of the shortbread cookie, then sipped her coffee. Now, that helped.

"Aren't these so good together?"

"They are. I haven't had shortbread cookies for so long. That's something else that's going to change."

Charlotte laughed. "So you left a husband who doesn't love

you, you're starting a brand-new job tomorrow, *and* you're eating shortbread cookies now. It's like a total makeover."

Marilyn laughed out loud.

Marilyn and Charlotte continued to visit for another hour but kept the conversation light. Then Charlotte excused herself because she had to get up at sunrise for work. Marilyn's day didn't start until 9:00 a.m. They said good night, and Marilyn headed back to her room and closed the door.

As soon as she did, she realized how exhausted she was. She walked over to the dresser to get her cell phone. It was probably safe to call Michele now; she was likely home from her date with Allan. On the dresser was a picture frame, the only one she'd brought from the house. It was an 8-by-10 photo of her three children the last year they'd all lived in the same house, when Tom was a senior in college.

She'd definitely been happier then, but it had nothing to do with Jim. It was the kids, all the busyness and activity they brought into her days. For the most part, home was a pretty happy place until Jim got home. The minute he walked through the door, the whole atmosphere changed. The Head of the House was home, with all his Bible verses and lectures, his narrow-minded views about every facet of life.

She looked at Tom's face in the photo. Sadly, he seemed to be taking right up where his father had left off. He'd always looked up to Jim, even as a boy. Marilyn could see that Tom was modeling his life as a husband and father after Jim's example. She'd wanted to scream at him to stop. That's not God's way, not how a husband should treat his wife and kids. But it was like a wall had sprung up between them. Tom was out of reach.

Since becoming a teenager, her daughter Michele could see how unhappy Marilyn was. She talked about it sometimes, though Marilyn was always careful not to join in too much. Jim was still Michele's father, after all. And Marilyn didn't want to fuel the fires of her bitterness and drive Michele further away from Jim than she already was. Michele had made it clear that she would be looking for a man the direct opposite of her father. And she'd found him in Allan. Marilyn was happy about that.

And then there was Doug, still so young. But even he had started pulling away the last few years. He didn't seem to be choosing sides. If anything, Doug was for Doug. Whatever made him happy, that's what he pursued. He'd either lose himself in his music or video games or look for any opportunity to spend time outside the house with friends. She didn't know how to reach him or what to say. But still, she had to keep trying to close the gap.

She picked up her cell and texted Michele to see if this was a good time to call. As she waited for Michele's reply, she couldn't help but wonder what Jim was doing right now. She was actually shocked he had left her alone all evening. Her cell phone beeped; it was Michele. The text said: *The movie still has thirty minutes. Can I call you when I get home?*

Marilyn texted back: *That's okay. I'm really tired. Think I'll go to bed. Let's just talk in the morning.*

She walked over to the bed, turned down the bedspread, and lay down, grateful for once that sheer exhaustion had overtaken her, making it almost impossible to think.

Jim had woken up groggy the next morning. He'd taken a sleeping pill last night. Had to—his mind kept racing through a dozen imaginary conversations with Marilyn. All of them ended in a fight. He still couldn't believe she'd done this. The anger he'd felt last night was right there to greet him before he'd even gotten in the shower.

What in the world did she have to be unhappy about?

He'd called her after fuming about it in the shower for twenty minutes but once again had gotten her voice mail. He didn't leave a message, afraid he'd make things worse if he did. At the moment, he was outside on the veranda, eating a bowl of stale Cheerios instead of the two eggs, turkey bacon, and rye toast she normally made him. His coffee was horrible. She always made the coffee; he had no idea what scoops-to-water ratio she used.

His shirts were all wrinkled, which meant he'd have to leave his suit coat on all day . . . in July! And he had an important client to see at eleven, a doctor who was toying with the idea of creating a second office in River Oaks. Marilyn was the fashion guru. She always picked out his shirt-tie combinations for important meetings. Jim needed to impress this guy. He'd be looking at a four-thousand-square-foot unit that had sat empty for eighteen months.

Jim heard the garage door close and Doug's car zip down the one-lane road out back. He was going to be late for school . . . again. He'd rushed around the kitchen, complaining about how Mom hadn't woken him up on time. "She always comes and gets me when I miss my alarm," he'd said. "What's she doing, sleeping in?"

Jim had decided not to answer. He didn't want to get drawn into a conversation about where Marilyn really was at the moment. He hadn't figured out what to say yet to Doug or Tom. Speaking of where Marilyn was . . . Jim still didn't know. He glanced at his watch, picked up the phone, and called Michele. To his surprise, she answered.

"Hey, Michele."

"Hi, Dad."

Jim sighed. *Don't get into it with her.* "Sorry to call you so early."

"Had a rough night?" she asked.

"To be honest, Michele, I'm feeling kind of stuck here. It's only been one day. There's so many things your mom does for Doug and me, I don't know where to begin. The thing is, I found her note." He waited a moment. Michele didn't reply. "Last night I asked you where she was staying. You seemed to think the note would tell me. Well, it didn't. All it said was, she was staying somewhere in River Oaks. It didn't say where, or with who."

"You mean with *whom*?"

"You're going to correct my grammar now?"

"I'm sorry. Obviously, you still think she's seeing someone else."

"Well . . ."

"Dad, there's nobody else. You should know Mom better than that by now."

"All right, listen, I don't want to get into that right now. The point is, I don't know where she is."

"And you expect me to tell you?"

"I don't think that's an unreasonable request. I've been providing for and protecting your mom all these years. Now she's out there somewhere, and I'm just supposed to be okay with that? Not knowing where she is?"

Michele paused. He could hear her breathing. "My problem is, if she didn't tell you where she's staying, she must have a reason. I don't feel right telling you without talking to her first."

"Then can you call her?"

"I will, but not right now."

"Why?"

"Because I need to finish getting ready for school. And I don't even know if she's up yet. I can tell you this, she's staying somewhere safe. I mean, c'mon, Dad, you know River Oaks. Nothing ever happens there."

"Can you at least tell me if she's staying in someone's house, or an apartment? Is she . . . alone?"

"We're back to that?"

He had to calm down before she hung up on him again.

"I'll call her later, see what she says. I can tell you this much. She's not staying in anyone's house. And she is with someone, but—"

"I knew it."

"Now stop! Let me finish. She's staying with a single lady, renting a room from her. There's no other man in her life. That's not what this is about."

Jim wished he could believe her. "Well, I need to talk to her.

As you know, I didn't see this coming. There's all kinds of things around here that need taking care of. Things I don't have time to do." Jim heard her sigh. "I'm going to have to call Maria," he continued, "the lady that used to come in here to clean. I don't know her number. Your mom handled that. I don't even know her last name."

"Well, Dad, that *is* a big problem." The sarcasm was evident in her voice. "My guess is, you probably paid her by check, right? Do some digging. I'm sure you'll find her last name with a little effort. Look, I've gotta go. I'll call Mom later, see what she says. If she wants me to tell you where she is, I'll call you back." She hung up.

Jim lifted his phone up and for a moment imagined himself tossing it into the pool. Just then, it rang. He looked at the screen. It was his son Tom. He pushed the bowl of mushy Cheerios away and answered the phone.

"Hi, Dad, it's Tom. What's going on? Did you ever find Mom? You never called us back."

"Sorry about that." He tried to sound business-as-usual. "Your mom's fine. We just . . . misfired in our communication. I should have called you guys back. Didn't mean to make you worry."

"I'm glad to hear it. I tried calling her but just got her voice mail."

"Well, don't worry. Are you on your way to work?" Change the subject, Jim thought.

"Yeah, it's a nightmare out here, as usual. Bumper to bumper. Must be nice having an office a few blocks away."

"Are you guys ever going to move closer to where you work?" Jim already knew the answer.

"Not anytime soon," Tom said. "You know the real estate market better than me. We're totally upside down in this place."

Jim knew that too. He'd tried to warn Tom not to buy that

house when he did; the price was so inflated back then. "Well, listen, I've got to finish getting ready. Will you be home tonight? I need to talk to you about something."

"Uh . . . I think so. You can probably call anytime after seven—we should be done with dinner by then. Is everything okay?"

"Yeah, well . . . it's nothing to worry about. But I'd rather talk to you tonight when I'm not in such a hurry."

"Sure, we'll talk then." Tom paused. "You sure everything's okay?"

"Yeah, let's just talk tonight. Call you around seven."

They hung up. Jim picked up his bowl and coffee mug, walked them back inside to the sink. He wasn't in a hurry, but he needed time to figure out how he was going to explain this to Tom and Doug.

Right now, though, he had one goal in mind: figure out where Marilyn was staying. It was just wrong that she and Michele would keep this from him. But Michele had given him enough information to point his nose in the right direction.

If Marilyn wasn't staying at someone's house, then her car was probably not hiding in a garage. If she was renting a room from a single lady, then she was probably staying at one of the many apartments spread throughout River Oaks. He knew the area. It wasn't a big town. And most apartment complexes, including the units above all the storefronts, only allowed tenants two parking places each.

He didn't actually have to be in the office till a few minutes before his first appointment at eleven. He would call his secretary, tell her something had come up. Between now and then, he'd drive all around River Oaks. He didn't need to wait for Michele to call him back later.

He'd find out where Marilyn was staying himself.

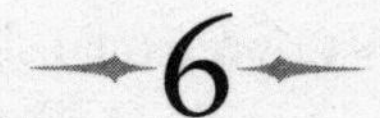

6

Marilyn pulled her car into a back parking lot, behind the row of stores that occupied the north side of Main Street. She smiled as she read the sign: Employee Parking. That's who she was, an employee. She lifted her purse off the passenger seat and closed the door, looking for another sign . . . the back entrance to Odds-n-Ends.

As she walked toward the door, she tried to remember the last time she'd worked for someone other than Jim. It had to be over twenty-five years ago, before Tom was born. Jim had insisted she quit her job when she was six months pregnant. They had both wanted her to be a stay-at-home mom, although outside the high-society circles they belonged to, it was mostly frowned upon. She was grateful Jim's job had made it possible.

The trouble had begun years later, when all three kids were gone most of the day to a private school. After doing every chore and errand she could think of, she'd sit around bored out of her mind until they came home. By then, Jim's business was booming, and they had moved several notches up the social ladder. This included leaving their old church to join one with a more prestigious clientele. That's how it felt to Marilyn anyway. Every relationship and social connection they formed seemed to revolve around Jim's business.

Had he ever once asked her where she would like to attend church or what kind of friends she might want to have over? Of course not. She also knew that never standing up to him had actually fed his self-centered outlook on life.

She remembered a TV commercial slogan: "Image Is Everything." That could have been the Anderson family motto. Jim had turned down her repeated appeals to get a job, even one that ensured she'd be home when the kids got home from school. In recent years, with Tom married, Michele in college, and Doug in high school, he had still turned her down. "I don't think that's a good idea," he'd said, with that polite harshness he was famous for. When she'd pressed him further, he finally snapped, "No wife of mine is going to work in a retail store!"

Well, she didn't have to put up with his harshness anymore. *And I never should have*, she thought. But it was so hard to confront him. She hated confrontation in general, with anyone. But especially with Jim. A fierce expression would instantly come over his face, and before she'd finish what she was trying to say, he'd overwhelm her with a barrage of words, making her feel stupid for even bringing up the matter. Then later he'd make her pay for it, ignoring her for hours.

She sighed and tried to shake off these dark thoughts as she rang the doorbell beside the steel door. Looking at her watch, she was relieved to see she was ten minutes early. Feeling nervous and excited, she stepped back when she heard footsteps coming.

"Hi, Marilyn, so glad you're here. Come on in." It was Harriet, the store owner. She stepped aside to let Marilyn by, then closed the door and said, "Follow me. You can put your things in our little employee room here." She turned in to the first doorway on the left. "It'll just be you and me until eleven-thirty. Emma will be coming in then to help with the lunch crowd."

Marilyn had never seen Harriet without a smile. She had gray hair, nicely styled. If Marilyn guessed right, she was in her midsixties, but she carried herself with the energy level of someone much younger.

"I've got your name badge right here," Harriet said, handing it to her. "I'm going to go open the front door. Customers will start trickling in. I'll man the register. You can just wander around the store, greet customers, and study the merchandise. After a week or so, believe me, you'll know where everything is. But for now, if someone asks for something you can't find, just tell them you'll go check, then come ask me. If there are no customers in the store, come on over to the counter, and I'll start showing you how to use the cash register."

"Sounds great, Harriet." Harriet left to unlock the front door. "And thanks so much for giving me this job," Marilyn added.

"You are most welcome. Glad to have you with us."

And that was how Marilyn spent the next two hours at her first job in twenty-five years. She couldn't have asked for a more enjoyable environment. It was one of her favorite shops in the downtown area. The whole store was filled with wonders. Charming knickknacks, a wide variety of ceramic collectibles, artsy greeting cards, humorous gifts and signs, a wall full of prints done by local artists, and a separate Christmas room stocked with over two hundred ornaments, miniature houses, and nativity figurines. All the while, the most pleasant and soothing music played in the background.

Every now and then a chime sounded, signaling a customer

had come into the store. But really, over the first two hours, that chime didn't ring often, which allowed Harriet to cover cash register basics with Marilyn. This came in handy at eleven o'clock, when the back doorbell rang.

"Do you think you can handle the register for about ten minutes?" Harriet asked. "It's one of the delivery trucks. He's not supposed to come until after lunch. Guess he arrived early."

"I think so," Marilyn said. At the moment, no customers were in the store. She hoped it stayed that way.

Less than five minutes later, the front door chimed. Marilyn froze as she saw who came in. It was Sophie Mitchell with another woman she didn't recognize. Sophie was a long-standing member of the church she and Jim had attended the last ten years. Marilyn had never liked her. Mainly because she was a snob and seemed to enjoy manipulating and intimidating people.

True to form, Marilyn suddenly found herself wanting to hide. For a moment, she thought about taking off her name tag and pretending to be just another shopper in the store. But she had to stay behind the register.

She kept her eyes on Sophie and her friend for the next five minutes as they strolled leisurely through the store aisles, picking up this thing or that. They seemed to be having a marvelous time. During those moments, Marilyn got hold of herself. She decided she didn't care what Sophie thought. Why should she feel embarrassed working at a retail store, or anywhere else for that matter? She needed the money because of her . . . new circumstances. But even if she didn't, she was enjoying herself. She'd been wanting to work here for months.

Finally, Sophie appeared from the last aisle in the store, carrying one of the many collectible angels, and headed toward the cash register. She was still talking with her friend when she looked up and saw Marilyn. A startled look came over her face. She looked up and down, as if to persuade herself that she really was seeing Marilyn Anderson standing behind the cash register. Her eyes zeroed in on Marilyn's name tag. "Marilyn," she said as she set the figurine on the counter. "What are you doing here?"

"I'm working here. Just started today, as a matter of fact."

"Really." Sophie's eyes widened, forming little wrinkles on her forehead. She quickly recovered and forced a smile. "How nice."

"Sophie," her friend said, "I think I'm going to go back and get that other angel we were looking at." She walked back to the last aisle.

Sophie leaned over the counter and said quietly, "I heard Jim's business has been struggling lately, from things Harold said." She left the next sentence unspoken, but Marilyn was sure it was supposed to be, *But I had no idea things were this bad*. Harold was Sophie's husband. He served on the deacon board with Jim, and they occasionally golfed together.

"Actually, Sophie," Marilyn replied in the same quiet tone, "me working here has nothing to do with Jim's business. It's something I wanted to do. And I might as well tell you—you're going to find out soon enough—Jim and I are separated."

The look on Sophie's face was priceless.

Just then, her friend came back with her angel. "Will that be all for you ladies?" Marilyn said. She rang up their purchases, hoping she did everything right at the register. Not another word was said. At least not until the two women exited the store. Immediately after, Marilyn saw Sophie through the front window, her mouth moving a mile a minute, certainly filling her friend in on the news.

Harriet came walking from the back hallway, carrying a small stack of boxes. "So how did your first sale go at the register?"

"I think it went . . . just fine," Marilyn said, smiling. A few lines from that song "Something to Talk About" began playing in her head.

For the past two hours, Jim had been roaming the streets and apartment parking lots throughout River Oaks in search of Marilyn's car. It seemed absurd that he hadn't found it yet. He began to wonder if she might have lied about staying somewhere in town.

His search had brought him back to Main Street, where he was now stopped at a traffic light. Two well-dressed, middle-aged women crossed the intersection in front of his car. At first, he didn't recognize them. When they reached the sidewalk, one of them turned and hurried back to his car, waving.

"Jim Anderson," she said. "I thought that was you." She talked so loudly, he heard her through his closed windows. It was Sophie Mitchell, his friend Harold's wife. He could stomach time spent with Harold, as long as they had a round of golf between them. But Sophie was another matter. She had always been Marilyn's responsibility. He looked up at the light, wishing it would turn green, then lowered his passenger window. "Hi, Sophie."

"Well, look, I know you've got to go. Just wanted to say how sorry I am about you and Marilyn. Does Harold know?"

"What?"

"You and Marilyn, you know, being separated. So sorry to hear it."

This was just great. "Uh . . . when did you hear that? From who?"

"Just now, over there." She pointed to one of the stores. "From Marilyn at Odds-n-Ends, where she works."

The light turned green, and the man in the car behind him tapped his horn.

"Better go." Sophie waved and hurried back to the sidewalk.

Great, now the whole church will know. It was only Friday, couldn't even wait till Sunday. Jim sped through the light but looked for the first parking place to pull into. He put the car in park and got out, looked across the street at Odds-n-Ends. *Guess that's how she plans to earn her own keep*, he thought. *Working at a retail store.*

Why should that surprise him?

He was wrestling with himself about walking right over there to confront her when his phone rang. It was Lynn, his secretary. "Oh shoot," he said, noticing the time. "Hey, Lynn."

"Mr. Anderson, Dr. Franklin is here. Do you see the time?"

"Yes, how long's he been there?"

"He just got here a few minutes ago."

It wasn't like Jim could say he'd been held up in traffic, not in River Oaks. "Tell him I'm so sorry. I'm just around the corner and will be there in three minutes. Offer him some coffee and chat with him till I arrive. Can you do that?"

"I suppose so."

"Great." He hung up. The confrontation would have to wait.

Later that evening, after grabbing a bite to eat at a Burger King, Jim pulled up to a Starbucks in Lake Mary. He couldn't believe he had to eat his dinner at a fast food place, another consequence of Marilyn's selfishness. Doug's red Mazda was already in the parking lot. Jim was meeting him and Tom. That morning, when Jim and Tom had talked, Jim said he'd call Tom tonight. But as the day wore on, Jim decided this was something he should tell his sons in person.

Of course, Doug had pitched a fit about it. "Why can't you just tell me now?" he'd said when Jim called him an hour ago. "And where's Mom, anyway?"

"That's what this is about," Jim had said. "Just be there. Grab something to eat someplace and I'll pay you back." Doug still hadn't gotten a part-time job. Another thing Jim had been after him about. Doug had grown up when their cash flow was running high. Jim realized now they had been way too easy on him. Doug was having a hard time accepting the idea that he was going to have to start paying his own way. As Jim walked into the Starbucks, Doug got up from a nearby table, his smartphone in hand.

"Hey, Dad."

"Is Tom here?" Jim asked.

"Not yet. Wait." Doug looked out to the parking lot. "There he is. His car just pulled in."

"Guess we can get in line," Jim said.

"You paying?"

"Yeah, I'm paying."

"Uh . . . can you pay me back for dinner too? I ate at the mall food court. It was eight bucks."

"Let me get some change when I pay for the coffee."

"Hi, Dad," Tom said as he joined them in line. "Sorry I'm late. Had to help Jean get the kids ready for—"

"You're not late," Jim said. "Go ahead and order. Looks like I'm buying." They stepped up to the counter. Well, he and Tom did. Doug was somewhere else, his face glued to his cell phone: texting, Twittering, or Facebooking someone. "Doug, would you put that thing away?"

"What? Oh."

"You're not going to be on that thing the whole time."

"No, I just had to—well, never mind." He got behind Tom.

After they'd gotten their drinks, they settled back at the table in the corner Doug had picked out earlier. "This won't take long, guys," Jim said. "We'll probably be done before you get a chance to refill your coffee."

"They don't give out refills on caramel macchiatos, Dad."

"You know what I mean."

"Sounds like something big is up," Tom said. "Are you okay? Is something wrong with Mom?"

Something was definitely wrong with Mom. "Well, let's start with, I'm not okay. It's nothing physical. Nobody is dying. But . . ." He looked down at the floor. How should he say this? "It's about me and your mom."

"You guys getting a divorce?" Doug blurted out.

"No," Jim said, looking back up. "We're not getting a divorce. At least . . . not now."

"What?" Tom said. "Are you and Mom having some trouble?"

"That's one way to put it," Jim said. "The truth is, well . . . I came home yesterday to find she'd walked out. She's left me."

"You're kidding," Tom said.

"I wish I was."

"That's why she hasn't been around the past two days?" Doug said.

Jim nodded.

Tom shook his head. "Where'd she go?"

"I don't know very much at the moment. She left me a note, asked me to give her some space."

"What does that mean?" Tom asked.

"I don't know."

"But you guys are both believers," he said. "Why would she leave you? Have either one of you . . . started seeing someone else?"

"I haven't," Jim said.

"You're saying Mom has?" Doug said.

"No . . . I don't know," Jim said. "Michele said there's no one else."

"C'mon, Dad." Doug set his drink down. "Mom would never go out on you. There's no way."

"I hope not," Jim said. "But I can't figure out why she'd leave like this, with no warning."

"You guys haven't been fighting or anything?" Tom asked.

"No. No more than an occasional spat. Small stuff, like every couple has."

Tom sat forward in his chair, released a sigh. "Wow. This is pretty intense. I'm glad neither of you are sick. That's what I was expecting. But this . . ."

"It's very intense," Jim said. "I know."

"So where's Mom now?" Doug asked.

"I don't know. Michele said she's staying with a single woman somewhere in town. An apartment somewhere."

"She won't talk to you?" Tom said.

"No. Not now anyway. I'm waiting on a call from Michele. Hopefully, she'll at least tell me where she's at."

"So Michele's taking her side, I guess," Tom said.

"Looks that way."

"I guess that's no surprise," he said. "You want me to call her? See what I can find out?"

"You mean your mom?"

"No, Michele."

"That might help," Jim said.

"Then again," Doug added, "it might backfire. You know Michele."

All three of them sat in silence a few moments, and each took a few sips of their drink. "This is really something," Tom finally said. "Definitely didn't see this coming. Jean's not going to believe it."

"I'm having a hard time believing it myself," Jim said. "The only thing I know is, she says she's been pretty unhappy for a long time."

"I knew that," Doug said. "You couldn't tell?" He had almost a look of disgust on his face. Jim decided to let it drop.

"Well, I didn't," Tom said. "I don't see what she has to be unhappy about."

Doug just shook his head as if to say, *Whatever*.

Jim knew Doug and Tom weren't the best of friends. Tom had made it pretty clear he thought Doug was a lazy, spoiled brat. He had appealed to Jim several times, saying he didn't understand why he and Marilyn coddled Doug so much. They had been a lot stricter with him and Michele growing up.

"Well, that's about the size of it," Jim said. "Needless to say, we could use your prayers."

"Where do we go from here?" Tom said. "Is there a next step?"

"Honestly, Tom? I have no idea. I'm playing it totally by ear."

"Do you think she'll agree to go to counseling?" he asked.

"Not at our church," Jim said. "In her note, she said she was going somewhere else for a while."

"Man," Tom said. "I just can't believe it."

Doug stood up. "Well . . . I guess I can. So are we done here?"

"Hey, Doug," Tom said in a reprimanding voice.

"That's okay," Jim said, shaking his head. "Yeah, we're done."

Doug picked up his caramel macchiato and turned to leave. He stopped, turned around, and said, "I'll tell you one thing. There's no way Mom is seeing someone else. I'll never believe that."

8

Marilyn got out of her car and walked toward the riverfront park. It was Saturday morning around ten-thirty, and the morning's cooler temperatures still prevailed. She didn't have to be at the store until one, then she'd work until they closed at nine. Last night, she'd slept wonderfully, probably due to being on her feet so much yesterday, something she wasn't at all used to.

But she'd get used to it. She was having a great time at Odds-n-Ends—it hardly felt like a job. After Emma had arrived yesterday, Harriet had shown Marilyn how to restock the candle and knickknack aisles and taught her a little about her reordering system. Before Marilyn knew it, it was six o'clock, and she was off.

Her first day of paid work in twenty-five years.

She stepped from the sidewalk onto the park's main walkway, which was lined with decorative pavers. The whole riverfront park was amazing. There to greet you in the center, fairly close to the road, was a magnificent fountain. At the top, water poured out and down the leaves of a sculptured palm tree, into three layers of stone bowls, each a little wider than the one above.

The entire park was shaded by ancient live oaks. Manicured walkways wound their way in and around the trees, with ample seating provided by ornamental iron benches.

Along the river itself a sea wall had been built, and just beyond it a small beach area. Parallel to the river, the widest walkway in the park ran the full length of the downtown area. But the place Marilyn was most interested in was a large grassy area on the farthest end. A small gazebo had been set up there, and she thought it would be the perfect place for Michele's wedding.

As she cleared the fountain, she saw Michele already there, taking large steps in a straight line, as if measuring the distance. "What do you think?" she yelled as she got closer. "Isn't this perfect?"

Michele didn't reply until she'd gotten to the end. "I think it's beautiful," she said. Michele's wedding wasn't till the end of September, two months away. "I was just trying to get an idea of how many rows of chairs we could fit."

They hugged. "Have you and Allan come up with your guest list yet?"

"Almost, just needs some tweaking."

"How many people so far?"

"About 220," Michele said. "Of course, that number might shrink considerably, depending on what happens between you and Dad."

"I'm sorry, Michele. I picked a lousy time to leave your father."

"Don't apologize, Mom. The ones we'd be taking off the list are people I'd rather not have at my wedding anyway."

"You mean people from our church?" Marilyn said. "My old church?" The wedding ceremony had been planned at the church she and Jim had attended together. It had a gorgeous sanctuary, but neither she or Michele felt comfortable having the wedding there now. Besides, Michele had pretty much left the church when she'd gone off to college. That's why she'd thought of the park. People did weddings here all the time, weather permitting.

"I'll have to go over the list with you soon," Michele said, "so I can get the invitations printed and mailed. We should have had them out several weeks ago, but now I'm *so* glad we didn't send them."

"Let's sit over there," Marilyn said. They walked across the grass and sat on one of the benches positioned symmetrically on each side of the gazebo. Marilyn handed Michele a piece of paper.

"What's this?"

"A girl named Emma works at the store with me. She had her wedding here three years ago. That's a link to a bunch of her wedding pictures online. She thought it would help give us some good ideas."

"That's great," Michele said.

"She goes to a church that meets in the high school. I'm going to start going there tomorrow."

Michele sighed.

"What's the matter?"

"That's another snag. I don't really want Pastor Hagen to do the ceremony now." He was the pastor of their old church. "But I don't know who else we can get to do it. I wish my pastor in Lakeland could do it, but he'll be out of town."

"I asked Emma about it," Marilyn said. "She thought her pastor might be willing to do the service, but she knew he'd insist you and Allan go through some premarital counseling with him first."

"Hmm," Michele said. "That could be a problem. Allan and

I have already been doing that with our pastor in Lakeland. We're almost done."

"Well, maybe not. I'm sure Emma's pastor is mostly concerned that you're getting that kind of help. Maybe the two pastors can talk so her pastor can find out what's been going on. I'll see Emma in a little while at work and ask for his phone number."

"You could text it to me," Michele said.

"Then that's what we'll do."

"Do you know his name?"

Marilyn shook her head. "I don't know him at all. But she says he's really nice. Kind of young, midthirties, I think."

"That's not that young, Mom."

"I guess."

Michele looked up, her eyes scanning the trees.

"Are you worried about the heat? I know it can still get pretty hot in September, but your wedding's in the late afternoon. I think these trees will provide plenty of shade."

"No, I was wondering about something else. Do you think they'll provide any protection if it rains?"

That was the only problem Marilyn had thought about with this plan. September was still officially hurricane season. They hadn't had one come through central Florida for almost ten years, but thunderstorms were always a possibility here. "Well, you and Allan should be fine. You'll be under this gazebo with the pastor."

"But I don't want everyone else getting all wet."

"We'll put a few words at the bottom of the invitation, asking everyone to bring an umbrella, just in case."

"I suppose," Michele said. "Maybe we could do the ceremony at the reception hall . . . as a plan B. We can watch the weather and decide a few days beforehand, then alert everyone through the internet if a storm system is moving in."

"That might work," Marilyn said. She looked at her watch. She was doing okay with the time.

Michele shifted and turned to face her. "So how are you doing with all this?" she said.

"You mean about leaving your dad?"

She nodded. "Does it bother you to talk about all this wedding stuff with your marriage . . ."

"Falling apart?" Marilyn sighed. "I'm okay. This doesn't bother me, because I know you're marrying a great guy. Someone who'll make you truly happy."

Michele smiled. "Allan really is . . . perfect. For me, I mean." They sat in silence a few moments. Finally, Michele said, "Were you and Dad ever this happy, like Allan and I are? I've never seen you that way. You know, *in* love. I'm sure Dad loves you, but it's almost like . . . I don't know, like you both have these totally defined roles. He's the head, the breadwinner, the one who makes all the decisions. You're the dutiful, submissive wife who keeps the house and manages the social calendar."

Marilyn had to fight a wave of unexpected emotions that suddenly rose to the surface. She hated the way Michele had described her and Jim's relationship, but that pretty much summed it up. She looked away a moment to get control.

"I'm sorry, I didn't mean to get you upset. You don't have to answer that."

She looked back at Michele. "No, it's okay. I guess the answer's a little complicated. I thought we were happy when we were dating. Even for most of the time after we got engaged. But something seemed to click, in a wrong way, almost as soon as we were married. Like our relationship had been set on some kind of rail. Your father would probably say we had the perfect Christian marriage. But I feel like we've been on the wrong track ever since. I loved your father back then, that's for sure. But I'm not . . ." A tear escaped down her cheek. "I'm not so sure he ever loved me. Not the same way."

"I'm sorry, Mom." Michele leaned over and hugged her.

"But, Michele, I don't think it's going to be that way with you and Allan. It's obvious he loves you every bit as much as you love him. And I'm very happy for you, for both of you."

Michele reached in her purse and pulled out a tissue, handed it to her mom. Marilyn wiped her eyes.

"You know, this feels a little weird for me, talking with you like this," Michele said. "It's almost like a scene from *Sense and Sensibility* or some other Jane Austen movie. Like somehow you got stuck in an arranged marriage and you're urging me to marry for love."

Marilyn smiled. "I guess the arrangement, at least for your father was . . . you love me, and I'll love me, and we'll get along just fine."

"That's terrible."

"Yes," she said. "Yes, it is." She looked Michele square in the eyes and took hold of her hand. "But that's not going to be your story, my darling daughter. If marriage should be about anything, it should be about love. You loving each other more than yourselves, and I can already see, Allan loves you like that."

Jim selected his seven-iron for the fifteenth hole, a beautiful par three on the River Oaks Golf Course. He lobbed it up nice and high, and with a little backspin it came to rest just ten feet from the pin. Although his whole life had been turned upside down the last few days, it didn't seem to affect his golf game.

"Nice shot, Jim," his friend Harold said. "I'll be lucky to clear that water trap in front." When Jim had seen Harold's wife Sophie yesterday on Main Street, he'd forgotten the two of them were playing golf this morning. They played most Saturdays, but Jim had been a little distracted, for obvious reasons.

"Just forget the water's there. You can nail this. I've got faith in you." That wasn't entirely true; Harold had already sunk three in the water so far this round. Jim stood off to the side to watch. He wondered when Harold was going to bring up the big news. The round was nearly over. There was no way Sophie hadn't blabbed to Harold about him and Marilyn being separated. But so far, their conversations had remained light and superficial, as always.

It was starting to get pretty hot out. Jim was grateful the

course was covered with so many trees. Lots of shade to hide under. Harold wasn't as happy about the trees. With his chronic slice, half his drives wound up in the middle of them.

"Rats!" That was about as close to swearing as Harold got.

Jim suppressed a smile as Harold's ball went nice and high but came up short and plunked right in the water.

"I think on the next one," Harold said, "I'm just going to pick the stupid ball up and throw it in the water myself."

They walked back to the golf cart, put their clubs in the bags, and hopped in. Harold was driving. The breeze from the moving cart felt nice. "Don't sweat it. I think you just tense up every time you see water."

"With good reason," Harold said. "How come you never do?"

"I don't know. I just pretend it's not there."

"You've got great mental discipline," Harold said. "Nothing ever seems to get to you out here."

Out here, Jim thought. Yeah, out here, he was still in control. They weaved around the cart path then came to a stop near a cluster of cypress trees, the green just up ahead. Jim got out.

Harold did not. "Say, Jim, I was talking with Sophie yesterday . . ."

Here it comes. Jim took off his glove, pulled his putter out of the bag.

"Is everything okay between you and Marilyn?"

"What? Why . . . what did Sophie say?"

"Not too much. Just that she bumped into Marilyn at one of the downtown stores. She said Marilyn was behind the counter."

"Yeah, she started working there this week. Just something she's been wanting to do, to keep busy."

"So, you guys aren't having any financial troubles?"

"Not really. You know my cash flow's been a little tight these past few months but, really, we're doing fine."

"Any . . . other kind of troubles?"

Jim looked back toward the tee, to make sure the next group of golfers hadn't arrived. "We're going through a rough patch, to be honest." Jim wanted to say as little as possible; he figured Harold wasn't interested in these kinds of details anyway. Most men hated getting personal. Harold likely just needed to be able to report back to Sophie that he'd inquired. "Marilyn's just wanting a little time for herself, that's all. And I'm letting her have it."

Harold stepped out of the cart. "So you two aren't . . . separated?"

"What? No, not legally. It's nothing like that. She's just having a little midlife crisis. Our daughter's getting married in September. Doug's home, but he's mostly on his own these days, doesn't really need his mom that much anymore. I think Marilyn's just trying to figure out the next step. You know, what she's supposed to do with her life now."

Harold got out of the cart, walked back to get his putter. "Well, that's good to hear." He grabbed another golf ball from his bag, walked around the water trap, and dropped it on the side closest to the green. "Mind if I play it from here?"

"No, that's where I'd play it," Jim said. Of course, that wasn't true. Harold should have dropped the ball on the other side, closest to where it went in the water. But Jim knew that wasn't going to happen. He doubted Harold's score would even reflect all these water shots. But hey, who was he to judge? If it got Harold in a better mood and off this touchy subject, Jim was all for it.

But Jim knew he was only playing for time. Tomorrow was

Sunday. With Sophie on the prowl, the whole church would know Marilyn had left him before the weekend was over.

Jim got cleaned up then grabbed some lunch with Harold before leaving the country club. As expected, Harold hadn't said another word about Jim's marriage troubles. On his way home, Jim drove down Main Street, slowing as he rode past Odds-n-Ends. Marilyn was probably in there, although he didn't see her car parked on the street.

That's right, he thought, she was an employee now. He drove around to the back parking lot, and sure enough, there was her car. He fought with himself about going inside; he had every right to. It angered him that he still didn't know where she was staying. She was his wife, for crying out loud, and she was treating him with such disrespect. He wasn't eating well, not sleeping well—had to take another sleeping pill last night. She may have cost him a new client yesterday, making him late to his appointment with that doctor.

The meeting with the doctor had gone well, though, once he'd gotten there. The man seemed genuinely interested in the space. And he'd said the price Jim quoted was in the ballpark. Jim had then taken him to one of the finest restaurants in River Oaks for lunch. When they'd parted, the doctor said he'd definitely be in touch but had a few more properties to see first.

It would mean a big improvement in their situation if that doctor came through. Jim sighed as he thought about it. Big improvement. What difference did that make now? He drove his car back around the front, slowed once more as he came to the store. There were no open parking spots. He took that as a sign to keep going.

When he pulled onto the one-lane service road behind the house, his heart sank. "Great, that's just great," he said aloud. He brought the car to a quick stop and waited. Should he back up? It didn't look like he'd been seen yet.

Parked there in the center space in front of his garage—looking totally out of place—was a vintage yellow '68 Chevy Impala with a black vinyl top. Which could only mean one thing. Sitting in the driver's seat was an elderly, balding man, equally out of place.

Uncle Henry.

10

It was no use. The car door opened, and Uncle Henry stepped out onto the driveway, looking his way. Jim quickly pulled his Audi forward, as if he hadn't stopped a few doors down to conjure up some escape plan. Uncle Henry wasn't *that* bad, he reminded himself, then realized the words weren't his; they were Marilyn's. She'd thought he was harmless, a little eccentric maybe. "He's just . . . unique."

But for Jim, Uncle Henry was over the top. He seemed to perpetually live out in left field, always offering perspectives and ideas about life that didn't fit anywhere in Jim's world. And ever since Jim's father had died, Uncle Henry had gotten it into his head that Jim needed an uncle in his life.

Uncle Henry was his father's little brother. Considered the black sheep of the family in his father's day. He was the hippie who'd found Jesus after almost dying of a drug overdose at Woodstock. He'd gotten cleaned up, then used the family money to graduate from Purdue with a master's degree in American history. He'd spent the better part of his working life teaching high school and fiddling with antique cars.

"Hey, Jim," Henry said, waving as Jim pulled his car into the driveway. "Just getting in from a round of golf?"

Jim drove into the open garage, turned off the car, and got out. "Yes."

"How'd you do?"

"Pretty good, shot a seventy-nine."

"Pretty good," Henry repeated. "Seven over par? That's a little better than pretty good."

"I guess." He walked back to the trunk, pulled his golf bag out, and set it in its place.

Uncle Henry walked up behind him. "Didn't I used to beat you pretty regularly?"

"Maybe when I was thirteen," Jim said.

Henry smiled. "That long ago?"

"You play anymore?"

"Not if I can help it," Henry said. "Golf for me now is like that guy said, a good walk spoiled. If I'm going to pay that kind of money, I've gotta have more to show for it than a sore back and a lousy disposition."

Jim smiled and thought of Harold's efforts that morning. "So what brings you over this way? Not exactly in the neighborhood." Uncle Henry lived in New Smyrna Beach, about a forty-minute drive from here.

"Actually, I kinda was. Buying a part for our old '65 Midas mini motor home from a guy in Altamonte Springs. I'm restoring it, hopefully in time for Myra and me to make a trip to the Keys before hurricane season starts. I had to drive right past here on I-4. When I was praying this morning, I got a feeling I should stop by. Thought I'd come and see how you and Doug were faring."

Me and Doug, Jim thought. He didn't mention Marilyn. Did

Uncle Henry know what was going on? Part of his eccentricity was his relationship with God. Uncle Henry and Jim both went to church. They both believed in God, read the same Bible. But Uncle Henry always seemed to get these strong impressions when he prayed, and then he'd feel the need to act on them.

"You know, I told your father before he died that I'd look after you."

See, it was saying things like that. Jim was certain his father wouldn't have asked Uncle Henry to do something like that, especially considering he had never looked after Jim himself. Jim stood there in the garage, trying not to look his uncle in the eye. He was about to fabricate a story that would keep him from having to invite his uncle into the house. Better do it quick, he thought. It was getting pretty hot standing there in the garage. "Well, Doug and I are doing fine. I'd be doing a little better if he'd get a job like I've asked him to a hundred times."

"Your business still pretty slow then?"

"Yeah, but that's not it. It's just . . . he needs to learn some responsibility."

"Responsibility's a good thing," Henry said.

"Yes, it is. Say, Uncle Henry, I'd invite you in but—speaking of business—I've got to see a client in a little while, show him one of my properties. I just came home to get changed so I can head back out."

"That's all right. I've gotta get going in a few minutes anyway. So . . . how are things with you and Marilyn these days?"

"What? Why do you ask?"

"Well . . . I tried reaching you this morning, but I guess you had your ringer off while you were playing golf. So I called Douglas."

Now Jim understood why Uncle Henry had left Marilyn's name out before. "And what'd he say?"

"Not too much, just the one big thing."

"He told you Marilyn has left me." Why hadn't he told Doug not to tell anyone about this yet?

"He was pretty upset about it," Henry said. "And I was too, after I heard about it. You and Marilyn have been together for so long."

"And we're still together. She's just . . . taking some time off." If Doug was upset, why didn't he talk to him?

"Taking some time off? That's something you do with work, Jim, not a marriage."

"Look, I don't know what to tell you. I think this empty nest thing's just starting to hit her. You know, with Michele's wedding coming up."

"Doesn't Michele mostly live at school these days?"

"Yeah," Jim said, "but after the wedding she'll be gone for good. And Doug, well, she and Doug aren't all that close now that he's gotten older. He mostly hangs out with his friends, plays his music, or stays shut up in his room playing Xbox."

"So that's all you think this is, her struggling with an empty nest?"

"Yeah, I'm sure she'll come running back here in a few days."

Uncle Henry took a deep breath. Jim felt sure he was about to unload a mini-sermon. But to Jim's surprise, he just stood there a few moments, didn't say a word. Then tears welled up in his eyes. What in the world?

"I've really got to be going, Uncle Henry."

"I know," he said, blinking back the tears. "It's just, I get a sense in my heart that what Marilyn's going through is a lot deeper than that. I think you ought to prepare yourself that this thing's not going to end so quick."

"What are you talking about?"

"I think you're going to need some help on this thing, Jim. That's all. You know God gives grace to the humble, the Bible says that a number of times. We Anderson men aren't known for our humility."

Humility? What's humility got to do with this? "We're just having a few bumps, that's all. Every marriage has them."

Uncle Henry backed a few steps toward his car; Jim was glad to see it. "Well, you know I'm here to help if you ever want to talk this out with someone."

"There's nothing to talk out. But thanks anyway."

"Okay then." The tears welled up in his eyes again. "Me and Aunt Myra will be praying for you two." He opened the door to his Chevy.

"Prayer never hurt anyone," Jim said.

"But you know, if what I'm sensing is true," Henry continued, then paused. "Well, you remember what I said about humility, Jim. It's always the right first step. But it's a hard lesson to learn, especially for a man. We don't like to ask for help, or even admit we need it. But we all do, every day. I've been working on that myself, asking for help. Not just from God but from the people he sends my way. Humility isn't complicated. It's really just returning to the way God set things up in the beginning. He designed us to need him all the time, and each other."

There he goes again, Jim thought, talking like some hippie guru. "Thanks, Uncle Henry, you have a nice afternoon." Jim breathed a sigh of relief when his uncle got into his car and closed the door.

11

I'm out here, Marilyn."

Marilyn looked toward the voice; it came from the apartment balcony. One of the French doors was opened a crack. Charlotte was apparently enjoying the night air. Marilyn walked across the living room carpet and opened the door the rest of the way.

"There you are," Charlotte said. "Come on out and join me." She was sitting in a wicker chair, drinking a glass of iced tea with lime.

Marilyn noticed she was wearing pajamas. Outside. She was sitting outside in her pajamas.

Charlotte noticed her noticing. "You're wondering about this?" She pointed to her outfit. "Nobody can see us out here. It's too high up, and the railing blocks the view for the most part." Marilyn looked at the other apartments on the same level. All the balconies were empty.

"No one ever comes out on their balconies," Charlotte said. "It's like they're just for show. Go get comfortable, pour yourself some tea, and c'mon. I ran out of lemons, but I had a lime in the fridge. Hope you like limes."

Marilyn smiled. "I do." She closed the door and headed to her bedroom. What a fun idea, something she'd never think of doing. As she changed, she was aware of how tired she was, and her legs felt sore from standing most of the day. But it was a good tired, and her aching legs didn't bother her too much. She looked at a clock on her dresser. It was 9:45, Saturday night. Tomorrow morning she planned to go to church then be back at the store at two. She hoped the service didn't start too early. After pouring her iced tea and adding a wedge of lime, she joined Charlotte on the balcony.

"Can you close that the rest of the way?" Charlotte said. "I just left the door open so you'd hear me when you got home. Might as well save a little on the electric bill, right?"

After closing the door, Marilyn sat in the other chair. There was really only room for two of them and a little round wicker table tucked in between. It felt strange being outside in her pajamas. Another first in her life.

"Isn't this nice?"Charlotte said. "I love sitting out here at night. You wouldn't think with all those people walking around in the street down there that it'd feel so private. But no one ever looks up here. They're all looking in the store windows, chatting to each other. And there's such a nice breeze up here."

"The downtown area looks beautiful at night," Marilyn said. "It always does, but from up here even more." She imitated Charlotte and rested her feet on the lower part of the rail. Looking down through the rungs, she saw a young couple strolling by one of the storefront windows, holding hands. They were about Michele and Allan's age and obviously in love; you could see it on their faces.

"Love is in the air," Charlotte said, watching the same couple.

Marilyn nodded. "So Charlotte, how did you come to be here in River Oaks?"

"Same way a lot of folks from up north did, I guess. I came down on vacation several years in a row with friends. You know, mostly going to Disney and the other theme parks. Then we'd spend a few days lounging around on the beach. After a while, I started thinking I should move here. Usually after a lousy winter. When Eddie started college, I asked him what he thought about moving down here when he graduated. He said he'd love it, so I figured, I'll come down first and get set up, you know? Why should I stay up there through four more winters? It's not like I was seeing him anymore once school started."

Marilyn sipped her tea. "But how did you end up in River Oaks? There's lots of places in Florida you could have moved to. Especially being an RN."

"It just worked out," she said. "The timing, I mean. I was down here on another vacation. My lease was up on my apartment, so I got the newspaper, started reading the want ads. They had just opened the Urgent Care center, so I called, and they said come over for an interview. I came an hour early so I could check out the area." A big smile came over her face. "Well, you know what happened then. One slow drive around this place and I was hooked. I called Eddie all excited, telling him I'd never seen a cuter town in all my life. It was like living in Disney World."

Marilyn thought about her first tour of River Oaks. It had been enchanting, almost unreal. She thought the people living here had to be the luckiest and happiest people on earth. Every home was gorgeous. Every property perfectly kept. So many parks and fountains and shady trees. The downtown area looked like a movie set from the fifties, except in vibrant color.

"After my interview," Charlotte continued, "and I knew I got the job, I spent the rest of the afternoon touring the model homes. It was just for fun, of course. Not like I could ever afford to live in one of those places. But I was all dressed nice for the interview, figured the realtor didn't know that. So I walked around, asked questions, pretended I had money and might be interested." She shook her head. "Some of the most beautiful homes I'd ever seen. Can't imagine what it would be like to live in any one of them. Unless maybe I had died and gone to heaven. Hey, I'm sorry, hon. What's the matter? Did I put my foot in my mouth?"

Marilyn didn't realize her expression had soured, hearing Charlotte go on about all the beautiful houses in River Oaks. She'd lived in one of the nicest homes in town. Hadn't Charlotte known that? She felt sure she'd told her. "It's nothing, Charlotte. You're right. The homes here are lovely."

"Oh my, that's right. You lived in one, didn't you? I'm sorry. Listen to me going on like that. It's just . . . you're out here on this little balcony with me . . . in your pajamas . . ."

"Don't quite look the part? Don't worry about it. But you know, having a house like that, even in a town like this . . . doesn't guarantee you'll be happy. I know a lot of miserable couples who live in big homes all around here. We used to invite some of them over for my husband's business parties." A few names came to mind, some of the nastiest people she'd ever spent an evening with. "I'm having much more fun sitting out on this little balcony with you."

"Really?" Charlotte said. "That's nice of you to say. 'Course, I think we could be having just as much fun sitting on one of those big wraparound front porches instead."

Marilyn looked around at all the empty balconies in sight. She wasn't so sure. "You know something, Charlotte? I can't recall the last time I even sat out on our front porch. And you know something else? I can't recall ever seeing any of my neighbors sitting on their big wraparound porches, either. Not even once." She thought about it a little more. "I can't remember ever seeing anyone else on their porches when I've driven around the different neighborhoods."

"Really?" Charlotte said.

"Really."

"What a waste."

"Isn't it?"

"Why do you think that is?" Charlotte asked.

"I don't know. Why doesn't anyone ever sit out on their balconies?"

"Good question." She sat up, looked around. "I never see anyone out here."

It was the oddest thing. It had never dawned on Marilyn before. That big wraparound porch was one of the things she'd liked best about the house on Elderberry Lane, and all the other houses in her neighborhood. It gave her a really nice feeling. Like it was the kind of neighborhood from ages past, when people really did spend time together on front porches, talking, laughing, drinking iced tea.

But now she realized it was just for show.

The house, the neighborhood . . . this entire town. All just an illusion of happiness. She'd had it all, the best the American dream had to offer. And here she was, sitting out on this tiny balcony, in her pajamas, drinking iced tea with Charlotte.

She hadn't been this happy in years.

12

Marilyn looked up from her table under the awning at Giovanni's, a little Italian café on Main Street. Michele should be there any minute. The sun had begun to set, but it was still warm outside. She hoped not too warm to enjoy their dinner together.

She was still wearing her outfit from work, glad she didn't have to wear a uniform. When she took the name tag off she was all set for a casual dinner out. She'd gotten off at six o'clock; the store closed early on Sundays.

That morning she had a pleasant experience at Charlotte's church, the one that met in the high school. She felt a little odd going to a church service in a school, especially the same one her son attended. The congregation was much younger than she was used to, but the people were so friendly it didn't seem to matter. The worship music was loud, performed by a contemporary band with drums, guitars, and an electronic keyboard. They were quite talented, especially the singers. The enthusiasm of the congregation soon drew her into the experience.

Once the pastor began preaching, she'd quickly forgotten

how young he looked. He talked for just over thirty minutes and never bored her once. But perhaps the best part of the experience was the fact that no one knew who she was or any of the problems she was going through. No one judged her. No self-righteous eyes to deal with or fears of what people were saying behind her back.

She glanced up again. Still no sign of Michele.

Marilyn looked beneath the table. Beside her purse was a little bit of foolishness, something she'd bought that afternoon. She couldn't wait to show Michele. It had been calling to her since her first day at Odds-n-Ends, just sitting there on a glass shelf. It was beautiful. Every time she saw it, it had stirred wonderful memories. These days, wonderful memories were hard to find. She glanced down at the box through the opening in the bag.

"Mom?"

She looked up. It was Michele, waving as she walked along the sidewalk toward the café. Marilyn got up to give her a hug.

"That's a nice outfit," Michele said.

"I've had it awhile, but it's been in the back of my closet. I actually wore it to work this afternoon."

Michele smiled. "I'm still not used to that, my mom working a real job."

"Motherhood's a real job," Marilyn said.

"You know what I mean."

The waiter walked up. "Can I take your drink orders while you look over the menus?"

"Sure," Marilyn said. They took turns telling the waiter what they wanted. After he left, Marilyn said, "Speaking of work, I bought something this afternoon I'm dying to show you."

"What is it? Something for the wedding?"

"No, something just for me."

"Really?"

Marilyn was reaching down for the bag when the waiter walked up. "Here's your drinks, ladies. Do you still need a few more minutes to look over the menus?"

"I'm sorry," Marilyn said. "We've been just gabbing away. We'll look at them now."

"No problem, I'll be back in a few."

"My treat, by the way," Marilyn said to Michele.

"Mom, you can't do that."

"Why not? I'm out with my daughter, we're doing wedding things. If your dad and I were together, I'd be doing this very thing on this very day."

"But isn't Dad going to be upset when he gets this bill?"

Marilyn thought a moment. "He might be. I'll tell you what, I'll pay for it myself."

"With what?"

"I'm working now."

"But you have bills now too. Just let me pay for my own dinner."

"No, it's my treat. Besides, I'm all paid up on my bills for the first thirty days. Now let's stop talking and read these menus before that nice young man comes back."

Marilyn smiled and opened the menu. After a few minutes, the waiter returned with their drinks and took their orders. Marilyn ordered a seafood manicotti dish. She was able to talk Michele into the item she had clearly been staring at but avoiding because of the price: beef braciole in a red wine tomato sauce. After the waiter left, Marilyn bent down and put the Odds-n-Ends bag on the table. She had to set it on its side to slide the gift box out.

"What is it?" Michele asked.

"Wait till you see." Marilyn carefully pried open the lid and lifted the shiny wooden box out.

"Is it a jewelry box?"

"Just wait." She opened the lid, revealing a figurine of a beautiful girl in a flowing blue dress. The girl had auburn hair and porcelain smooth skin. She spun slowly in the center of the box, her arms swirling above her head.. Music began to play. But not just any music. "Do you recognize the song?" Marilyn stared at the dancing girl. Michele didn't answer. Marilyn looked across the table. Tears welled up in Michele's eyes.

She did remember.

"'Somewhere My Love,'" Marilyn said softly. "Remember? It was 'Lara's Theme' from the movie *Dr. Zhivago*. I saw it in the store, and the dancer instantly reminded me of you. A customer asked to hear the song, so I turned the key and I couldn't believe what came out."

Michele reached for the linen napkin and dabbed her eyes.

"Remember how we used to dance together in the living room to this song, when you were taking dancing lessons?" Marilyn said.

"That was . . . so much fun," Michele said. "You'd push all the furniture off to the side, roll up the oriental rug, and we'd spin around and around."

"Just in our socks on the wood floor," Marilyn added, then sighed. "I was awful, but you danced beautifully."

"What are you talking about, Mom? I was a clumsy twelve-year-old. *You* were the dancer. I loved watching the way you moved."

Marilyn shook her head. "I don't think we're having the same memory, darling." She suddenly realized the music box was a little loud for the space, even though they were outside. Several women at tables nearby were staring. "I better close this."

"No, not yet," said a petite elderly woman at the table to her right. "Please. Not till the song finishes." She sat next to another woman, about her same age. Both finely dressed. "My late husband, he was such a great singer. He'd sing that song to me. We'd turn the music up loud and swirl across the floor."

"You two were like Fred Astaire and Ginger Rogers," her friend said. She looked at Marilyn and Michele. "I'm not exaggerating."

"I'd love to be able to dance like that," Marilyn said, her eyes shifting to the dancer in the music box. "But I never got the—" She was suddenly overcome with emotion. She reached for her napkin. Michele leaned over and patted her hand.

"It's never too late to learn," the elderly woman said.

Yes it is, Marilyn thought. She was much too old to try something like that. And besides, who would she dance with? Michele? Her daughter wasn't a little girl anymore; she had Allan now. Marilyn had no one.

Not now and really . . . not ever.

Michele seemed to sense what she was feeling. "She's right, Mom. I remember how we danced. You really are a natural. I'm sure with a few lessons—"

"I'm not a natural." She looked across the table. "But thanks for saying it." The song ended, and she closed the lid. "But I have this music box now. And I can play it whenever I want . . . and remember how much fun you and I had together . . . a long time ago."

"Well," the older woman said. "Thank you for sharing your music box with us. Brought back a lovely memory for me too."

"You're welcome," Marilyn said. She lifted the music box and set it back in the gift box it came in. She looked up. "I better get this off the table, the waiter's coming with our salad." She set the bag gently on the floor beside her purse. When she looked up, the elderly woman reached out her hand.

"I'm going to leave you two alone to enjoy your dinner, I promise. My sister and I need to be going. But here, take this card, just in case you change your mind."

Marilyn took it and read the words "The Windsor Dance Studio."

"That's not our studio," the woman said, "well, not anymore. But I still go there sometimes to help out. They have all kinds of classes for every kind of dance, including ballroom. That's my favorite. There's a new beginner's class starting up this week, and it's reasonably priced too."

"But I'm too old to start—"

"No, you're not. Excuse me, I don't mean to interrupt, but honestly, more than half the people who take these classes are your age or older. And the studio is right here downtown, on the ground floor of one of the buildings right around the corner on Oak Lane."

Marilyn looked at the card again as the waiter came up carrying a big bowl of salad.

"C'mon, Mom," Michele said. "Do it. You'd have so much fun."

Fun, Marilyn thought. Was that reason enough to do anything? It was such an unfamiliar concept. But then, isn't that why she had left Jim? To finally do things she wanted to do, things he'd never allow her to even try? "I don't know," she said.

The elderly woman stood up. "Well, just think about it. And thanks again for allowing us to intrude on your time together. That's a lovely music box, by the way."

Yes, Marilyn thought, looking down at her purchase.

Yes, it is.

13

Marilyn and Michele had decided to take some of the delicious Italian food home in containers, so they could leave room to split a large slice of tiramisu. "Here," Michele said, handing her mother a list of names. "We better get this over with before the waiter brings the dessert."

Marilyn looked over Michele's wedding invitation list, immediately noticing all the crossed-off names.

"They're all from your old church," Michele said. "I left some of the nicer people on there, the ones you seem to get along with. But you better give it a look, make sure I didn't go too far. I don't want to get you in too much trouble."

Marilyn took a sip of coffee and finished scanning the list. "I'm not the one you have to worry about, it's your father." She looked up. "I don't have a problem with a single name you crossed off." She was a little concerned about what Jim's reaction would be when he heard they were having the wedding in the park instead of the church.

"Well," Michele said, "when he sees the final list, we can

emphasize how much money he'll be saving now. He's always stressing about money these days."

She was right about that. But Jim cared about image even more. "Well, he doesn't tell me everything going on with his business. I know he's lost some major clients the last couple of years. He lost another one last week. But, I'd say go ahead and send the invitations out to all those left on the list. Tomorrow morning, after your father is safely off to work, I'm going to sneak back in the house to get a few things. I'll put this list on his dresser with a little Post-it note, so he can see who we're still inviting. But be prepared, he may insist we add back a few names."

The waiter came up and set the tiramisu between them. "I've brought you two new forks," he said. "Would you like a separate dessert plate?"

"That's okay," Marilyn said. "We'll just share it."

He refilled their coffee cups and left.

"I was just thinking, Mom. Let me redo this list first, so I can delete all the crossed-off names. It might be worse if Dad actually saw the names crossed off. Do you have a printer where you're staying?"

"I've seen Charlotte use one to print coupons. I'm sure she won't mind if I borrow it." She reached her fork over and snatched a bite of dessert. "Oh my, this is delicious."

Michele took a bite. A strained expression came over her face.

"You don't like it? We can order something else."

"No, it's delicious. I was just thinking . . . is there any chance Dad would . . ."

"What? What's the matter?"

"You don't think Dad will refuse to pay for the wedding now. Now that you guys are separated."

"No, I'm sure he'd never do something like that."

"I've been pretty hard on him over the phone the last few days. He knows I'm on your side in this."

Marilyn thought a moment. "How hard?"

"I don't know," she said. "I haven't yelled or screamed at him. But I've definitely been talking to him in a way I never have before. You know, just telling him like it is."

Marilyn wished she had been talking to Jim like that, for a long time. He needed a strong dose of telling-it-like-it-is. The closest she'd come was the letter she'd left on her dresser. She was relieved he'd honored her request and left her alone. She hadn't really expected him to. At some point, though, she'd have to face him in person. "Well, maybe you better lighten up a little, Michele. I don't think he'd do anything rash, like not pay for the wedding. But still, he is your—"

"Do you guys still have the money for the wedding with all of Dad's business problems? Can we still use the budget we talked about a few months ago?"

"What? Yes. If there's one thing your father's good at, it's budgeting and finances. He set the money aside for your wedding quite a while ago. I looked at the account before I . . . did this. It was all there."

"Do you think he'll still walk me down the aisle?"

"Of course he will, honey. He still loves you. That's never going to change." Marilyn said this with an air of certainty.

But if she was so sure, why had it just popped into her head that they could always ask Michele's brother Tom if they needed to?

Jim dried off from his shower and dressed in casual clothes. He'd showered once already this morning, but it had been a scorcher out on the golf course today. Playing later in the day didn't help. Even in the shade, there was no escaping the humidity. He didn't normally play on Sunday afternoons, but he figured, why not? It wasn't as if Marilyn would be upset.

He'd played with a group of strangers. He wasn't in the mood to call Harold or any of his regular golfing buddies. Most went to his church, and then he'd have to explain why he'd skipped out that morning. He'd wrestled over the decision. Part of him felt he should be there; his presence might offset all the gossip about Marilyn leaving. But, he realized, it would probably go on just the same. Being there, he'd feel the sting of every stare.

Wasn't gossip supposed to be wrong? When did it become okay to talk about people behind their backs, in church, no less? It made him angry as he thought about it, everyone talking about him and his problems, led by their queen, Sophie Mitchell. They'd speculate about all the reasons why Marilyn had left. Most of the blame would be put on him.

He was the man, after all, the head of the house. Hadn't God blamed Adam for all of Eve's sins? And why would a reasonable woman move out of such a gorgeous house to live in some dinky apartment, unless her husband was some kind of ogre? But Jim wasn't an ogre. He knew plenty of husbands who were—even at church. Guys who yelled all the time, barked out orders, with everybody walking on eggshells whenever they were around.

Jim wasn't like that. He never yelled at Marilyn, or Doug. They had conflicts sometimes, but who didn't? He always made it a point to keep his volume under control. She had no right to put him in that light, give all those people reason to think he was the bad guy here.

After putting his shoes on, he stood and walked to the mirror, made sure hairs weren't sticking out where they didn't belong.

He heard something downstairs and for a moment thought it might be Marilyn. Stepping into the hall, he heard Doug's voice talking loudly on his cell phone.

Now there was an idea, maybe he and Doug could get some time together. He was starving. As he got to the bottom of the stairs, he saw Doug heading toward the back of the house. "Hey, Doug, hold up." Doug turned around. "Thought maybe you and I could get something to eat together. What do you say?"

"Uh . . . sorry, Dad, I can't. Didn't you get my text?"

"Text? No. What's going on?"

"I sent it this afternoon while you were out golfing. A bunch of the guys are showing up at Jason's for pizza in about . . ." He glanced at his watch. "Ten minutes from now. We're having a big Xbox tournament."

"Oh."

"Maybe another time. Gotta go or I'll be late."

"Okay." He sighed. "Don't be out too late, it's a Sunday."

"Yeah, but there's no school tomorrow—it's summertime, remember?"

"That's right. Well . . . have fun."

"I will. See ya." He turned and headed out the patio door toward the garage.

Jim heard the sound of a car out front, then the engine turning off. A car door closed. Who could it be? He walked into the living room and opened the sheers a few inches.

Oh no. Anyone but him.

It was Mort Stanley, the head deacon of their church.

14

Jim decided to wait for the doorbell. He didn't want Mort to think he was sitting around with nothing to do. Once it rang, it dawned on him . . . he didn't have any refreshments in the house. That was Marilyn's department. He waited a few moments then opened the door. "Mort, what a surprise. Come on in."

"Evening, Jim." Mort walked in, dressed in a suit and tie.

Mort Stanley was an extremely successful attorney in town. Jim rarely saw him when he wasn't dressed like this. He couldn't read Mort's mood by the expression on his face, but that wasn't unusual. Mort had a great poker face, which came in handy leading a board of deacons made up of businessmen and professionals.

"Can I get you some coffee? I'd have to make it, but I'd be happy to put—"

"I can't stay long enough for coffee, Jim." He walked farther in, past the foyer into the living room.

"Well, have a seat then," Jim said. "You can talk freely, by the way. We're alone."

"That's mostly why I'm here," Mort said. "You being alone."

"What?"

"I'm sure you know what I've come here to talk about."

Jim did, but he said, "No, I'm not sure."

Mort sat in a stuffed armchair. Jim walked over and sat on the leather sofa closest to him.

"C'mon, Jim, it's about you and Marilyn. Four or five people came up to me this morning at church. 'Have you heard about Jim and Marilyn?' Of course, I hadn't, so I said no each time. And of course, they went on to tell me. To be honest, I would have preferred hearing something like that from you."

"You mean about Marilyn leaving?" Jim regretted saying it. Of course, that's what this was about. Mort Stanley was an intimidating presence at a board meeting, much more so in a man's living room.

"So it's true."

"Well . . . yes and no," Jim said. "She's not here now, and we are apparently having some difficulty."

"What I heard is that the two of you are separated."

"Not legally," Jim said. "And I don't think it's going to come to that. She's just a little upset about something, and she's taking a few days to cool off. I'm sure this whole thing will blow over very soon."

Mort stared at him a few moments. "You're not lying to me, Jim. Trying to spin something here, are you? Are either of you seeing someone else?"

"No," Jim said. "There's no adultery in play here, Mort. I can assure you of that." He was at least sure of his part.

Mort took a deep breath, looked down at the floor a moment then back at Jim. "You need to get this situation back in hand. Very soon. Terrible timing for something like this to occur.

We've got that big board meeting coming up in two weeks, and that office space of yours is a big item on the agenda. Have you forgotten about that?"

Jim felt sick. He had forgotten. Completely. The church was seriously considering leasing one of Jim's properties to serve as the seniors fellowship center for the next year, until they raised the necessary funds to expand the church building.

"It might be on the chopping block if you can't reel Marilyn in. Sam Hall is one of the people who came up to me today."

Sam Hall. Of course. Sam was also on the deacon board and would love nothing better than to see Jim lose this opportunity. He had a property in the running, but his was smaller and farther away.

"You know I've been going to bat for you ever since this idea first got introduced. I've already drawn up a lease agreement for our next board meeting—had one of my staff attorneys write it . . . at my expense. I was hoping we could get everything settled that night. Maybe even sign the papers. But if you and Marilyn are splitting up, I—"

"We're not splitting up, Mort."

"Is Marilyn here?"

"No."

"Where is she?"

"I . . . I don't know."

"You don't know?"

"She's not talking to me at the moment, but I know she's staying in an apartment for the time being, with a—"

"She won't even talk to you? Jim, that's not good."

"I know it's not, but believe me, it's not that serious. My daughter Michele knows where she is."

Mort released a sigh, his poker face slipping. "Is that supposed to sound reassuring? Your *daughter* knows where your wife is?"

"I'm going to find out, tomorrow. I promise. I know where she works."

"Jim, I'm a lawyer. I've watched couples split up for decades. I don't think you're living in reality. Your wife has left you. She won't talk to you. You don't even know where she is, and let me guess, she doesn't want you to find her. She wants you to leave her completely alone. Am I right?"

Jim didn't want to agree.

"Am I right?" he asked again, with a little more edge.

"Yes."

He shook his head. "That sounds pretty serious to me. Sam said this morning he wants us to call an emergency deacons' meeting this week, to take another vote on this property matter. He's already spoken to a few of the other deacons—men who voted our way the last time. They're saying if you and Marilyn are splitting up, it would definitely affect the way they'd vote this time around."

This was great, just great. "I'm telling you, Mort, Marilyn and I are not splitting up. We're just having a difficult time. Is that not allowed in our church? Are you telling me that none of the other deacons have ever hit a rough patch in their marriage? They all get along with their wives a hundred percent of the time?"

"No," he said. "But none of their wives have ever walked out on them like this. Jim, we're not just talking about losing the lease opportunity on your building here. To be a deacon in this church—and I'd venture to say, any church in our denomination—you can't have a scandal like this going on behind the scenes. It's a moral thing too. Deacons are held to a certain standard, even the Bible says that."

"So what are you saying?"

"I'm saying, if you can't get Marilyn to come back or maybe sit down with a marriage counselor, you're probably going to have to resign from the deacon board too."

Jim sat back against the cushion, totally deflated. Look at what Marilyn's foolishness was costing them. She probably had no idea. She was off trying to find herself, spread her wings, or some other stupid thing going through her head. And now he was about to lose another significant income source for their family. Not to mention the humiliation she was creating for him at church. The ripple effects of something like this could be devastating to his business and reputation.

"I'm sorry to have to say things like this to you, Jim. Honestly, I am. There's still time to turn this thing around, if you can get Marilyn to snap out of this soon. I can hold Sam off for a little while, but you know how these things work. Politics aren't pretty, church politics especially." He stood up. "You've got to figure out what's bugging Marilyn and do something to get her happy again."

"How much time do I have?"

Mort walked toward the front door. "I think I can buy you two weeks, tops. Till that board meeting we already have on the calendar. But if you can't turn this thing around, at least get her to move back in here while you work things out . . . I don't know. You need to be prepared for the board going with Sam on this property thing, and asking you to resign."

"Would I have to leave the church?"

"No, nothing like that." He looked at his watch. "Look, I've got a dinner I need to get to downtown. I'm really sorry to have to come here like this, but I didn't feel right talking about such things over the phone."

They were standing by the door now, so Jim opened it. "I appreciate that, Mort. I really think you all are making way more out of this than the situation calls for. I'll do my best to get things turned around in time."

"You do that, Jim. I'll be pulling for you." He walked through the door onto the porch then turned around. "A word of advice?"

"What?"

"Don't be driving down to where Marilyn works and make some big scene. This is the lawyer in me talking now. You don't want that. You confront her there, in front of a bunch of witnesses? Not good. Believe me. That'll only make things worse."

15

"I have to do this, Jean. I can't just sit back and do nothing, watch my family fall apart." Tom Anderson started searching every horizontal surface in the house. "Know where I put my keys?"

His wife Jean walked up, holding them in her hand. "Two things. First, they're right here. You left them on the dinner table. If you'd put them in the same place every time, you wouldn't have to go through this frantic search whenever you leave the house. And second, *your* family isn't falling apart. We're your family, remember? Me, Tommy, and Carly. That's what we did on our wedding day." She tapped a framed photograph of their wedding that was hanging in the hall. "We started a new Anderson family unit."

Tom walked over and took the keys. "I know that, and you know what I mean."

"I'm not sure I do," she said. "I don't see why you think you have to go out another night and leave me by myself to take care of the kids. What happened to our heart-to-heart chat last week about you coming home from work on time more often and giving me a break?"

"I'm still going to do that."

"When? You've been out the last five nights in a row."

"I have not. You were with me the last two."

"Okay, and the other three you didn't get home from work until almost eight o'clock."

"I got paid overtime."

"That's not the point. The kids are in bed by then, and I had to do everything myself. I asked you about it, nicely, and you said on Monday—remember Monday?—that you'd be home on time, you'd help me with the kids. Then the two of us would relax together on the couch, just like old times. Remember?"

"I remember, but that was before my mom decided to walk out on my dad. Besides, I'm not going to be gone that long." He turned and walked toward the front door.

"The Starbucks you picked for your little family meeting is an hour away."

"It's only forty-five minutes this time of night. I had to pick someplace in the middle. I couldn't ask Michele to do all the driving."

"What about Doug?"

"He said he was coming." Of course, Tom had to bend his elbow to get him to agree.

"Couldn't you just talk to them on the phone? You're not going to be home till after the kids' bedtime . . . again."

"Come here," he said gently, holding out his arms. She came and he hugged her. "I'm sorry. I don't want to go out again. I'd rather stay here with you and the kids. But this is important. It's not the kind of thing you can do over the phone. We need to talk this out. I thought if anyone would understand what I'm trying to do, you would." Jean's parents had divorced four years ago, right after the two of them had gotten married.

"All right," she said, looking up at him. "Go on, go fix it."

"I don't think I can fix this. I'm just hoping to get the three of us on the same page." Tom hoped Doug wouldn't bail out on him. Michele said she'd be there, though she wasn't happy about the idea. "Look, I promise I'll be home after work on time tomorrow, and we won't go out anywhere. And if you want, we can skip our home group meeting on Wednesday night, make it two nights in a row."

"Don't promise," she said. "Just do it."

"Give me a kiss. I've gotta go if I'm going to be there on time."

Tom drove through Orlando, the traffic on I-4 was crowded, but it kept moving. He made it through without losing his temper once and got off the exit for Celebration. He'd picked this location for their meeting mainly because it was halfway between where he lived and Lakeland, where Michele went to school. And because it had a nice Starbucks with an outdoor patio.

He liked Starbucks, but Michele loved it. He thought it might help her overcome her reluctance to meet. And she loved Celebration. She said it reminded her of River Oaks "without all the baggage." Doug, on the other hand, wouldn't have been happy no matter where Tom had set the meeting.

Although Tom and Michele weren't that close, he felt more optimistic about her future since she and Allan had gotten engaged. Allan was a solid guy. But Doug? Tom had real concerns about his little brother. And this thing going on between his folks now only magnified those concerns. As Tom drove through the neighborhood streets toward the downtown area, he was reminded of just how similar Celebration and River Oaks were.

He admired the magnificent homes on both sides of the street—another thing both towns had in common. It reminded him of another thing: how impossible it was for him and Jean to ever afford a place like one of these. He'd never reach his dad's level of success, not at this pace. Why had he bought that stupid house when he did? The mortgage payment was killing him every time he wrote out the check. It would take years for the equity to get to the break-even point, even if he sold it. Why hadn't he—

No, he had to stop thinking about it, stay focused on his time with Doug and Michele. He turned down Celebration's version of Main Street and started looking for a parking space. The Starbucks was just around the corner on the right. There were no spots on the street, but he was glad to see Michele's and Doug's cars as he drove by. He pulled into the parking lot behind the building.

Just as he turned off the car, his phone rang. Glancing at the screen, he saw it was Uncle Henry. He looked at his watch. Should he answer it? He liked Uncle Henry, but sometimes he could talk. It rang two more times. "Hello."

"Hey, Tom, it's Uncle Henry. How ya doing?"

"I'm doing fine, Uncle Henry. How about you?" He should tell him right away he couldn't talk.

"Listen," Uncle Henry said, "I'm sure you know about the troubles your mom and dad are having."

"Yeah, actually—"

"I'm just calling because I've left messages on both their machines, but neither of them have called me back." Tom decided not to point out that people didn't use answering machines anymore. "Do you know how they're doing?" Uncle Henry continued. "Aunt Myra and I've been praying for them and your whole family. Wish there was something we could do."

"To be honest, I'm not sure what any of us can do. I'm just about to have a little meeting with Michele and Doug at this coffee shop."

"Are you? That's good. You tell them we said hi."

"I will," Tom said. "Maybe I'll know a little more after our meeting. I think Michele knows more than anyone what's going on. She's the only one Mom will talk to."

"That's too bad," Uncle Henry said. "Not that she's talking to Michele, I mean. I just wish your mom would let someone else get involved, like a pastor or a counselor. I'm a little concerned about Michele getting stuck in the middle."

"I am too," Tom said. "But look, I've got to go. They're in there waiting for me."

"Well, you go on then. Tell them Aunt Myra and I are praying for you guys."

"I will." Tom got out and closed the car door. Prayer, he thought.

Yeah, they could definitely use some prayer here.

16

Tom walked around the corner toward the Starbucks and noticed through the wrought-iron fence a few empty tables in the café area. A moment later, a hand waved at him. It was Doug sitting next to Michele at a table under a green umbrella. Tom came around through the opening and joined them. They didn't have drinks. "You guys aren't thirsty?"

"We're plenty thirsty," Doug said. "We don't have jobs."

Tom laughed. "So . . . I'm paying?"

"You're the one that dragged us down here," Michele said. She was kidding.

"Guess it's my treat then," Tom said.

Michele told him what she wanted and said, "I'll stay here and keep the table."

Doug began giving Tom his order. "Uh-uh, little brother. I can't carry three cups back here."

"Just ask for those little cardboard containers," Doug said.

Tom shook his head. "Off your butt, c'mon." They walked through the glass door and stood in line. "You know, I would have given you a ride." Doug still lived at home, which was a little farther out than where Tom lived.

"I know," Doug said. "But I was already more than halfway here. Met some friends this afternoon for a movie at Universal City Walk. Then we grabbed a bite to eat."

"Good to know you have money for some things."

"Yeah, but not much. Dad's cut my allowance in half this summer."

They stepped up to the counter. Tom ordered his drink and Michele's, Doug ordered his. After paying, they stepped around to the side counter and waited. "Weren't you supposed to be getting a job this summer?" Tom said. "You know, that's how most people solve their money problems."

"Now you sound like Dad."

"You say that like it's a bad thing." Tom smiled. Doug made a face. "What are you, seventeen now, Doug? You don't even shave yet."

"I've been shaving for over a year, almost two."

"All right, the point is, you're at the awkward age between being a kid and becoming a man."

"Oh, man. Really? This is how you're gonna make me pay for the coffee?"

"This isn't a lecture," Tom said. "I'm just saying, you're used to Dad always paying your way. I get that. Did the same thing myself once. But in the real world, things don't work that way. We've got a word now in society for guys that refuse to grow up, who live with their folks forever and won't take responsibility for themselves. Begins with an *L* . . . a big *L*."

Doug's face confirmed he knew the *L* was for *loser*. "Okay, big brother, now you sound even worse than Dad. First off . . . as you pointed out, I'm only seventeen. I'm not 'living with my folks forever.' Second, I'm not refusing to grow up. I'm not grown up, not yet. Just got my driver's license a year ago. I can't drink alcohol. I can't even vote."

"Here's your drinks, guys," the barista said. They walked over to another counter to fix them.

"Good points, Doug. I came on too strong."

"Apology accepted," Doug said. "But I didn't get to my third point. You've probably heard, the economy isn't so good."

"No, I hadn't heard," Tom said sarcastically. "So you've been out there beating the bushes every day, trying to find a job, and you keep getting turned down. Is that it?"

A long pause.

"Guess that answers my question," Tom said. "C'mon, Doug, lighten up. I'm not ragging on you. I just know the reason Dad keeps bugging you about getting a job is that his business isn't doing so well. Did you know that?"

"No, he never mentioned that."

"It's like you said, the economy isn't doing so good. Dad's lost a lot of clients. He's having to pay mortgages on a number of properties with no rent coming in."

"Really?"

"Really. He doesn't have the kind of money flowing in he had a few years ago."

Doug put the lid on his caramel macchiato and took a sip. "He told you that? Why didn't he tell me? All he does is nag me and make me feel stupid."

Tom thought a moment and realized that Dad hadn't told him about his finances, not in so many words. Tom figured it out by piecing different parts of conversations together. "You know Dad, he doesn't share his thoughts and struggles that easily."

"That's an understatement."

"The other thing is, with Mom walking out like this, I'm sure he's worried about what that might do to their finances. But let's hold up on that until we sit down with Michele." He opened the door for Doug. They walked out and sat at the table.

"Here you go." Tom handed Michele her drink. "You like it how it comes, right?"

"You remembered." She took a sip. "So . . . what's on your mind? Obviously, it's about Mom and Dad."

"Guess we'll skip the small talk," Tom said.

"I already did my small talk in line," Doug added. "Tom knows I shave now."

"That's great." Michele took a sip of her latte.

"Well," Tom said, "I just thought the three of us should meet, make sure we're all on the same page about what's going on with Mom and Dad."

"The same page?" Doug said. "What page is that?"

Tom sat back. "Just that we're all in agreement, we want Mom and Dad to get back together as soon as possible, and we don't want this thing ending up with them getting divorced."

"Divorced?" Doug said. "Are things that bad?"

"I haven't heard Mom talk about divorce, Tom," Michele said.

"Maybe not. But you know how these things go. She's moved out, Michele. Dad said she won't even talk to him."

"I know that. But she told me she just wants a little time away, to sort out how she feels."

"Okay . . . and what if after a little time away, Mom decides she feels like she doesn't want to be married anymore? She wants to make this permanent. What then?"

"You're taking a big jump," Michele said. "She's only been gone a few days."

"You've said it yourself, Mom's unhappy," Tom said.

"Real unhappy," Michele added.

"Like enough to move out," Doug said.

"Right." Tom sat forward and reached for his cup. "And unhappy people are usually depressed. And depressed people are often vulnerable. They might do all kinds of things they wouldn't normally do to break out of their depression."

"Like what?" Michele said.

"Like . . . what if some man starts showing her a little interest. Sees her as an available single woman? She's pretty attractive for her age. If Mom's been unhappy a long time—"

"There's no *if*. She has, Tom. A very long time."

"You're just strengthening my point, Michele. All the more reason for us to try and do what we can to push her back toward—"

"We can't push her, Tom. Not now. Believe me, that would definitely backfire."

"All right, push isn't the right word. I mean . . . try to influence her not to let this thing drag on too long, before something happens."

"Guys," Doug said. "I don't see Mom going out on Dad. She's not like that."

Tom looked at him. "Anyone is capable of doing anything when they're unhappy, Doug, believe me." Both gave him a look that said, *What are you talking about?* "I'm not saying I know firsthand," he quickly added. "Well, in a way I am. That's how I got stuck buying this inflated house we're in right now."

"Buying an overpriced house is not in the same league as adultery," Michele said. "Mom has a strong walk with God."

Tom looked at her. "Michele, tell me you think there's no way something like that can happen. You know Mom better than any of us. Are you absolutely sure?"

She didn't answer.

"See?" he said. "You know it's possible. And even if that doesn't happen, it's still not good for them to be apart like this. We need to do whatever we can to help her see that. At least get her to be willing to see a marriage counselor, get the two of them talking again."

"I don't have a problem with what you're saying," Doug said. "But I don't see how I can make any difference. What can I do? She's not even in the house anymore."

"I don't know," Tom said. "Start praying, for one thing. Ask God to start softening her heart."

"You mean both their hearts," Michele said. "I'd say Dad's heart's even harder than hers."

Tom doubted that. "He's not the one who walked out."

"No, but do you understand *why* she walked out? Have you spent any time thinking about how unhappy she must have been to do something that drastic?"

Tom realized he hadn't. But to him, it didn't matter. You don't walk out on your marriage. Period. "I don't see Jean ever walking out on me like that," he said. "Short of me being unfaithful . . . which isn't going to happen."

"Are you *absolutely* sure?" she said, somewhat mocking the question he'd asked a few moments ago. She set her coffee down. "Like you said, people are capable of doing anything when they're unhappy."

17

It was Tuesday evening, a little after six-thirty. Marilyn and Charlotte had just finished eating another Lean Cuisine dinner. Marilyn had worked during the day today and had intended to come home and fix them both a real dinner. But she still wasn't used to being on her feet so long. She knew as soon as she'd walked through the front door, she didn't have the energy to start cooking.

She came out of the bathroom after brushing her teeth and stopped a moment in front of her dresser to admire her music box. She must have polished it three times already since bringing it home.

Home . . . it felt funny thinking of this little apartment bedroom that way. She couldn't resist it, so she lifted the lid of the box. The music started playing, and the beautiful dancing girl started twirling around.

"I love that song! From *Doctor Zhivago*, right?"

Marilyn looked up to see Charlotte's happy face in the doorway.

"All right if I come in?"

"Sure."

"I saw that sitting on your dresser yesterday, and I wanted to open it in the worst way. I thought maybe it was a jewelry box, so I didn't."

"Isn't it beautiful?" Marilyn said. "I got it at Odds-n-Ends, with my employee discount." She felt silly saying it so proudly.

"She's gorgeous," Charlotte said. She began humming the melody. "She's not really a ballerina, though. The dancing girl."

"No, she's not. I think that's what caught my eye," Marilyn said. "Besides the song. She's dressed more like she's doing a waltz. She reminds me of my daughter Michele when she was younger."

"Does she dance like that?" Charlotte asked.

"Not really. When she was a little girl she did." Marilyn told Charlotte all about how she and Michele used to dance together in the living room. When she was done, Marilyn noticed the business card the elderly woman had given her at the restaurant, sitting there on the dresser beside the music box. She picked it up.

"What's that?" Charlotte said, standing right next to her. "The Windsor Dance Studio . . . where have I heard that name?"

"An elderly woman gave it to me Sunday when I was eating dinner with Michele at Giovanni's. She heard the music playing, and we chatted a little while. She loved the song too. She said she and her husband used to dance to it, before he died, and he'd sing the words. She was so cute. I think they used to own the studio. She still goes there to help out sometimes." Marilyn closed the music box.

"That's right. That's where I heard the name. A young girl came into Urgent Care a few days ago with a sprained ankle.

It happened at that studio, and she was trying to get them to pay the bill."

"Oh my."

"The owner came down—I guess the new owner—he was a real looker, I'm tellin' ya. Think his name was Roberto. Tall, dark, and handsome." She smiled. "All the nurses were talking about him after he left. Can't repeat some of the things they were sayin', if you get my meaning. But I was thinking, I could just see him out there on the dance floor. Kind of reminded me of that Latin actor, you know, what's his name?"

"Antonio Banderas?"

"That's it. Only this Roberto guy was taller. Listen to me, like I know how tall Antonio Banderas is."

"So this girl sprained her ankle dancing?" Marilyn said. She didn't like the sound of that. She had actually half-talked herself into giving it a try.

"Yeah, she made quite a scene. Roberto wound up covering her bill, but he made it pretty clear he didn't think his studio was responsible."

"Do you know what kind of dance she was doing?"

"It was a swing class. But this Roberto said she was showing off, doing all kinds of moves that he wasn't asking them to. Her partner was apparently flipping her all over the place. Through his legs, over his head, things like that."

Well, that was some relief. Marilyn had no interest in anything that radical.

"Why, you thinking about taking lessons?"

"Maybe. Michele thinks I should."

"Have you ever taken lessons before?"

"Are you kidding? Jim would never let me do that."

"You serious? He would actually forbid you?"

"Well, maybe not *forbid* me. But I never felt like I could even bring up something like that. I already told you how much he hated dancing. So why would I even consider it? Besides, who would I dance with?"

"Obviously not with him, but seriously, Marilyn, you should do it. Dancing's back in vogue these days. You see all those dance shows on TV. People of all ages are learning how."

"But I can't do something like that . . . alone."

"Who says?" Charlotte started walking toward the doorway, then turned. "It's not like you'd be going out on Jim. It's a dance studio. There's probably lots of people there without partners. Dancing with someone isn't the same as dating or getting into a relationship. You just do it for the fun of it. Just because you want to. What's the harm?" She shrugged her shoulders. "I'm making some decaf, want some?"

"I'd love some."

Charlotte walked out. Marilyn set the business card on the dresser beside the music box and reread the information. Could she do something like that, take dance lessons? By herself? It was a crazy idea. It was probably too expensive anyway. She had to start being careful with her money now.

Just then Charlotte poked her head inside her door. "You know what? They're probably open right now. Most people work during the day and take lessons at night. Why don't you call down there, get some more information?"

"You really think I should?"

"I definitely do. Sounds like your daughter thinks so too."

Marilyn picked the card back up. "But I wasn't thinking about taking swing lessons, at least not at first."

"I'm sure they teach all kinds of dance styles down there.

Swing, ballroom, country western . . . probably even the polka. Give them a call. Can't hurt."

She was right. It couldn't hurt to call. Charlotte walked out again. Marilyn got her phone out of her purse and dialed the number. It rang two times, and she hung up.

I can't do this, she thought. Who am I kidding?

18

The following day, a Wednesday, Marilyn worked the daytime shift again at Odds-n-Ends. She was beginning to feel more comfortable in her new role there and was actually able to answer about half of the customers' questions without seeking Harriet's help. And she'd become a whiz on the cash register.

In idle moments throughout the morning, she'd been mulling over her conversation with Charlotte about taking dance lessons. The desire to "give it a try" had formed into a decision to do so when a woman about ten years older came into the store and fell in love with the same music box.

The woman set it down on the counter and lifted the lid. "Isn't this just the most beautiful thing?" she said. "And I just love that song."

Marilyn rang it up on the cash register. "I bought this same music box just the other night."

"My oldest granddaughter is eight," the woman said, "and she just started taking dance lessons. I'm going to get this for her."

"She's going to love it," Marilyn said.

"By the way," said the woman, "was I wrong to bring this one up? Isn't it a floor model?"

"No, we keep all our stock on the shelves."

The woman leaned forward, as if telling a secret. "This was the last one."

"That's okay," Marilyn said. "You can buy it. I ordered two more, they should be in this afternoon."

"Oh good," the woman said. "I didn't want to have to come back. I live over an hour away."

Marilyn wrapped it carefully for the woman and set it in the bag. After the woman left, Marilyn heard the back door open and close and turned to find Emma coming in from the hallway. She glanced at her watch. "Oh good, Emma, you're just in time to relieve me for lunch."

Emma set her purse behind the counter. "I just finished eating mine on the way in. It was delicious, a chicken salad wrap. I almost died when a big splotch of honey mustard fell out of it. Fortunately, it dropped on the steering wheel, not on my blouse. Going anywhere special?"

Marilyn smiled. "Kind of," she said. "But not to eat." She picked up her purse and started walking from behind the counter.

"Well, are you going to tell me?" Emma said.

She almost didn't want to say. "I'm going over to a dance studio to see about signing up for some lessons."

"Really?"

Really, Marilyn repeated in her mind. Was she really going to do this? "I think so. If it's not too expensive."

"I'd love to do something like that."

"Why don't you?"

"I can't. Between school . . . and work . . . and homework."

"What kind of lessons would you take if you could?"

"Probably swing. But I also like the Latin ones. You know, the rumba, the cha-cha, the mambo." Marilyn had heard of them but couldn't tell one from the other. "What are you hoping to learn?" Emma said.

"I have no idea," Marilyn said. "But I better go. Gotta be back in thirty minutes."

Marilyn had looked up the Windsor Dance Studio's website last night and was surprised to find it was only two blocks away from the store. It was a nice day, so she decided to walk. It occupied two large storefront suites on Oakland Avenue. She walked past the big glass windows, happy to see the view inside was mostly blocked by curtains, except for the area by the front door. She didn't cherish the idea of all those people on the street looking in at her like she was some fish in an aquarium as she hobbled her way through dance lessons.

She stood at the door, took a deep breath, and opened it. A little chime rang above her head, but there wasn't anyone sitting at a desk by the carpeted entrance. To the right, a large wooden dance floor took up most of the space, but the place was empty. The lights were off except over the desk. She looked around, but there was no little bell to ring. Should she leave?

"Oh, sorry to keep you waiting."

She looked up into the smiling face of, yes . . . a tall, dark, handsome Latin man with wavy hair. He stepped into the reception area through a doorway on the back wall. She smiled, thinking of what Charlotte had said. "You must be Roberto." Marilyn held out her hand.

"Yes, I'm Roberto. A pleasure to meet you, Miss . . ."

"I'm Marilyn—Mrs. Marilyn Anderson."

He shook her hand. "And how can I help you? Do you wish to learn how to dance?"

"Well, yes, I guess I do. But I can come back another time if you're closed."

"No, we're open. But there are no lessons scheduled at the moment. Have you ever taken lessons before?"

"No, but I used to take my daughter to a dance class."

"I see. Come over here and have a seat." He pointed to some cushioned chairs set in front of the desk while he sat behind it. "What kind of lessons did she take?"

"Some ballet, and something like jazz, but I forget what they called it."

"We have a ballet class for young girls here at two today. One of my dance instructors teaches it. I only work with adults. What kind of lessons are you interested in taking?"

"I'm not totally sure. I was thinking of ballroom, I guess. Like the waltz."

"Perfect," he said with a big smile. "We have a beginners class that meets in the evenings once a week. We learn the waltz, the tango, the foxtrot, several others. The next class is tomorrow night, right here, at seven."

"Really? So soon?" She didn't know why she said that. She was only planning on getting some information at this point.

"We'd love to have you join us."

"Is it . . . very expensive?"

"Not at all. We have very competitive prices. I could say we are the least expensive studio in River Oaks, but then we're also the only studio in River Oaks. Here, take this." He held out a brochure. "This explains all our classes, the schedules, the prices." She took it from him. "We're running a special now for beginners. Your first two classes are absolutely free. Just a way for people to try it first, see if they like it, before making a longer commitment."

Marilyn opened the brochure and looked at the inside pages a moment, trying to work up the nerve to ask her next question.

"So what do you say? Can I expect you tomorrow night?"

"Maybe," she said, then looked up. "Does anyone come who . . . doesn't have a dance partner?"

"Yes, yes. Many times. Particularly those who are . . . a little older." He looked at her hand. Marilyn thought he noticed the ring on her finger. "It's not uncommon for one spouse to want to learn how to dance and yet another one to not be . . . as interested."

That would be putting it mildly in my case, she thought.

"So, shall I expect you? If you don't thoroughly enjoy yourself—which I'm sure you will—you don't have to return."

"Okay," she said. "I think I'll come."

"Great," he said.

She looked at the clock behind the desk. "I better go, my lunch break is almost over."

"I'll see you out." He came around the desk and opened the glass door for her.

"Thank you," she said, smiling. "Have a nice day."

"See you tomorrow night."

Jim sat across the street in his Audi, parked several stores down, glaring at Marilyn. He had followed her here from Odds-n-Ends. At the moment, she appeared to be standing in a doorway, flirting with some Latin or Italian-looking man at a dance studio. The guy was easily ten years younger.

Earlier, as Jim had sat across the street from her store, he'd wrestled with the idea of walking right in there, demanding that she meet with him and talk, even though Mort, the head deacon, had advised against it. But how else could he get her to see him? Just as he was about to get out of the car, she had come out of Odds-n-Ends and started walking down the sidewalk. He'd watched her until she turned the corner. He'd backed his car out and followed her. The trail had led here.

Now she was walking back the way she came. What was Marilyn up to? And who was that man she was laughing and flirting with?

19

I'm sorry, Dad, I forgot to ask her."

"What do you mean, you forgot, Michele?" She didn't answer. Jim had to calm down. He knew he was in danger of getting hung up on again. He couldn't believe he had to play such games . . . with his own daughter. He was on his way home from work. It was Thursday evening. He had just called her—once more—to find out where Marilyn was staying.

"We mostly talked about my wedding," Michele said. "You're still coming, aren't you?"

"Of course I am." What a thing to say. "Okay, listen. I understand you've got a lot going on right now. I remember how crazy things got when we got this close to Tom's wedding. But Michele, your mom's been gone more than a week now. I've done my best to give her some space. You can ask her. I haven't called or bothered her in any way. But I think it's a little ridiculous that I still don't know where she's living . . . or any of her plans for the future."

"She's not making plans for the future. I know that for a fact."

"I don't mean long term," Jim said. "I mean day to day. A

pretty big thing has come up, something that could really make a difference in our finances, and she needs to know about it." He was thinking about the two-week deadline Mort Stanley had given him for the deacons' meeting. He now had about ten days left.

"So that's what you want to find Mom for, to talk about finances? Not a good idea, Dad."

She could be so exasperating. "That's not the only thing," he said. "I know you can't appreciate how important things like this are, since I've been paying your way all these years. But believe me, you and Allan will know exactly how much money matters after you walk down that aisle."

"Believe me, I already know. At least some. Allan and I were working on our budget just last night. Things are going to be very tight."

"Well, they've been pretty tight for us the past few years," he said. "Tighter than they've been since our early years of marriage. But I've got something brewing that could really give us some breathing room. Your mom leaving me like this could ruin it."

"Uh . . . how could Mom leaving you have anything to do with one of your financial deals? You've got a client that's actually asking about your marriage?"

"Well, yes, as a matter of fact. This one cares. They care a great deal." He really didn't want to get into this with her. "The thing is, I need her back in the house for this deal to go through. And I've got less than two weeks."

"What? Dad, that sounds absurd. You need her to be there to host one of your business parties?"

"No, it's nothing like that." He turned his car down the service road behind Elderberry Lane.

"Then what is it? Who would make such a ridiculous demand?

Your personal life is no one else's business. Why should your marital status affect someone interested in renting one of your properties?"

Jim sighed. "It's the church, okay? The church your mom and I—the church we were *all* attending as a family—for over ten years. They're the client. And they definitely care about my marital status."

"The church," she said, a tone of disgust in her voice. "Let me guess, Mr. Stanley paid you a visit."

How could she know that? "Yes, he did. But I don't want to get into all of this with you. They have standards, Michele. All churches do. They can't have a deacon representing the church whose wife has walked out on him."

"I don't see how that should matter whether or not they rent a building from you. That's not a moral decision, Dad. I'd be surprised if half the construction workers who built that building even go to church. Why should they care?"

"It's complicated, Michele. Okay? The thing is, they do."

"And so you want Mom to move back in—right now—to put on a good show? Is that the deal?"

"No . . . it's not to put on a show." Jim pulled into his driveway, pushed the garage door button.

"It's not? Okay, Dad. Let me ask you this . . . did Mr. Stanley even ask you how you were doing? Spiritually?"

"What?"

"Did he spend any time taking an interest in your soul? Ask you any questions about how Mom is doing or what you thought might have caused her to leave?"

Jim wanted to say yes, and was just about to. But, he realized, it would be a lie. "Well, Mort—Mr. Stanley—is not a pastor. He's a deacon. He's more in charge of practical matters."

"Oh . . . I see. He's not a pastor. He's just a deacon. So that means he couldn't take a few minutes to care about you as a person. That's the pastor's job." The comment reeked with sarcasm.

"It's not like that." Jim turned off the car. The garage door closed behind him.

"Dad, it is too. That's why I hated that church. Why I'm never going back. Whatever happened to being your brother's keeper? Mom is hurting big-time right now. I bet you are too. And all he came to talk to you about was the embarrassment your family life is causing the church."

"That's not all. I'm sure he cares about us. But he's got a job to do."

"A job," she said. "That's right, Mr. Stanley, the deacon. Well . . . whose job is it to care about people going through a crisis? The pastor? Okay, Dad. Has the pastor called you then? Has he come over to see how you're doing? How Mom's doing? I'm sure he knows she's left. That church is so full of gossips, I'll bet everyone knew before the Sunday service was over."

Now Jim wished he had never called. "The pastor's a very busy man."

"I'm sure he is."

Neither said anything for a few moments.

"You know what, Dad? Our pastor's a busy man, and he's already met with Allan and me four times for premarital counseling."

"Well, I'm glad to hear it."

"Have you looked over the list yet?"

"What list?"

"Our wedding invitation list. Mom said she would leave it on your dresser."

Jim remembered seeing it there. "No, I haven't yet. I will though, soon."

"I guess I should warn you," she said. "I've left most of the folks from your church off the list."

Oh great, Jim thought. Just great. What should he say? "Michele, that's not going to help matters, doing something like that. Most of these people have known you since before you were a teenager. And you're kind of shooting yourself in the foot too. They'd give you and Allan some wonderful presents if they—"

"Dad . . . I don't want their presents. I want our wedding day to be pleasant, and we want all the people there to be either family or friends. *Real* friends."

Another long, awkward pause.

"Speaking of money," she said. "Are you . . . can you still pay for the wedding? You said things are really tight right now. If you need us to cut back, we can. Allan and I have talked about it, we can—"

"No, Michele. Don't worry about the money. I saved for years for your wedding and set the money aside in a separate account. You guys do whatever you were going to do before your mother . . ."

He just didn't want to say the words again. Why, Marilyn? he thought. Why did you leave me? And why now?

"I'm sorry, Dad." He heard her crying softly on the other end. "I'm sorry all this is happening. Sorry for what you're going through too. I'm especially sorry you've got no one to help you, no one caring for your soul. I know you can tell, I'm mostly on Mom's side in this, but you know I love you, right?"

He felt his own emotions welling up.

"Are you . . . are you still going to walk me down the aisle?"

"What? Of course I am, Michele. No matter what happens

between your mom and me, you're still, and you'll always be my little . . ." Tears began falling down his cheeks. "My little girl," he said. He took a deep breath. "But hey, I've got to go."

"I will ask Mom about telling you where she's staying," Michele said. "The very next time I talk to her."

"No, don't worry about it," he said. "I've got to go. I love you too."

He hung up and got out of the car. He wouldn't wait for Michele to get around to talking to Marilyn when it suited her. He'd find out for himself. This very evening. He glanced at his watch. She had worked all day at Odds-n-Ends—he'd driven by that morning and saw her car in the employee parking lot—which meant she should be getting off in the next hour or so.

Jim got back in his car, turned it on, and pushed the garage door button.

20

Marilyn was so nervous. She was actually doing it.

For the first time in her life, she was going to learn how to dance. She closed her car door in the parking lot of the Windsor Dance Studio. It was set behind a row of stores and second floor apartments on Oakland Avenue. Although it was still light out, she knew darkness would set in by the time class was over. But River Oaks was safe, in general, and the parking area had an abundance of streetlights installed.

She put her cell phone back in her purse. She had just called Michele, hoping she could talk her into going through with this. "You should definitely do it, Mom," she'd said. "Especially if they're giving you the first two classes free. What do you have to lose? If you hate it, just don't go back."

As she walked across the parking lot, she glanced at her low-heeled leather shoes, glad she already had a pair in her closet. The brochure had recommended them, but she didn't have the money for a new pair, so she'd snuck back in the house on her lunch break. While there, she grabbed a pleated skirt and close-fitting blouse, which the brochure had also recommended.

Up ahead, three middle-aged couples, the women dressed in similar attire, walked through a breezeway to the street entrance. She followed them. As she walked past the big glass studio windows, she was alarmed to find the curtains had been pulled back. Now everyone walking or driving by could see inside.

One of the husbands held the front door open for her.

"Do they keep those curtains open during class?" she asked.

"All the time," the man replied. "Roberto only closes them when no classes are scheduled. He said he opens them because we all need to get used to the idea of people watching us when we dance. Because after he's taught us well, 'no one will be able to keep their eyes off you as you glide across the dance floor.'" He said this last part in a mock-Spanish accent. "I think he does it for the free advertising."

"Thanks," she said and stepped inside. Great. Now she was even more nervous.

The studio looked as it had yesterday, except all the lights were on. The wood floor glistened, and light music played in the background. A row of cushioned chairs had been lined across the seam where the carpet and dance floor met. Eight to ten people were already sitting in the chairs, and soon the three couples she had come in with had joined them. She did the same. That's when she noticed. She looked around once more to be sure. But there was no doubt about it.

Marilyn was the only one there without a partner.

Roberto had lied to her, or else he'd wildly exaggerated. He'd said people without partners came in all the time. But she was the only one alone. He had gotten the average age right. Most were her age or older, except two younger couples on the end, who looked to be in their twenties. But how could she learn to dance without a partner?

She wanted to leave, to get up right now and walk out the door. Roberto hadn't come out yet. Just then, an elderly woman walked through the front door. But what good would that do? Was she supposed to dance with this woman? That would look silly. And Marilyn was at least six to eight inches taller, which meant she'd probably get stuck playing the man's role. How could she learn her part if she had to figure out the man's steps?

No, this wouldn't work. This was a mistake. It was time to leave. She was about to bend down for her purse when several people sitting on chairs began greeting the woman like she was a dear friend.

"Audrey, how nice to see you."

"Audrey, you came. I'm so glad."

"Hello, Mrs. Windsor, are you staying for the whole class?"

The woman responded to the greetings as she set a big black purse on the desk.

Mrs. Windsor? Marilyn thought. She turned around to get a better look at the woman. She did look familiar. Then she remembered. This was the woman she'd met at Giovanni's last Sunday, when she'd eaten with Michele, the one who'd loved her music box and gave her the card about the studio.

"Oh, hello, Audrey. So nice of you to come." It was Roberto. He peeked his head in from the office doorway. She nodded and smiled at him. "Class, I'll be right there. Sorry I'm running a little late. Did everyone sign in? If not, make sure you do. The clipboard is right on the desk. Audrey, would you be a dear and show them? And everyone, make sure you make a name tag for yourselves. I'll be back in a few minutes, and we'll get started." And he was gone.

Three or four people stood, so Marilyn did too. This was

her chance to slip out. They went one way around the chairs toward the desk; she went the other way toward the front door.

"Oh, hello there."

Marilyn looked. Audrey was speaking to her.

"I'm so glad you came. I'm sorry, I don't remember your name. We've met, remember? At the restaurant. What was it, Sunday evening? You had the music box, right?"

Marilyn smiled and walked around the chairs toward her, holding out her hand. "I don't think we actually exchanged names. But you gave me the card to the studio."

"That's right." Audrey shook her hand. "I guess you know my name's Audrey."

"And your last name is Windsor," Marilyn said. "This used to be your studio?"

"Yes, well . . . me and my late husband's."

"He was a great singer," Marilyn said.

"And a fabulous dancer," Audrey replied. Her eyes momentarily drifted upward as if catching a brief memory floating by.

"My name is Marilyn. Marilyn Anderson."

"Very nice to meet you, Marilyn. Are you enjoying that music box?"

"Very much. So, do you come here often?"

"A few nights a week anyway, just to watch or help out if I can. Here, let's go have a seat." She walked toward the line of chairs. Marilyn followed. Her plan of escape had been thwarted, at least for the moment.

They sat beside each other. People began chatting. Marilyn decided to be bold. "Can I ask you something?" She spoke just above a whisper, hoping Audrey would get the hint.

Audrey leaned toward her. "Sure, anything."

"I don't know if you've noticed, but I'm the only one here

without a partner. Except you, of course. Roberto told me lots of people come without a partner, but look . . . it's not true."

Audrey bent forward and looked down the line of chairs. "Well, it doesn't look like he had that one right. Not tonight anyway." She sat back. "If he told you 'a lot of people,' that might have been an exaggeration. But I've been here when people have come alone. Even some of these couples will have a reason to come alone some nights. One of them might be sick or have to work."

"But what about a night like tonight?" Marilyn asked. "Will I just be sitting here watching everyone? Roberto doesn't expect you and I to dance together, does he?"

Audrey smiled. "No, I don't think so. But you don't have to worry about it tonight, anyway. Usually, he starts off showing everyone how it's done, then he'll have the men and women come up separately to work through their steps with him. My guess is, there won't even be time after that for the couples to do the steps together. I could be wrong, but why don't you just wait and see?"

Marilyn sat back, only slightly encouraged. That might be okay for tonight, but what about the rest of the time?

"Okay, ladies and gentlemen . . . I'm back." Music began filling the studio, and Roberto literally whirled past them onto the dance floor, holding the hand of a beautiful young woman. Everyone watched in amazement as he spun her around and then led her in the most beautiful waltz Marilyn had ever seen. It was breathtaking, like something she'd only seen before on TV.

Audrey leaned over and whispered, "Like I said, Roberto likes to start off showing everyone how it's done. That's Angelina, a stage name, I think. She's one of the jazz instructors. She'll probably leave right after this dance."

Sitting in his Audi across the street, Jim glared through the big picture windows at the scene.

Marilyn was sitting next to an older woman and seemed mesmerized by some handsome Latin man on the dance floor.

She couldn't take her eyes off him.

21

After "showing everyone how it's done," Roberto introduced Angelina to the class then released her to go home for the night. After she left the room, he said, "Please don't be intimidated by my dance with Angelina. That was not my intention. In fact, it's just the opposite. I want to encourage you to believe in yourself and in your own potential for the days to come. There was a day when Angelina and I were both in your shoes, sitting nervously in chairs, awaiting our first dance lesson. Everyone starts at the beginning."

Marilyn heard him but still felt intimidated.

Her anxiety was relieved a bit by what he said next. "Since we're at the beginning, our ballroom dance class will start with the waltz, but we'll play a slower number than you just heard. And we won't start off dancing as couples. May I have all the men on my right side across the back, and all the women on my left?"

Audrey Windsor leaned over and whispered, "See? I knew you had nothing to worry about." Marilyn smiled and stood, along with everyone else except Audrey. She looked down at Audrey. "You go on," Audrey said. "I already know these steps."

Over the next hour, Roberto stood in front of the class, his back facing the street. He alternated between the men and women, demonstrating the basic dance steps for each. Then he challenged the class to imitate what they had just seen. After, he had just the men get up and worked with them. In about ten minutes, he said he'd do the same with the women.

Marilyn was absolutely loving it.

The whole atmosphere was light and cheery with plenty of laughter. Mostly people making fun of themselves after getting something wrong. And there was plenty of that going around, which made her feel even more at ease. Roberto weaved through the men, giving specific comments and encouragement. He showed tremendous patience, especially with one elderly man who appeared to have no sense of rhythm. No matter how many times Roberto repeated the steps, he didn't get it.

"Move on to the next one, Roberto," the man's wife said from the chairs. "Gordon's hopeless. That's why I'm wearing steel-toed shoes." Everyone laughed.

Finally, Roberto said with a smile, "Nice, Gordon, you just keep working on that."

The music stopped. "Okay, men, have a seat. Ladies, your turn." Roberto walked back to the office to restart the music loop.

As soon as the music began, Marilyn could feel her legs wanting to do the steps. She was getting it; she was actually getting it! Roberto walked to the front and mimicked the ladies' part. "Nice, ladies, very nice." He watched them attempt to repeat his example. "Right foot back, left foot to the side, closing on three. Right foot down, left foot up. Good, now left foot back, right foot to the side, close on three. Very good, now keep it going." He began walking between them. "Feel the music, that's right. You're all doing just fine."

When he walked by Marilyn, he said, "You're a natural, Marilyn. Look at you. Beautiful, just beautiful." He said nice things to some of the others, but nothing as strong as that. She kept flowing with the music, counting her steps, as his words repeated in her head. He meant you're dancing beautifully, she said to herself. He wasn't talking about how you look. Was she that desperate for a compliment that she had to even wonder about this?

She looked at Audrey still sitting in her chair. She was listening to Gordon explain something but looked up and saw Marilyn, nodded then smiled. Marilyn glanced back at Roberto as he made his way through the group toward the front. When he walked past her, he said, "Splendid, Marilyn. Just splendid."

See, he was talking about your dancing, not your looks. But he kept looking at her as he reached the front; then he smiled as if he was holding back something he had wanted to say. *No, just stop it. That's not what's going on here*.

"We're almost out of time, everyone. So ladies, you may take a seat." They stopped dancing and turned toward the chairs. "Except you, Marilyn, if you don't mind. Would you stay up here, please?"

Marilyn was shocked, but she obeyed. What was going on? What did he have in mind?

He walked toward her. "I thought it would be a good idea, class, if I gave you a clear picture of what this first, basic step looks like as a couple dancing together. That way you can practice between now and next week at home. Marilyn, would you step up here, please, and join me?"

"Me?"

"Yes, I noticed you already have these steps down pat." He raised his left hand in the air. "Gentlemen, we begin by raising our left hand in the air like this. Marilyn, would you grasp my hand with your right hand, gently. There, very good."

She couldn't believe it. She was holding another man's hand. She was about to dance with someone . . . for the first time since she and Jim had begun to date over twenty-seven years ago.

"And now I put my right hand around her shoulder blade, like so. Marilyn, if you'll step just a little closer."

She did. She was so nervous.

"And now, rest your left arm on mine. Just like that." He looked toward the class. "Do you see this, everyone?" He looked back at Marilyn. "Now just one step closer, Marilyn, and we're ready to begin."

She carefully took that step. She could feel the warmth of his body, even smell his cologne. "Don't be nervous, my dear. You'll see, this is as easy as eating pie." He turned toward the class again. "Now she will simply do the exact same steps she was doing on her own, but in response to me." He began to move, and Marilyn followed. "Step, side, close. Step, side, close. Step, side, close." Just that quick, and they were already across the dance floor. He stopped, let go of her hands, and faced the group again. "Do you see how simple it is?"

Marilyn stood beside him, unsure what to do next. She was suddenly aware that every eye in the class seemed focused on her.

"Of course," Roberto said, "I have many other things to cover with you, which we'll pick up next time. But essentially, we keep following these same steps all the way through the song." He turned toward Marilyn. "And how about my partner, ladies and gentlemen? Didn't she do a wonderful job? Let's give Marilyn a big hand." Everyone clapped.

Marilyn looked away, embarrassed by the attention. That's when she saw him. To her left, through the big picture window closest to the front door. She saw a mirrored reflection of the dance studio, but through it, there standing under a streetlight, his arms folded . . . was Jim.

He was glaring at her.

She knew that look. She hated that look.

"So class, that's it for tonight," Roberto said. "You all did a wonderful job. Keep practicing these basic steps, over and over, until they become second nature to you. And if you can, practice them together, just like Marilyn and I did a moment ago. If you don't have any music at home like this to dance to, we have a CD you can buy. All the songs you danced to tonight are on it."

He looked at Marilyn again. "You were wonderful, my dear. I notice you don't have a dance partner with you. Didn't you ask about this when we first met?"

"Yes. I'll be taking the classes alone, but I guess that's not going to work. Looks like I'm the only one without a partner."

"Nonsense," he said. "You dance beautifully. I'll be your partner."

Marilyn didn't know what to say. "Really?"

"It would be my honor." He looked over at a group standing by the desk. "Now I must go. It looks as though a few people want to buy the music CD." He reached for her hand as if he was about to dance again, lifted it, and kissed it gently. Then he walked away.

Marilyn's eyes snapped toward the picture window.

Jim was gone. She was relieved. Maybe he didn't see. She heard the front door open and looked.

It was Jim walking into the studio.

22

That's it! Jim thought. Enough's enough.

He'd sat there almost the entire time watching the dance lesson, first in his car, then by the sidewalk. He'd suspected something was brewing between Marilyn and someone. Watching her and that Latin guy flirt outside the studio the other day seemed to confirm it. But during the first half of the dance class, Jim had talked himself out of it. She was just out there on the dance floor with the rest of the ladies. Then he noticed how every time the instructor got near Marilyn, he said something that made her smile.

It got worse—all the other ladies sat down. Except one.

Watching Marilyn dance with this guy, the way they looked at each other. It was too much. And then that kiss.

As Jim walked through the glass door, he told himself to calm down. Like Mort Stanley said, blowing up in front of a bunch of witnesses would only make things worse if this ended in divorce. But she was all done putting him off. If there wasn't anything going on with Mr. Latin Lover, she should have no problem telling Jim where she was living. At the very least, she had to agree to go with him for counseling. Anything less than that? Well . . . he might have to get in this Latin guy's face, after all.

He turned to find her in the crowd. People were gathering their things. Some were talking to the instructor, who sat behind the desk. There she was, looking right at Jim, her face almost in a panic. Guilty eyes.

"Jim," she said.

He forced a smile. "Can I have a word with you, Marilyn?" He let out just a little edge.

She picked up her purse and walked toward him. "What are you doing here?"

"I just want to talk. Maybe we should go outside." He looked around quickly. Except for one old woman, no one noticed them. He turned and went back out the door, certain she would follow. He heard her footsteps behind him.

A young couple, holding hands and Starbucks cups, walked by on the sidewalk. He nodded and smiled. A small group of college kids walked the other way. Turning around, he saw her standing a few feet from the door. He remembered the breezeway a little farther down in the row of storefronts, just beyond the studio. Pointing to it, he said, "Let's talk there."

"I don't know if I want to," she said.

Her words sounded firm, but he saw the same panicked look in her eyes. He took a few steps toward her. "If you don't want me to make a scene here, you'll follow me to that breezeway." He turned and started walking. He heard footsteps behind him again. Good. When he got halfway down, he stopped and faced her. "So, what's going on?"

"What do you mean, what's going on? Nothing's going on. I just attended a dance class."

"I mean between you and that . . . Latin guy."

"What? You mean Roberto?"

"Oh, it's Roberto."

"Of course, it's Roberto. That's his name."

"So there's nothing going on with you two, is that what you're saying?"

"Of course not. Don't be absurd." The panicked look was gone.

"Marilyn, I saw him kiss you."

"On the hand, Jim. It's a culture thing. You're being ridiculous."

"A culture thing. I saw you two yesterday, alone over there by the front door. During your lunch break. And now at the class, with all the women he could pick, he singles you out to be his partner?"

"Oh, so what, you're following me now?" She raised her voice.

"No . . . but what do you expect me to think? You take off last week with no warning. I have no idea where you've gone, where you're staying. Michele won't even tell me. You don't mention anything about it in your note."

"As I recall, what I said in my note was, I wanted you to leave me alone, to give me some time to myself. But instead of respecting the one thing I asked, you start following me?"

"Keep your voice down," he said sternly. "If you want to turn this into a shouting match, two can play at that game. I'm trying to keep this civil."

"I'm not shouting," she said, then sighed. "I can't believe you're doing this."

He looked up. Two couples from the dance class entered the breezeway. They stopped when they saw them. "Come on, we need to get out of here. The dance people are coming." He tried to say it calmly.

"Well, that's because this is the easiest way to get to where our cars are parked."

"Let's talk by your car then," he said. "Where is it? Back here?" He walked toward the back parking lot.

"I'm not going with you."

He turned around. "Marilyn, this will only take a minute. I'm not going to stop trying until you talk with me. You owe me at least that much after twenty-seven years of marriage."

She turned around and saw the two couples standing by the entrance of the breezeway. "Okay, we'll talk. For a few minutes. But you wait until all these people get in their cars and leave."

"I can do that." He walked into the parking lot and quickly spotted her car under a streetlight. A few moments later they were standing on either side, Marilyn on the driver's side. The two couples came through the breezeway and headed to their cars.

One of the older men said something to his wife then walked toward them. "Is everything okay, Marilyn?"

"Everything's fine, Gordon," she said. "This is my husband, Jim. We're fine, just having a little chat."

He stood there a moment. "Well, if you're sure."

"We're fine, really. See you all next week."

The man waved, then turned and joined his wife. The two couples left. Over the next five minutes, a number of others came through the same way. They all waved to Marilyn, some shouted out pleasant good-byes.

"I think that's everyone," Marilyn said. "Now let's get this over with. I've got to get home."

"Home," he said, disgusted. "What do you mean, home? You've left your home."

"Right, I did," she said. "Do you want me to make this permanent, Jim? I told you in my note, that's the one thing that—"

"No, I don't want you to make it permanent. I want you to come home . . . now."

"Well, I'm not going to. I'm not even close to doing that. You coming here like this? Makes me want to—"

"Marilyn, if you'd tell me where you're staying, I wouldn't have to come here like this."

"So that's what this is about? That's what you expect me to believe? And if I tell you, I'm supposed to believe you're going to be fine with that? Then you'll leave?"

He didn't respond. What should he say?

"I didn't think so." She put her keys in the car door.

"So now you're just going to drive off? Just like that? What has gotten into you?"

"Maybe you should read my note a few more times, Jim. I said everything I wanted to say when I wrote it. I want some time away. I want you to leave me alone. What's so hard to understand?"

"Marilyn . . . I don't understand how you think it's okay to just walk away from our marriage like this. Without any warning, you just—"

"Without any warning? I've been trying to talk to you about our marriage, about how unhappy I've been for months. No . . . years."

"When?" he said. "I don't recall you saying anything about being *this* unhappy, enough to just walk out. You haven't even given me a chance. We haven't even tried counseling. You know what the Bible says. God hates divorce."

"I haven't said anything about divorce."

"No . . . well, where do you think things like this lead? You've only been gone a week, and you're already flirting with this dance instructor. You say there's nothing going on, but that's how these things happen, Marilyn."

Her eyes seemed to fill with hate. She opened the car door. "This conversation is over."

"Wait," he said.

"No, I won't wait." She bent down to get in the car, then stood back up. "For your information, there's absolutely nothing going on between me and Roberto. He's just a dance instructor, that's all. He singled me out for two reasons. First, I was the only one who didn't have a partner. And second, because he actually thought I might be a good dancer someday. But what would you know about that? You wouldn't even dance with me at our wedding."

Tears filled her eyes. Angry tears.

"Is that what this is about?" he said. "You want me to dance with you? Okay, then, I'll take these stupid dance lessons with you, if that's what it takes. I'll come back with you next week."

"Don't you dare," she said. "If you do, I'll leave and never come back." She got in the car, slammed the door, and turned the car on.

"Wait," Jim said, backing away.

She backed the car out and drove off.

23

Watching all this unfold in the shadows behind a ficus tree in the breezeway was Audrey Windsor. She had noticed the man walk into the studio; he had a troubled look in his eyes. When she saw how Marilyn Anderson had reacted to him, she immediately guessed he was her husband.

And that they weren't doing very well.

She had followed the last group of dance students out, then waited in the breezeway to make sure Marilyn was okay. Now that she had driven off, Audrey decided the coast was clear. But the man still stood there in the empty parking space under the streetlight, staring at Marilyn's car as it disappeared around the corner.

Her own car was nearby. She waited a few moments to see if he'd leave, but he didn't. Now he was staring at the ground, looking more sad than angry.

Oh no. He was walking this way. His car must be parked in front. *Just act natural. Walk toward your car; you'll be fine.* Just then she felt a nudging in her soul she'd come to recognize over the years, like the still small voice of God. Then this marvelous, familiar peace, as if the Lord was telling her not to be afraid.

But it was more than that; a sense of boldness came over her.

She stepped out from the shadows toward the parking lot. He was only a few yards away. He looked up, noticed her. A strained smile on his face, but his eyes didn't match the smile. He nodded as he noticed her watching him.

"You're Marilyn Anderson's husband, aren't you?"

"What?" He stopped walking.

"I'm sorry, I don't mean to be nosy, but my car is parked out here." She pointed. "Right over there, two spots beside where Marilyn parked. When I got to the end of the breezeway here, I heard the two of you arguing, so I stayed back."

"Well, I hate that you had to hear it. We don't normally argue like that, certainly not in public."

They stood there a moment. Audrey silently prayed for direction. "The two of you are separated, I take it."

"Yeah, we are. That was the first time I've talked to her in a week."

"By the sound of it, things didn't go the way you hoped."

He looked down. "No, they didn't. Not even close." He suddenly looked back in the direction Marilyn's car had gone, like he'd just remembered something. "I can't believe it. She *still* didn't tell me where she's staying."

Audrey realized this was something she could find out; Marilyn's address was probably written on the sign-up sheet. But she decided to leave it alone. "How long have you two been married?"

"Twenty-seven years."

"That's a long time. My husband Ted and I made it to fifty-one before he passed away last year."

"Well, I doubt we'll get that far the way things are headed. How do you know Marilyn? Are you taking dance lessons? I saw you in there a few moments ago."

Audrey smiled. "Not exactly. It used to be my dance studio. Well, Ted's and mine. My name's Audrey Windsor, by the way." She held out her hand.

"Jim Anderson," he said as he shook it gently.

"The year before Ted died, he got pretty sick, so we put the studio up for sale. But I still like to visit as often as I can. The new owner, Roberto, doesn't mind." She leaned forward as if telling a secret. "As long as I stay out of his way, that is."

A disgusted look instantly appeared on Jim's face.

Audrey remembered something he'd said. "You know, your wife's telling the truth about Roberto. I don't think there's anything going on between them, certainly not on Marilyn's end. Roberto's just a first-class flirt. He likes to play up that whole Latin-lover persona. Thinks it enhances his image."

This was something that really annoyed Audrey. Roberto had given no hint of this during their negotiations; he had been the perfect gentleman. Nor that he would start introducing all the sensual dance moves that had become so popular lately, since those dance shows started appearing on TV. She had tried talking to him about it, but he'd basically told her—minus the Spanish accent—to butt out.

"I saw the way he looked at her," Jim said. "Then how he singled her out from the class, the way he kissed her hand."

"What, that? That doesn't mean a thing. Your wife is an attractive woman but, it's like I was telling you, Roberto is all image and show. So far, I haven't seen signs that he means any harm. And believe me, I've been watching." Before Ted died, he had the foresight to put a morals clause in their contract. If

Roberto did anything too scandalous, he'd have to change the dance studio's name.

"Maybe not, but . . . Marilyn is so vulnerable right now. And to be honest, she's a bit naïve about these things."

Audrey knew what was really bothering him. He was afraid he was going to lose her. But maybe that was a good thing. Maybe a little bit of that kind of fear could be useful. "I think you're wise to be concerned. It's never a healthy thing for a husband and wife to be separated very long."

"I agree. I want her to come home now, but she won't even talk to me. How are we going to fix this if we don't talk? I think we should get some counseling."

"Counseling can be a very good thing," Audrey said. "But . . . if you don't mind me saying, I think something like that's a little ways off. The problem is . . . you've lost her heart."

He looked at her as though she'd started speaking another language. "What?" he finally said.

"You've lost her heart, don't you see? Right now, she doesn't want to hear anything you have to say. My guess is . . . she's been trying to talk to you about how unhappy she's been for a long time, but you haven't been listening." Maybe she was coming on too strong here.

"Did she tell you that?"

"Why, no . . ."

"That's exactly what Marilyn said in her note, almost word for word."

Audrey didn't have the heart to tell him, it didn't take a brain surgeon to come up with that. A woman who's been married for twenty-seven years—especially a Christian woman—wouldn't just walk out on her marriage unless she'd been trying to fix things a good while and had finally given up hope. "Has she ever talked to you about attending a marriage retreat with her, maybe suggested some marriage books the two of you should read together?"

He thought a moment. "Maybe . . . yeah, I guess. I don't know. If she did, it was a long time ago."

"Well, my guess is, she probably tried a number of things. Is it possible you've been too busy and missed her signals? Maybe you've been distracted by things at work? I know men tend to get preoccupied with things. During football season, especially during the playoffs, I'd have to stand right in front of the television to remind Ted that he even had a wife."

Jim smiled. "I'm sure it's possible. My business has been going through a tough time lately. I guess there's a lot of that going around. Seems like it's taking all my energy just to stay afloat." He looked up toward the stars a moment. "I don't know if we'll even make it financially if she winds up leaving me for good."

That bold feeling came over Audrey again. "Do you love her, Jim?"

"What? Of course I love her."

"Does she know that?"

"Of course, she—" He paused, released a sigh. "I don't know. She should know."

"How?"

"What?"

"How should she know?"

Another pause, a longer one. He looked right at her. "You said you think I've lost her heart? You seem to know a little bit about these things. Any idea how I can win it back?"

Thank you, Lord. "I might," she said. "How hard are you willing to try?"

"I'll do just about anything at this point."

"Just about?" Audrey said.

"Well, I mean . . . why? What do you have in mind?"

An idea that had begun forming a few minutes ago suddenly became crystal clear. It was something Marilyn had said to him, just before she had driven off. "How would you like to learn how to dance?"

24

Did she say . . . *dance*? "What?" Jim asked.

"Would you like to learn how to dance?" Audrey said again. "You said something to your wife about being willing to learn how to dance if it would get her to come home. I think your exact words were, 'I'll take these stupid dance lessons with you, if that's what it takes.'"

Did he really say that? He must have. But how could dancing matter? Marilyn wouldn't leave him over something as silly as that. Besides, he needed her to come home *now*. That's what Mort said. They needed to be in counseling before the big deacons' meeting in ten days. "Dancing lessons would take too long," he said.

Audrey looked confused. "Too long? How do you know they'd take too long?"

"Well, I'm sure they will. I have less than two weeks. There's no way you could teach me to dance by then." He sighed. "Nobody could. You probably also heard her say I didn't even dance with her at our wedding. I didn't dance then and haven't danced since. That was twenty-seven years ago. I don't dance, Mrs. Windsor."

Audrey's look of confusion grew stronger. "Please, call me Audrey."

"Audrey, then," he said. "The point is, there's no time for me to learn how to dance. And besides, I don't see what good it would do if I could learn. She won't even talk to me. How am I going to get her to dance?"

"I don't understand the urgency. What's going to happen in two weeks?"

"Less than two weeks. Really, ten days."

"Okay, ten days. What's going to happen then?"

"I'd rather not get into it. It's kind of complicated. I appreciate the offer, but honestly, I can't see how me learning how to dance helps our situation. I don't know everything that's eating her, but I can't imagine dancing is high on the list."

"It's the first thing she mentioned," Audrey said. "I think that's significant."

"Maybe. I think she just came out of a dance lesson. If she was coming out of a theater, she'd have said, 'You never take me to the movies anymore.' Our problems aren't going to be solved by me learning how to dance."

"I agree." Her confused look was gone.

Now Jim was confused. "You do?"

"Your marriage problems are much bigger than your unwillingness to dance."

"It's not that I'm unwilling. I don't know how. I stink at it."

"Well, we can talk about that later. But I agree, you learning how to dance isn't going to make your marriage problems go away. Not your biggest ones, anyway."

"Then why did you bring it up?"

"Because it just might soften Marilyn's heart. Think about it. You said she left a week ago. And what's one of the first things she does now that she's free from you—I'm sorry. That's a terrible thing to say." Jim shrugged. "She signs up for dance lessons. A few minutes ago, she brings up the fact that you've never danced with her, not even at your wedding."

Jim thought a moment. "You think it really matters?"

"It might," Audrey said. "Back when Ted and I hit the twenty-five-year mark, we weren't getting along at all. Our kids were grown, it was just the two of us, and we realized we didn't have anything left. He didn't like me, and I definitely didn't like him."

"But did you leave him?"

"No . . . but I wanted to. I was certainly thinking about it. About that time, some friends at church—a couple our own age—came alongside us and helped us out. They told us some things we'd never heard before. It didn't happen overnight. If I recall, it took several months, but things began to improve once we started doing what they said. It's sad when you think about it. People get married all the time, but we don't have a clue about what makes marriages work. Looking back, I don't think I was happy with Ted for most of those first twenty-five years. Maybe certain moments here and there. But we stayed together, year after year, banging our heads against the wall. And here the doorway to being truly happy was just a few steps down the hall. We never knew. If those precious friends hadn't shared with us what they did, I think Ted and I would have split up."

Could this lady be on to something? He had been pretty happy before all this, had been for most of their marriage. But Marilyn wasn't . . . sounds like for a long time. He definitely related to the "banging our heads against the wall" part. Felt like he'd been doing that all week. "So what does all this have to do with me learning how to dance?"

"I'm sorry. I got off track. I wasn't talking about dancing then. Well, in a way I am." She paused, as if she had more to say, then changed her mind. "The point is, if you're willing, I'd be willing to teach you how to dance. Six lessons, one each week."

"I don't know, Mrs. Windsor—I mean Audrey. I don't think that's something I'd be interested in. Besides, like I said, I don't have six weeks. I have less than two."

"I understand." Suddenly her face became very serious. "Well, Jim . . . I *don't* understand. I don't understand what your less-than-two-week deadline is all about. I do understand your marriage is in serious trouble. If you really want to win Marilyn's heart back, you need to consider how much effort you're willing to put into it. Seeing where she is now, I'm not even sure you can win her back at all, let alone in two weeks . . . excuse me, *ten days*. There's no quick fix when it comes to relationships."

It felt like she'd thrown cold water in his face. He knew what she said was true. He had no idea what it would take to turn things around with Marilyn. Not in ten days, two weeks, or two months. What if it was already too late? What if he had lost her for good?

Audrey's face softened. "I can't teach you very much in ten days, Jim. But if you'll give me six weeks, I'll not only teach you how to dance, I'll share some of those things Ted and I learned from our friends. You'll learn some dance steps and a whole lot more. And you'll see your marriage in a whole new way. Over the years, we helped lots of couples make a fresh start. Some whose marriages were as bad off as yours."

Was their marriage really as bad as that? *Listen to yourself. Of course it is. Marilyn all but hates you now. Maybe she does hate you.* Then another thought repeated in his mind. *You've lost her heart.*

This was true too. Marilyn wanted nothing to do with him. She couldn't even stand to be in the same room with him. He remembered the last words she'd said, just before she drove off. After he'd offered to take those "stupid dance lessons" with her.

"If you do, I'll leave and never come back."

He was fooling himself. He had absolutely no idea what it would take to win her back. He still had no clue why she'd even left. What did he have to lose? "Where would we do this? These . . . dance lessons?"

"In my home," she said. "I still occasionally give private lessons, so I cleared all the furniture out of our family room and made a nice little studio there."

"Would we be alone?"

"Just you and me."

"How much would this cost?"

"I won't charge you a dime."

"Really?"

"Really," she said, handing him a card. "My phone number and address are on this. Call me after you've had some time to think about it."

He took the card. "I might take you up on this."

"Well," she said, "don't say yes too quickly. It's not going to be easy. I can already see that. In fact, you might find these to be some of the hardest lessons you've ever learned."

"Because I'm such a lousy dancer?" he said, smiling.

She smiled back, pulled her keys out of her purse. "I wasn't talking about the dance part."

25

The weekend passed without any more confrontations with Marilyn. Jim had decided to back off after the heated exchange last Thursday night at the dance studio. If he kept pressing her, she'd be convinced he had begun stalking her, which, of course, was absurd. All he wanted was to find out where she was living. It didn't seem like such an outrageous request.

It was Monday night; he'd gotten off work about an hour ago, stopped off on the way home to get some Chinese takeout for him and Doug. They had settled into an odd routine over the last week or so, now with Marilyn firmly out of the picture. Jim didn't like it, but he didn't know what else to do about it at the moment. The new format had them spending even less time together than before. With Marilyn in the house, he and Doug would connect at the dinner table, at least to some degree. Doug would mostly keep to himself as he wolfed down whatever she'd cooked, offering short answers to Marilyn's attempts to ask him about his day.

Now Jim had even less interaction than that. He'd set the boxes of Chinese food on the kitchen counter. Doug had figured out which ones were his and said a quick "Thanks, Dad" as he'd headed back to his apartment over the garage. Jim wanted to yell after him and insist he come back and eat with him. But what was the point? Doug would dutifully obey, the whole while he'd want to leave. They'd sit staring at each other, listening to each other chew. Jim could have tried to come up with topics they could talk about, but he knew what would happen. All the things that bugged them about each other would find their way to the surface, and they'd end up in a conflict . . . without Marilyn there to referee.

So Jim sat there on a bar stool, eating his Kung Pao chicken and fried rice, alone. His chopsticks were still in the bag. Doug had figured out how to use them. Well, there was something they could have talked about . . . for three minutes.

Jim looked at the digital clock on the stove. He had ten more minutes before he needed to get ready for his first dance lesson with Audrey Windsor. What was he thinking saying yes to this crazy idea? He'd wrestled with it all weekend. But every argument he'd come up with to cancel met one singular and much stronger argument to follow through . . . the words Audrey had said last Thursday night. *You've lost her heart.*

Jim had no other options. Even this option might fail. But he had to try, so he decided to give it at least a few weeks.

A few weeks.

That part bugged him too. Once he'd agreed to go through with this, he'd called Audrey on Saturday to set up a schedule, hoping to cram in as many lessons in the shortest time possible. But due to "other pressing commitments," she insisted she could only meet once a week, on Monday nights. Pressing commitments? Jim thought when he heard her say it. What kind of pressing commitments could she possibly have? She was retired, and at least seventy years old. He'd offered to pay her, thinking she was probably giving preferential treatment to her paying customers, but she'd said no. Money had nothing to do with it. Besides, she'd said, he would need the time in between each lesson for homework and practice.

Homework and practice? What could that possibly mean?

His phone rang, startling him. He reached for it across the counter. No, no, he thought when he saw who it was. Not him, not now. But he had to take the call, and he knew what he was calling about. "Hi, Mort, how are you?" It took some effort, but he tried to sound upbeat.

"Not bad, Jim. I'm on my way home from work, thought I'd give you a buzz. Our big meeting is one week from tonight."

"I remember," Jim said. He wished he could forget.

"How are things going with Marilyn? Any progress?"

"Some," Jim said. "We had a fruitful chat on Thursday night. Think I understand now a little more about what's bugging her. I'm working on a plan."

"So I take it she hasn't moved back in yet."

"Not yet, but I'm hoping we'll get—"

"Did she tell you why? What it's going to take to make that happen? There's not much time left."

"I know, I know."

"Did you offer to go to counseling with her? Most women respond pretty well to that."

How could he tell Mort they didn't get that far in their "fruitful chat"? Should he tell him that he still didn't even know where she slept at night? "I'm definitely open to that, Mort."

"But is she?"

"I'm not sure yet, to be honest."

"Not sure? Jim . . . did you even ask her?"

"No. I wanted to, but . . ." Jim should just tell Mort the truth. There was no way he'd get Marilyn back in the house or in marriage counseling before the deacons' meeting next week.

But he couldn't.

"Should I start preparing the board to go with Sam Hall's property? He's been calling me about it all week, brought it up again . . . yesterday at church."

That last remark was something of a jab. Jim had skipped out on church again yesterday. He'd planned to go, but at the last minute his stomach wouldn't cooperate. "Let's don't go there yet, Mort. Can't you give me a little more time? I'm still hoping Marilyn's going to snap out of this, any day now." He'd said it, but he didn't believe it.

There was a pause. "I guess I can wait until Friday. But seriously, Jim . . . if there isn't real progress with her by then, you need to come clean with me. I don't want any surprises at this board meeting."

"I'll definitely let you know by then."

"And by progress, I mean she's either moved back in or you've at least gotten her to agree to go to counseling."

"I understand."

"Well, let's keep in touch."

After he hung up, Jim berated himself for not being straight with Mort now. There was no chance Marilyn would agree to either of those things before Friday. Why hadn't he just said so? Glancing back at the clock, he realized he needed to get upstairs and get ready. That phone call ended his appetite anyway. He folded up the little white boxes of Chinese food and shoved them in the refrigerator, then hurried upstairs.

He didn't have that much to do, mainly just change out of his suit into some casual clothes. He'd asked Audrey what he should wear, and that's what she said. Nice casual, no jeans. He'd asked if he needed to buy dance shoes (he couldn't even believe the words had come out of his mouth), but she said no, not tonight anyway. Tonight was going to be a little different. Which, of course, made no sense, because he had nothing to compare the evening to.

After changing, he scrambled down the steps, then remembered he'd forgotten to tell Doug he was going out. He pulled out his phone then changed his mind. Doug would have his headphones on and probably wouldn't hear the phone ring; he never listened to Jim's voice mails anyway. It was his way of forcing Jim to learn how to text. Besides, Jim needed to work a little harder at having actual conversations with him.

He locked up and left the main house, then walked across the backyard to the garage. As he clicked the garage door opener, he tried to figure out what he was going to say. He climbed the steps, mentally rehearsing a few options. There was no way he was going to tell Doug the truth.

No one could ever know the truth. Not Doug, not Tom or Michele, and certainly not Marilyn. Jim would rather eat broken glass or drive his car into a drainage canal than tell anyone he was taking dance lessons.

26

Jim followed Audrey's directions to her house, which was still in River Oaks but in a neighborhood of smaller homes modeled in a bungalow style. They still had front porches, of course, but they didn't wrap around the side, and most were single story. But hey, Jim thought, she and her husband had to be doing okay at that dance studio before he died. Otherwise, they couldn't have afforded a place in River Oaks. Even in the bungalow section.

As he pulled up to the curb in front, he admired the house, small as it was. The word *quaint* came to mind. After that the word, *symmetric*. Even the modest landscaping on each side of the porch was a mirror image of the other. As he got out of his car, he looked around at the other homes on the block, happy to see no one was outside or appeared to notice him.

He was also grateful Audrey had no signs out front or by her door, announcing her private dance studio inside. As he walked up the steps, he realized the homeowners' association would never allow such a thing anyway. Which was great, because he didn't want anyone to know why he was there.

After a few moments, Audrey answered the doorbell. "Jim, so glad you made it. Right on time."

Jim quickly walked inside. He was freshly reminded of how young Audrey seemed for her age. If she and Ted had been married fifty years, she had to be in her seventies. But she looked so elegant and refined and stood with perfect posture. Maybe dancing all these years had kept her in such good health.

Her place was nicely decorated, although the furniture pieces were obviously from a different era. A strong aroma of air freshener or potpourri involuntarily filled his lungs. Pleasant music played from somewhere in the back of the house.

"Would you care for a cup of coffee or tea?"

"Coffee if you have it made," he said.

"I do. Follow me." She walked around a short stairway into the carpeted living area.

"I didn't realize these models had a second floor," he said. "From the outside, you just see that dormer in the middle. I thought it must be an attic."

"There's a couple of bedrooms and a bathroom up there, but I hardly go upstairs anymore. Fortunately for me, the master bedroom is downstairs, right over there," she said, pointing toward a closed door on the left side of the foyer.

They walked into a spacious dining room; the kitchen was off to the left. He could now tell the music was coming from a room on the other side of a set of double French doors.

"Have a seat," she said, looking at the dining room table, "while I pour us some coffee."

As she did, he looked through the French doors, noticed the shiny wood floor, and guessed this room was her little dance studio. Seeing it made him tense up.

"Are you a little nervous?"

"Terrified." He couldn't believe he said that.

"Good," she said. "That's the right answer."

What on earth could she mean by that? "You're glad I'm terrified?"

"Well," she said, "not glad, exactly. And I'm sure you're not exactly terrified. But I expect you have a reasonable amount of fear. And why shouldn't you? You're doing something totally out of your comfort zone."

"That's an understatement. I can't ever see me feeling comfortable about dancing."

She walked over carrying a tray with the coffee and everything to fix it. "No? Well, tell me something you do that you feel totally comfortable doing." She set the tray down and sat.

"Well . . . golf, I guess."

"Are you pretty good?"

He smiled. Pretty good wasn't being honest. If he could play more often, knock a few more strokes off his game, he might have a shot on the PGA senior tour.

"By that smile, I guess that's a yes," she said. "My Ted liked to play golf, back when he was healthier. So I know a little about it."

"River Oaks has a beautiful course. Is that where he played?"

"Most of the time." She stirred her coffee. "Do you remember the first time you ever played golf?"

"What?"

"The first time you ever played golf . . . do you remember how you felt before you started?"

Jim thought a moment. He did remember. An image flashed through his mind: he was following his father out to the driving range. Ten years old. Golf was his father's religion, very serious business. Their backyard bordered the sixth hole. His dad had just given him a lesson. He remembered how he'd felt, walking behind his dad that day. He was afraid he'd forget something and screw up.

And of course, that's exactly what happened. "I get it," he said. "People are always afraid of things they've never done before. So . . . are we even going to learn any dance steps tonight?"

"What if I said not exactly?"

"That would make me happy."

"Then you can relax. Tonight, we're only going to talk about dancing. This week is what my husband used to call the Introduction Week." She took a sip of coffee. "I wish he were here. He did such a better job explaining all this."

Jim was glad to put dancing off another week but now had no idea what to expect.

"So why do you think you're so afraid of dancing?" Audrey said.

"I'm not afraid of dancing. I'm just no good at it."

"Because you've never done it before."

"Right."

"Not even at your wedding." Her smile disappeared. It was more a statement than a question.

He didn't know what to say next. "I did get up, eventually."

"You danced with your wife at your wedding?"

"I wouldn't exactly call it dancing." He reached for his coffee cup.

"Do you have any idea how much young women look forward to their wedding day?"

"Not really, but I'm sure they do."

"They start thinking about it as little girls. They dream about that magical day when a man falls in love with them and proposes, and their father escorts them down the aisle. They'll say their vows, their fiancé places that ring on their finger, looks them in the eye and says—"

"We did all that, Marilyn and I. We said our vows and said I do. We even said some things during the ring part of the ceremony. I didn't mess up a single word."

"But part of the dream, Jim, is that first dance at the reception. I'll bet Marilyn even had a song picked out."

Jim remembered. She did. "Unforgettable" by Nat King Cole. But she knew he didn't dance. "Why didn't she ask me beforehand?" Jim said. "We never danced while we were dating or engaged. Not even once."

"I'm guessing she didn't think she had to. It's pretty customary for the bride and groom to dance."

Jim thought about it. What he wanted was to get up and leave, right now. He knew what was going on here. Audrey was trying to make him feel guilty for something that had happened twenty-seven years ago. "I guess not."

"I never have," she said. "But you know what, Jim? In a way, you and Marilyn did dance that day. And you've been dancing the same dance ever since, right up until almost two weeks ago when she walked out the door."

"I'm sorry. I have no idea what you're talking about."

She smiled. "And," she continued, "you already know all the steps to this dance. It's a dance almost every couple learns shortly after they get married."

Okay, she must be talking about some kind of metaphor. "I guess I'm supposed to ask, what's the dance?"

"Obviously, I'm using a kind of word picture. My husband Ted called it the Fear Dance. And my guess, Jim, is you've become pretty skilled at it already."

27

"The Fear Dance," Jim repeated. "The only thing I'm afraid of right now is Marilyn leaving me for good, causing us to go broke. We could lose our house, my business could be ruined—"

"I'm not just talking about what you're afraid of now," Audrey said. "I'm talking about other fears, fears you've had for a long time, even way back on your wedding day. And before that. Ted used to call them *core* fears."

What was she going on about?

"The thing is," she continued, "you probably don't know those fears are even there, or what they are. And you probably don't know what Marilyn's fears are, either. But you both have them." She took a sip of her coffee.

Jim did too. It was already lukewarm. "Okay," he said, "let's say I buy that. I'm not sure I do yet, but to make sure I'm following you . . . why do you call it a Fear Dance?"

"See, these core fears cause us to react in certain ways to others, especially people we're close to. When they push our fear buttons, so to speak. We get hurt when that happens, so we react. Our reaction often causes us to step on our partner's fears. Like stepping on their toes while dancing. Then they get hurt and so they react accordingly. All the while, neither one understands what's going on, because we don't know what's making us afraid inside, or what our spouse's fears are. So this Fear Dance keeps going, round and round. Two people just stepping on each other's toes. It's a funny sight to see on the dance floor, but in real life, it's very painful."

Stepping on each other's toes, because we're afraid? Jim wasn't all that excited to come here to learn how to dance, but this wasn't at all what he expected.

"Let me give you an example," she said. "A moment ago when I asked you if you were nervous coming here for your first dance lesson, what did you say?"

"That I was terrified."

"But when I asked you why you didn't dance with your wife on your wedding day, what did you say?"

Jim thought a moment. "I said . . . it was because I couldn't dance. But I wasn't afraid, I just didn't know how. That's not the same thing."

"You sure about that?"

What did she want him to say? "Pretty sure," he said.

"What would have happened if you had just said yes when it came time for the two of you to dance? What if you just did it because you loved Marilyn and wanted to make her happy?"

"Everyone would have laughed at me the moment they saw how badly I—" He stopped talking. He had been afraid. Afraid of being laughed at. This was actually starting to make sense.

"You were afraid of failure," she said. "Afraid you'd dance so bad you'd be humiliated in front of all those people." Jim nodded in agreement. "Fear of failure is a pretty powerful fear. I think it may be a core fear for you, Jim."

Could this be true? Was that when everything got offtrack with them, way back then?

"Do you know how powerful your fear of failure was on your wedding day?"

He looked at her, unsure of what to say.

"You love Marilyn, right? Loved her on your wedding day?"

"Very much. She's . . . she's the only woman I've ever loved."

"But see, this fear of yours was more powerful than your love for Marilyn. All of a sudden, she didn't matter. You left her all alone out on that dance floor, every eye watching her. The dream she had since she was a little girl was being crushed as each moment ticked by. Now she's not here, so I can't ask her, but I'd venture to say, she wasn't feeling too loved right about then, was she?"

Jim's eyes started moistening up.

"I wouldn't be surprised," Audrey continued, "if feeling unloved or rejected is one of Marilyn's core fears. And I imagine the two of you have been to a lot of weddings together since your wedding day."

Jim nodded. "We have."

"And probably, at every one of those, as couples got up to dance at the reception, your core fear kicked in, and the two of you didn't dance."

"I've never danced with her."

"So every time that happened, I'll bet she flashed back to your wedding day, and the pain would come back all over again, stirring up all those feelings of rejection."

He let out a deep, pent-up sigh. "Marilyn actually said something like that in her note, something about how this whole thing got triggered by a recent wedding."

"So see, in a way, Jim, you did dance with Marilyn that day. And many times since. It was the Fear Dance."

Jim felt awful.

He'd never realized any of these things before, but now they were painfully clear. And painfully true. He had been afraid of being laughed at on their wedding day. Afraid of destroying the athletic image he'd worked so hard to create in high school and college. So, to preserve that image, he had completely rejected his bride, forced her to play the fool instead, and totally crushed her girlhood dreams.

"My coffee's gotten too cold to enjoy," Audrey said. "I'm going to freshen it up. You want some more? It's decaf, won't keep you up tonight."

"What?" Jim looked up. "Yes, that would be nice. Thanks."

Audrey got up and walked into the kitchen to get the coffeepot. After she topped off their cups, she turned the coffeemaker off and set the pot back in its place. "I just remembered something I wanted to give you. Better go get it now, before I forget." She walked past him toward the living room.

"What is it?

"Just a little present for you. Something for next week." She stopped and looked down at his feet. "You're what, a size 10?"

"Yes, good guess."

"After teaching dance lessons for thirty years, you become a pretty good judge of people's feet. Wait right here." She hurried through the living room and out of sight. Moments later, she walked back holding a shoe box and set it on the table.

"What's this?"

"Open it. It's for you. Now, don't feel like you have to take them."

Jim opened the lid and saw a shiny pair of black leather shoes. "Are these dance shoes?" he asked.

"The best money can buy."

"How much do you want for them?"

"Nothing. They're a gift. From me to you. They were the last pair I bought Ted before he died. He got sick before he ever got a chance to use them."

"But Audrey, I can't . . . I can't take these."

"Of course you can. I want you to have them. Shoes this nice don't belong buried in the back of a closet. I want to see them spinning and swirling on the dance floor."

"I'm not sure that'll happen on these feet," he said.

"I am," she said with a smile. "I know they will."

They sat there a few moments in silence. Jim wasn't sure if they were done or what she planned next. She looked like she had something else to say. Finally she said it. "There's one last thing I need to mention tonight. As I got out the shoes I remembered it. Something Ted always talked about right after he'd tell folks about the Fear Dance."

Jim wasn't sure he was ready to hear any more. He looked at his watch. Had he only been here twenty minutes? It felt like two hours had gone by. "Will it take long?"

"Not at all. Won't take two minutes."

"What's it about?"

"Misplaced expectations," she said. "It has to do with the things we want, and how we keep looking in the wrong place to get them." She put a teaspoon of sugar in her cup and stirred, then tasted it. "Anyway, it's like when people dance. Sometimes they move forward together, sometimes they step back. But what happens when both partners step forward at the same time?"

"I guess they bang into each other."

"That's right. The same thing happens with our expectations. When couples get married, they have this wrong notion that their spouse is supposed to make them happy, to fulfill all their wants and desires. That was certainly true with me and Ted. The problem is, it works at first but only a little while. You know what happens after that?"

"We get disappointed." He guessed it was their age difference, but Jim couldn't help feeling like he was back in elementary school being quizzed by a teacher.

"Do you know why?"

"Because . . . our spouse can't fulfill all our expectations?"

She smiled. "You're catching on. I'm so glad. I haven't explained all these things to anyone since Ted died. And he used to do most of the talking. See, the truth is, God designed things so only he could meet the deepest needs in our hearts. But most people aren't used to looking to God that way. We put all our hope in the person we fall in love with. All these romantic movies and love songs don't help us very much here, either. They tell us over and over again that we'll be happy if we can just find the right person and fall in love. So when we find that special person, we get all excited. But do you know what happens not too far down the road?"

"We get disappointed." This seemed like the right answer to all her questions.

"And once that happens, we start looking for another partner. But see, all we've really done if we leave is find another person to dance that old Fear Dance with, and the vicious cycle starts all over again." She opened a manila folder and handed Jim a few sheets of paper stapled together. "Between now and next week, I'd like you to look these things over. It's a list Ted came up with, the most common core fears people have. Read it over when you're not in a rush and you have some time alone."

Time alone is all I have now, Jim thought.

Just then something she'd just said repeated in his mind. *We start looking for another partner.* Is that what Marilyn was doing now? Is that what this was all about? He had failed to meet her expectations, and now she was looking for a new dance partner?

28

Marilyn was beside herself. She couldn't remember when she'd ever had so much fun.

It was Thursday evening. They were just finishing up their second dance lesson at the Windsor Studio. She was sitting in a chair, almost breathless, wiping her face and neck with a towel. For most of the last thirty minutes, the class had danced the basic waltz nonstop to some of the most beautiful music she'd ever heard. She had danced with Roberto, and of course he had danced flawlessly. But other than a few missteps at the beginning, Marilyn had kept right in step with him the whole time.

She'd been practicing at the apartment all week, but only when she was alone. Charlotte was thrilled she was taking the lessons, but for some reason, Marilyn couldn't bring herself to practice with Charlotte there.

When she'd first walked in this evening, she'd felt a little lost. Audrey wasn't there and hadn't shown up to class all night. Marilyn wondered where she was. Once again, Marilyn was the only one there without a partner. But true to his promise, before the class began Roberto had come over and reminded her that she'd be his partner tonight. And several of the class members had greeted her by name and talked with her like old friends.

She was so glad now she'd signed up for these classes.

Just then, an unsettling thought came. She glanced at the big window, then felt instant relief. Jim wasn't there. She looked by the front door, remembering how he'd stormed in last week, the furious look on his face. He wasn't there, either.

"Watching you and Roberto dance tonight was really something."

Marilyn turned around to face the voice. It was Faye, Gordon's wife. He was the older man from last week who couldn't get the dance steps down. "What?" she said, although she'd heard what Faye had said.

"You and Roberto," Faye repeated. "You were such a joy to watch."

"Why, thank you."

"It was like you two were in a different league than the rest of us. Of course, you'd expect Roberto to be, but you were doing a good job there, holding your own. Gordon and I are just beginners, and we're not getting off to a great start, if you ask me." She was smiling.

Marilyn didn't know what to say. It was a fairly small room, so you couldn't help but watch everyone else as they danced. Flashes of the considerable number of times Faye had scolded Gordon came to mind, every time he stepped on her toes or got the steps wrong. She always did it in a playful tone, and Gordon always laughed after. "How are your feet holding up?" Marilyn said.

Faye looked down at them. "They're doing fine. You musta thought I was kidding about wearing steel-toed shoes." She looked up again. "I wasn't. I told Gordon when he kept pushing me to sign up for these classes, I ain't about to let you mangle my feet once a week. It's bad enough when we have to dance at weddings every now and then."

"Gordon was the one who wanted the two of you to take these classes?"

Faye nodded. "Ol' Gordon, he loves to dance. But I don't know why. He's awful at it. Course, I don't need to tell you that." She leaned forward. "The man can't even clap on beat. All these years we been married, every time there's a chance to dance, he drags me out there on the floor. Now don't get me wrong, I love to dance. And I love Gordon to bits. But those two things don't necessarily go together."

Marilyn wondered what it must be like to have a husband who loved to dance. And here he was, like Faye said, terrible at it. Gordon didn't seem to mind her playful jabs a bit. "Is he making any progress?" Marilyn said.

Faye looked over her shoulder. Gordon was by the desk, talking to one of the other husbands. "I tell him he is," she said. "But you know . . . I don't think so. I'm not sure these lessons are helping one bit. But I promised him I'd give it a try. See, we're celebrating our fiftieth anniversary in two months, and we're taking a seven-day Caribbean cruise. Gordon looked into it, and there's all kinds of opportunities to dance on these cruises. He's convinced himself all he needs is a few good lessons, and we'd be all set." She looked up at him with love in her eyes. "It's only week two, but I'm not that hopeful. Let's just say, I plan on packing these steel-toed shoes for that cruise."

Marilyn smiled. "Fifty years, congratulations. That's an amazing accomplishment these days."

"I suppose so," Faye said. "He's really a wonderful man when you look past his flaws, and pretty easy to be with. I'm the one that's a pill."

Marilyn wondered what it must be like to be married for fifty years to someone you still felt that way about. She and Jim had made it just beyond the twenty-five-year mark, and look where they were. She remembered how they had celebrated their silver anniversary, also on a Caribbean cruise. The ship had stopped at ports like San Juan, St. Thomas, and the Cayman Islands. But the trip had been her idea, not Jim's. When she booked it, she had high hopes it might stir fresh romance into their relationship.

That didn't happen. Not even close.

Jim had spent most of his time with his nose in his laptop or reading a bestselling business book he'd bought a few days before they'd left. "Can't wait to read this," he'd said with far more enthusiasm than he'd shown toward her about any aspect of the trip. She couldn't even get him to spend an hour going over the different excursions they could take together at the various ports of call. "You pick them out," he'd said. "Whatever you want, hon. I'll be fine with it." He didn't even look up from the computer screen.

But he certainly had loved the food. So had she. How could you not? Gourmet meals from morning till night, prepared by chefs. And plenty of it, all included in the price. It had turned out to be the high point of the cruise . . . for both of them. It certainly wasn't the dancing. Gordon was right about that. There were plenty of opportunities to dance aboard cruise ships. Marilyn knew better than to even bring that subject up with Jim.

"Excuse me, ladies."

Marilyn looked up into Roberto's smiling face. He was bending over, one arm leaning on the back of her chair.

"I hope I'm not interrupting anything too important."

"No," Faye said. "We're just yakking."

"Marilyn, could I have a word with you?"

"What?"

"A word? Won't take a minute of your time."

"You two go ahead," Faye said, standing up. "I've gotta get Gordon home in time for his meds." She smiled and walked away.

Roberto sat in her seat, right next to Marilyn. Someone by the front door yelled good-bye to him. He looked up and waved, then gave her his undivided attention. He had such penetrating eyes. Marilyn had noticed that when they danced. When Roberto looked at her, it was like the two of them were alone in the room. Just her. Just him. Gliding across the floor.

"I wondered," Roberto said, "if you'd allow me to take you to lunch tomorrow. There's something I need to discuss with you."

"You want to take me . . . to lunch?" Was he asking her out on a date? She instantly tensed up.

"You do eat, don't you?"

"Yes, of course I eat, but—"

"Then let's meet for lunch, anywhere in town. You pick the place."

"I don't know." Then she remembered. "I . . . I work tomorrow. During the lunch hour, I mean."

"Okay . . . then when do you get a break? Sometime in the afternoon? They must give you a break sometime."

"They do. I think it's around three o'clock."

"Well, then, how about coffee? I'll meet you at the Starbucks around the corner. Three o'clock. We can talk then." He smiled, then stood up.

"But . . ."

Someone called to him, and he walked away.

29

I don't know what to do, Charlotte. It just feels so wrong."

Charlotte had the day off. She'd worked late last night, so she'd slept in. It was almost noon on Friday. She was eating her breakfast, and she'd asked Marilyn to join her for a cup of coffee before Marilyn headed off to her job at Odds-n-Ends. "What feels wrong about it?" she said.

"I'm married," Marilyn said. "I shouldn't be going out with another man. I think I'm just not going to show up this afternoon." She took a sip of coffee; her hand was actually shaking.

"Doesn't sound like you're going out with him. Not like that, anyway. Aren't you just meeting him for coffee?"

Marilyn nodded.

"People do that all the time. With people they're not married to, I mean. You know, co-workers, neighbors, friends. Isn't that what you two are? Just friends?" She scooped a piece of fried egg onto her toast.

"I guess. I'm not even sure we're friends yet. Not really. He's my dance instructor. We're just dance partners." Marilyn went on to explain how Roberto had agreed to be her partner for the class since she was the only one attending without one. And how they had danced together for the last thirty minutes of the class last night. "It was the most fun I've had since I don't know when," she said.

"See?" Charlotte said. "That's all you were having . . . good clean fun, right? I mean, he didn't put any moves on you while you danced, did he?"

"No . . . I don't think so." Marilyn thought about the way he'd looked at her while they danced. It was almost mesmerizing, but it didn't seem lustful or romantic. She would have recognized it if it had been, wouldn't she?

"You don't think so?" Charlotte said. "I know you're kind of out of practice after being married for so long, but I think you'd know it if a guy was coming on to you. Don't you think?"

"No, you're right. He wasn't putting any moves on me. We just danced."

"So, why'd you hesitate when I asked? Don't get me wrong. I'm not trying to make you feel guilty about it. Just trying to be a friend."

"I'm just confused." She sat back in her chair. "This whole thing is so new for me. Dancing with someone who's not my husband. It feels like such a romantic thing, but I know it's really not. Maybe it's the atmosphere, the beautiful music, or the fact that we're holding each other while we're dancing around the floor. But really, he was a perfect gentleman the whole time."

"I'm sure it's nothing then. He just wants to meet for coffee. It's not like it's a date." Charlotte mopped up the last piece of egg with her last piece of toast. Before putting it in her mouth, she said, "If you get there and you feel he's starting to get the wrong idea, or if what he wants to ask you is the least bit inappropriate, you can just tell him to get lost."

Marilyn hoped nothing like that happened. There was no way she could finish her dance lessons if it did.

"If you want, I could go with you. You know, it doesn't have to look like we planned it. I could just show up for coffee there at the same time."

"Thanks, but I don't think that's necessary. I'm a big girl. I should be able to handle this. Besides, it's probably nothing at all. I'm just making a big deal out of nothing."

"I think you might be," Charlotte said. "Meeting a friend who happens to be a man for coffee is kind of in the same range as dancing. It doesn't mean there's anything romantic going on. Why don't you pray about it? Ask God to help you tell if this guy's starting to hit on you. And if he is, like I said, you stand up and tell him to bug off."

"You're right, Charlotte. That's what I'll do." She looked at her watch. "I really need to get going." She took a last sip of her coffee. "I feel so much better about this now. Thanks for talking with me."

"That's what friends are for," she said, smiling.

Marilyn hurried back to her bedroom and grabbed her purse. She really did feel better about the situation now. She said goodbye to Charlotte and headed out the door. As she made her way down the steps, another troubling thought surfaced. What if someone saw her having coffee with Roberto this afternoon? The Starbucks was in a central spot downtown, right out in the open. What if someone from her old church saw them?

What if Jim did?

Marilyn got in line at Starbucks, five minutes before three. She was relieved; Roberto hadn't arrived yet. She had a thirty-minute lunch break, and the café was only a five-minute walk from Odds-n-Ends. She left in time to get her cappuccino and find a seat before three. That way she'd make sure she paid for it herself, and that she only had fifteen minutes left to talk before she had to head back.

How much damage could be done in fifteen minutes?

The line moved fairly quickly. She placed her order then walked to the other side of the counter to pick it up. As she stirred in the Splenda packet, she heard the front door open. She glanced up to see Roberto walk through.

His face lit up. "Marilyn, there you are," he said in that marvelous Latin accent. Marilyn had to remind herself it was a put-on. "So glad you could come." He got in line. "But I wished you had waited to order. It was going to be my treat."

She noticed that both a young woman in line and one behind the counter instantly looked at Roberto *that* way. "I'm sorry, Roberto. Go ahead and get yours. I'll get us a table."

"Very well. I'll be there *un minuto*."

She picked a table in the corner of the outside section, set behind a half wall, the farthest one from the door. So far, she didn't recognize a soul. A few moments later, Roberto joined her.

"You look lovely, Marilyn."

Marilyn instantly felt self-conscious. "This is just something from the back of my closet."

He looked at her name tag. "Odds-n-Ends is a nice store. I've bought gifts there for people several times."

"It really is. I bought myself a gift there just last week. A beautiful music box. As a matter of fact, that little music box is the reason I'm taking dance lessons." Marilyn went on to tell him about how she'd met Audrey while playing the music box for Michele at Giovanni's.

"That's a wonderful story," he said. "My thanks to the maker of the music box then."

Marilyn smiled, took a sip of her cappuccino. Was he flirting with her or just being nice? He was just being nice, of course that was all it was. It was just the way he talked. And the way he looked at people when he talked. "So," she said. "What's this thing you want to talk to me about? We better get to it right away. I really only have a few minutes before I have to head back to the store."

"Oh . . . my loss. But really, this will only take a few minutes. I could have told you last night at the studio. But it seemed so impersonal."

"So this is something personal?" she asked.

"In a way, but not really. I just didn't want to say this in front of all the other class members. And I didn't want to put you on the spot, so to speak. Even now, please know, you *don't* have to do what I'm about to ask you. I don't want you to feel *any* pressure."

Whatever could it be? "Please . . . don't keep me in suspense."

"Well, I made this decision last night after we danced. Actually, I started thinking about this after last week's class. I could tell you were a natural the moment I saw you on the floor. But after last night, my decision was crystal clear."

"Roberto . . ."

"I'm sorry, I'm still keeping you in suspense, aren't I? The thing is, there's a regional dance contest at the end of September in Orlando. It's a very prestigious event. An opportunity for dance instructors throughout central Florida to put on display how well they're able to teach their students."

"I don't understand. What does that have to do with me?"

"Everything, my dear. The rules state each instructor must

select as his partner someone from a beginner's dance class. They absolutely have to be a novice. This is your first dance class, correct?"

"Yes."

"Because you'll have to sign an affidavit stating so. But Marilyn, you'll be perfect. I usually do this just for the extra publicity it brings to the studio. But my dear, with you on my arm . . . I think we have a chance of actually winning the whole thing!"

30

It was Sunday morning. Jim sat in the church parking lot, trying to work up the courage to get out of the car. He smiled as different members he recognized drove up, parked their cars, nodded then stared at him as they walked by. Probably trying to figure out what he was up to. Trying to put together in their heads which parts of the gossip they'd heard about him and Marilyn were true.

He was a pariah now, inside that building. He was sure of that. A man fallen from grace. If not from God, certainly from men. And in that building, what people thought about you was all you had. Your image, your reputation. He'd spent years crafting it, honing it to a fine edge. Making the right connections with just the right mix of people.

As he thought about it now, it seemed a bit like the pressures of high school, albeit a more sophisticated version. A religious version, where the popular crowd was still popular for some of the same reasons, and people like him had always felt on the outside trying to break in but never quite getting there. He was always on a treadmill, trying to keep the connections and acceptance alive. Knowing that at any moment something could happen—almost anything at all—to sever these fragile ties.

And if that happened, they'd cut you loose and you'd float away untethered like a balloon, as the crowd chatted and pointed at you until you faded from sight.

Jim sat there in his car, knowing that right now was such a moment for him.

If it had not already happened, it certainly would the moment he walked in the door and handed this letter to Mort Stanley. He decided to do it before the service. And he wouldn't stay for the looks, the stares, the fake smiles. No, he'd be heading back here to his car; the golf clubs were already in his trunk. He'd drive out of the parking lot before the choir had finished singing the second hymn.

The untethered balloon.

He held the letter up by the steering wheel and read it once more. No good reason to do that; he'd written and rewritten it a dozen times up to this point. Still, there was an itch to read it again. Just once more.

Dear Mort (and the rest of the deacon board),

Please accept this letter as my resignation from the deacon board, effective immediately. I won't be attending the scheduled meeting tomorrow night to discuss the proposal regarding the church leasing my property for its senior center over the next year. I understand my absence, this resignation, and the information I'm about to share will likely result in the church deciding to pass on the deal.

As you all have likely heard, my wife and I aren't doing well at the moment. To be more precise, we are separated. My efforts to bring about a quick resolve to this crisis have proved ineffective. We are no closer to reconciling our differences than we were the day she walked out two weeks ago. I still don't know what the main issues are, because she won't even talk to me.

But of course, these are my problems, not yours. And I no longer wish to be a hindrance to the board and the many important projects and plans you all must make for the church's future. It has been a distinct honor to serve with you men over the past two years.

Sincerely,
James Anderson (Jim)

He reread the last line, the part about it having been "a distinct honor" to serve on the board these past two years.

Had it been? Really?

On one level it had. He loved the feeling of being nominated by members of the church to serve in that honored role, and remembered the joy he'd felt the day he'd been voted in. He even loved the boring meetings, discussing the big issues, being a part of such an elite guild.

But the paper he held in his hand would end all that. And he knew—because he'd seen it happen to others over the years—one never rises once fallen from grace. Not in this church. Not with their standards and, yes, with their noses—as his daughter Michele used to say—raised so high in the air.

He got out of the car, trying not to think of how this decision would affect his personal finances. Three other board members had leased properties with his company, as well as two other prominent businessmen in the church. Fortunately and for now, their allegiance would hold by the lease contracts they had signed. So there wouldn't be any immediate drop in revenue. But would these men renew their leases again when the time came? Would Jim ever see a single new customer come from the members of this church?

He walked across the parking lot to the sidewalk. Would anyone in the church even reach out to him on any level after this?

A few might make perfunctory phone calls, those who still had a modicum of Christian charity alive in their hearts. But for most, he would simply cease to exist. He was the pariah now. The untethered balloon.

He opened the glass door, heard the organ begin to play. The door closed behind him. Three church members he knew—and a few weeks ago would have thought of as friends—stood by the entrance to the sanctuary. They looked his way just a moment. One said something to the others, and they quickly hurried inside.

As he reached the sanctuary door, he recognized the song the organ was playing: "Blest Be the Tie That Binds." He stepped inside, scanning the crowd for Mort Stanley as the choir began to sing:

> Blest be the tie that binds our hearts in Christian love;
> the fellowship of kindred minds is like to that above.

31

Jim pulled into his driveway, waited for the garage door to rise. Playing golf had always been good medicine for him, but especially today. His drives had actually gone several yards farther than his average. Probably had something to do with the short bursts of anger he released every time he whacked the ball. Different faces of people at church would come to mind, the ones he knew didn't like him or the ones he was certain were talking about him behind his back.

Why did people think that was okay? Especially church people? The garage door clicked into place, and he pulled the car inside. They did it all the time, at least at his church. He supposed he'd engaged in it himself from time to time, or at least sat there nodding dumbly while others did. Of course, it never bothered him so much before. He'd never been on the receiving end. At least not that he could tell.

He turned the car off and got out, stood there waiting for the garage door to close again. It certainly bothered Marilyn—the gossip, that is. And it really had bothered Michele. That was the reason she'd given for leaving the church altogether once she left for college. She had come back one holiday in that first year with a teaching outline from a new church she'd been attending near the school. She said members of this church had to make a commitment to resolve their conflicts by following something she called "Peacemaking Principles." Then she plopped the outline down, right there on the dinner table, insisting he and Marilyn hear her out.

"That's what's so wrong about your church, Dad. Can't you see? Look at all these Scriptures about gossip and slander. Do you see what this says?"

Jim looked down at the page. He was just humoring her, of course, knowing if he put up a fuss this thing would go on until his roast beef and scalloped potatoes had grown cold. She pointed out one verse after the other, in both the Old Testament and New, stating plainly how much God hated gossip and slander. How it was in the same list of serious sins as sexual immorality and stealing. And she read other Scriptures about how it destroyed relationships.

Jim already knew gossip and slander weren't good things. He didn't need his daughter ruining a good dinner by highlighting such a depressing topic. And he certainly couldn't see how it was as serious a thing as immorality or stealing.

Standing there in the garage now, he began to think there was something to what Michele had been trying to say. After putting his clubs and shoes away, he walked through the garage past the laundry room, when he heard loud music coming from the stairway leading to Doug's apartment. He headed up the stairs and banged on Doug's door. The music stopped.

"Hey, Dad, you're back. How was golf?"

"Pretty good," Jim said. "How was church?"

"What?"

"You said you were going with Jason's family this morning."

"I did. I've been home for over an hour."

Jim didn't like Doug's hesitation. Should he press harder? He wasn't in the mood to catch Doug in a lie and didn't have the energy to deal with all the tension. "Listen, I'm heading over to the house to take a shower and get cleaned up. Then I'm calling for a pizza."

"From Gabbie's?"

"Sure, we can get it from there. I'm guessing you want some."

"I'm starving."

"Pepperoni, as usual?"

Doug nodded. "But they'll do half, so make the other half Italian sausage or whatever you like."

"I will. Why don't you head over in about forty-five minutes. Should be here by then."

"Great. See you then."

Jim stayed a little longer in the shower than usual, allowing the hot water to pour down his neck and back. It seemed to soothe the savage beast inside. He realized that one of the faces that had not come to mind as he whacked those golf balls was Marilyn's. He was still angry with her for leaving him like this. None of these troubles at church would have ever started if she'd stayed home. Why did she have to do something this drastic to get his attention? Why hadn't she given him some kind of warning signal that she had reached the danger zone?

As he dried off, he thought about something Audrey Windsor had said when they first chatted last week in the parking lot. *My guess is . . . she's been trying to talk to you about how unhappy she's been for a long time, but you haven't been listening.* And then something else: *Has she ever talked to you about attending a marriage retreat with her, maybe suggested some marriage books the two of you should read together?*

Marilyn hadn't done anything like that. She'd just walked out. She'd written a note and walked out. A picture of the note came to mind. Something she'd said. He walked over to his dresser, pulled the note out from the top drawer. *You probably have no idea how many times in recent months I've tried to talk to you about how unhappy I am, how unhappy I've been. It goes right over your head. I've dropped hint after hint, clue after clue. None of it gets past that hard shell of yours.*

Had she really tried that hard? How was it possible? How could he have missed every signal? Nobody is that dull, he thought. He set his towel on the bed and started getting dressed, put on some shorts and a pullover shirt. It was still relatively warm out. He thought it would be nice to eat the pizza outside on the veranda. And it would be nice to get some time with Doug. Of course, Doug probably had plans for the rest of the evening. If not, maybe they could watch a DVD together, maybe a decent action film. Doug always knew a good one to pick out.

He went into his side of the closet to get a pair of deck shoes to wear. After setting them on the floor, he reached over to turn on the lamp beside the bed. It had clouded over that afternoon. As he pulled back from clicking on the lamp, his elbow caught the edge of his golf magazine and knocked it to the floor.

That's when he saw them.

It was a freeze-frame moment, as if some invisible hand held his head in place. Two books. Beneath them, a magazine. A wrinkled yellow Post-it note sticking out the top. They'd been there on his nightstand so long, they'd become part of the furniture.

But he saw them now. And he remembered.

He reached over and picked them up, looked at the covers, read the titles . . . as if for the first time. They were marriage books, both of them. Ones Marilyn had read months ago. Well, the first one. The second one possibly last year. And he remembered her asking him to read them. She said they were wonderful. Something else about how they'd really helped her understand some things about their relationship. She had given them to him, and he'd put them on his nightstand, without any intention of reading them.

He opened the cover of the first one, looked at the table of contents. There were checkmarks beside four different chapters. A flash of a conversation with Marilyn, after the book had sat by the bed for several weeks, untouched. "I know you're busy, Jim. And you hate to read books. Well, books like *that*. I checked off a few chapters that I thought might help. The book's written by a man, and he really seems to understand how men think. Do you think you could at least read those? It's less than forty pages."

Jim had assured her he would, just to get her to stop asking.

He picked up the magazine. It was a woman's magazine, for goodness sake. How did she expect him to read that? He opened it to the marked page. Saw a smiling couple holding hands, walking on the beach. The article was called "7 Ways to Put the Fire Back into an Aging Romance."

He closed the magazine, set it back on top of the books, and clicked off the lamp. Then he lay back on the bed and sighed. She had been trying to get his attention. For a good long while. As he lay there, other memories started coming to the surface. Snippets of conversations over the last year or so. Marilyn gently asking, sometimes almost pleading with him, about one thing or another. Each one, some aspect of their relationship.

Moments he'd completely missed.

Hint after hint. Clue after clue.

32

Jim pulled up to Audrey's home for his second dance class. It was Monday night. Just before heading over, he'd spent about an hour studying the list of twenty core fears she'd given him last week. He couldn't believe he'd forgotten to do this, and he was sure she'd ask about it tonight. He was surprised how easy it was to pick out one other core fear he had. Maybe he had more, but now he saw at least two.

Picking up the shoe box on the seat beside him, he headed toward the front door. He probably could have worn the dance shoes here, but he didn't want to scuff the leather soles walking on the pavement.

Audrey opened the door. "Come in, Jim. You came back."

"You didn't think I would?" He stepped through the doorway.

"I hoped so, but I gave you a lot to digest last week. Hoped I didn't scare you off."

"No," he said as he walked into the living room. "I'm still not sure you can teach me how to dance, but I said I'd give it a try, so here I am. Should I put these on now? We're going to actually dance tonight, right?"

"We are, so go right ahead. You can sit there on the couch. I'll go pour some coffee. I also have bottled water in the refrigerator for once we start the lesson."

Coffee, Jim thought. He hoped that didn't mean he was going to have to sit through another twenty-five-minute talk before they started the lesson. Still, he had to admit he had learned some helpful things last week. Of course, they'd have been a lot more helpful if Marilyn could have been there to learn these things at the same time. She certainly had her share of core fears. As he'd read over the list, he saw quite a few things that sounded a lot like Marilyn.

"So are you still feeling terrified?"

Jim looked up as he finished tying the laces. "Oddly enough . . . I'm not." He stood up. "I've dropped all the way down to just plain nervous."

"See?" she said. "Fear loses some of its power just by shining the light in its eyes. Did you get any time to look over that list I gave you?"

He walked toward the kitchen, noticing she'd set his cup of coffee on the dinette table. She followed beside him. "I certainly did."

"Did you answer the little questionnaire at the end?"

"I did that too." He picked up his coffee and took a sip.

"Spot any other fears besides the one from last week?"

"At least one," he said. "The one about feeling powerless or being controlled."

"That's another big one for men," she said. "In fact, those were my husband Ted's core fears. You actually remind me of him in some ways." She said it like a compliment. "Did your wife or kids ever talk to you about having control issues or being a—"

"A control freak?" he added.

She smiled. "That's the term."

"A few times," he said, returning the smile. "Well, quite a few, actually. But I never saw it as a bad thing before. I don't see myself as trying to control anyone. Feels like I'm just being responsible. The husband is supposed to be the head of his family."

She opened the French doors leading into the studio. "Well, being responsible isn't a bad thing, I agree. It's the fear in our hearts that corrupts it. That, and thinking more about what we want than what's best for the folks we're responsible for. But we can talk more about that later. You've got your dance shoes on—and they look very dashing on you, by the way. Let's go into the studio and I'll start the music CD."

Over the next fifteen minutes, Jim sat in a chair sipping coffee as Audrey explained the basic waltz and demonstrated the steps. First the man's, then the woman's. Then she turned the CD off and played a brief video of her and Ted dancing these same steps. It was really quite elegant, but Jim could never imagine himself dancing like Ted. He noticed Audrey's eyes welling up with tears as the video played. When it ended, he began to tense up. He knew what came next.

Audrey blinked back the tears and stood. "I'm sorry. I still miss him so much. So . . . are you ready?"

Jim stood. "No."

"Back to feeling terrified?"

"Maybe." He smiled.

"Well, take a look around the room. What do you see?"

Jim looked. "I don't understand." It was just a big empty room with a shiny wood floor. Floor to ceiling mirrors against one wall.

"We're alone. There's no one here who's going to see you mess up. Except me. And I'm certainly not going to make fun of you. So watch . . . I'll imitate the man's basic steps again. Then you imitate what I do." She did it, twice. Then walked over and turned on the music. "Now, your turn."

"Okay." But he just stood there. He couldn't get his feet to move.

"Want to see me do it again?" she said. "Here, watch my feet. It's really quite simple. Step, side, close. Step, side, close. See? Now you do it."

Now you do it. It's really quite simple. That wasn't the problem. The problem was, he felt like a complete idiot. The feelings and sensations from a hundred different memories rose up like an invisible wall he couldn't break through. All the times he and Marilyn had been at a party or a wedding or . . . that cruise, and he'd felt the pressure and guilt she projected his way for not being willing to dance. As well as all the imagined stares from people who'd make fun of him if he dared to even try.

Audrey walked over and turned off the music. "Are you okay?"

"Yeah. It's silly. I know I can do this."

"I know you can too." A look of concern came over her face. "But your hesitation actually gives me an idea. I've been trying to think of a way to bring this up anyway." She sat in a chair.

Jim sat down beside her.

"This is really our first dance lesson," she said, "since last week we just talked. Do you know what Ted titled this first lesson back when we used to teach couples at church?" Jim shook his head. "He called it 'the Power of One.' It's really the idea of taking responsibility for yourself and the things you do, without shifting the focus to anyone else. I think if you understood this principle, it might help you move those feet."

She sat there looking at him. Had he missed something? Had she asked him a question? "Okay," he said.

"See," she continued, "we always get preoccupied with what our partner's doing. Not just on the dance floor but in life. Something goes wrong and we blame other people or circumstances for the things we struggle with, when most of the time it's us. The things going on inside of us and our reactions to how people treat us. Can I ask what you're thinking right now? What do you think is keeping you from taking that first step?"

Jim thought about it, then he began to explain. Without meaning to, he quickly went beyond sharing the resentment and fears he'd felt about dancing. All sorts of things he struggled with came up, starting with Marilyn and the predicament she'd put him in. Then about Michele for taking Marilyn's side and all the disrespect she'd shown him since this ordeal began. About Mort Stanley and the stupid deacon board and all the gossips at church who judged him. Then about the economy and all the properties he owned that he couldn't get leases for.

As he talked, Audrey listened patiently, with nothing but kindness in her eyes. But it was like a message came through those kind eyes. Somehow he could also tell . . . in everything he shared, he had placed the blame—all of it, every single thing—on everyone and everything but himself.

When he finished, she paused, then said, "You're seeing it, Jim, aren't you? All of your problems, the way you see them anyway, are caused by others. Do you see how our minds work? If everybody would just cooperate and do things the way we want them to, our problems would disappear. We get totally focused on everyone and everything else but our own part." She smiled. "Tell me something, Jim. Can you fix any of this? Any of the people or the problems you just described? Can you control these people or change the way they treated you? Have any of your efforts helped? Even a little?"

He realized, not a bit. No matter how hard he'd tried, he hadn't fixed a single thing or solved any of his problems. "If anything," he said, "I've made things worse."

"And that makes you feel out of control, powerless."

"Pretty much."

"But see, that's a good place to be. Now you're getting close to understanding what Ted meant by the Power of One. You can't fix Marilyn or Michele or the people at your church or any of the problems you're facing. There's only *one* thing you can possibly control, with God's help, I mean, and that's yourself. The way *you* act, and the way you react to the people and things around you. When you understand this one truth, it will set you free from so many things. God wants you to be free, Jim. But that can never happen as long as you think you're trapped by your circumstances or what other people do. Including Marilyn."

Audrey stood up, walked over, and turned on the music. "I think this is what's holding you back from dancing, Jim. Don't focus on all these things you can't control. Focus on something you can change. God will hold up his end, but it's like Peter that time Jesus walked on the water. Peter had to get out of the boat." She showed him once more the basic dance steps for a man, then came back and held out her hand.

Jim stood up and took it.

She led him to the middle of the dance floor and let go of his hand. "Now, you do it. Don't think about anyone or anything else. There's just you here, and me. You can do this. Take the first step forward. Then slide the other foot out to the side, then close." She stood back.

Jim waited a moment, listened to the music. Then he did it. Step, side, close.

"That's it. Again, Jim."

Step, side, close.

"Once more."

Step, side, close. By now, he was at the other end of the room, so he spun around.

He couldn't stop smiling.

33

Tom, it's Dad." Jim hated doing this. "Is there any chance we could talk?"

"You mean now? On the phone?"

"No, I mean in person. I could drive over there."

"Is everything okay? You don't sound too good."

Jim sighed. "I'm . . . okay. I've just got some things bouncing around my head. I wish I could talk them out with your mother, but that's not possible. I talked to someone about it, and they suggested I talk with you guys."

"Me and Jean?"

"No, I mean my kids. I'll explain more when I see you. Is now a good time? It would take me thirty minutes to get there."

"Do you want to meet at the house?"

"I think I'd rather meet somewhere else."

"How about Panera? It's only a few blocks from here."

"Great, see you in thirty minutes."

"Sure, Dad."

"Really appreciate this, Tom. Apologize to Jean for me. I won't keep you very long."

Jim hung up, walked over to his dresser, and grabbed his wallet and keys. He couldn't believe he was doing this, but it was part of his second "homework assignment" from Audrey. She had all but insisted on it earlier tonight, before he left her house.

He stood there by his dresser, thinking about their parting conversation on the porch. It had happened less than an hour ago. "The lights are beginning to come on for you, Jim. I can see that," she had said. "But if you really want a breakthrough with Marilyn, you're going to need some help. Eventually, you need to hear from her, what she's feeling and thinking at a heart level."

"But how? She won't even talk to me."

"Not now, she won't. So you'll have to do the next best thing. Talk to your kids. They're all adults now, right?"

"My kids?"

"Didn't you say the youngest is a senior in high school?"

"Yeah, but—"

"Then they're not really kids. I bet you could get a big dose of reality if you'd open up and let them in. Get some honest conversation going on."

"You want me to talk to them . . . about all this?"

"It's called humility, Jim. It's a good thing. Not your strong suit, I know. But it's the doorway to experiencing wonderful things from God. Jesus was all about humility. And God gives grace to the humble. The Bible says that a number of times."

Jim remembered a conversation with Uncle Henry, when he'd stopped by the house a couple of weeks ago. Uncle Henry had said almost the exact same thing about humility.

What Audrey had said next was even more difficult to hear. "The reason you're chafing so much about doing this is it strikes a chord in that core fear you just learned. The one where you feel powerless and always need to control everything. I'm suggesting you open up your heart and listen to your kids. Make sure they know you really want to hear what they have to say, even if it hurts your feelings. And believe me, it will. It'll hurt plenty. But humility will bring you the strength to listen and really understand them."

Jim turned out his bedroom light. He had to do this. He walked through the empty house and headed toward the garage. He and Tom had always been the closest. He dreaded the thought of having this kind of conversation with Michele, or even Doug.

Talking to Tom was the best place to start. But still, Jim wasn't looking forward to it.

Not one bit.

As Jim drove to Panera, Tom had called saying he was running about twenty minutes late, something to do with one of the kids and poopy diapers. Jim was grateful. He was starving. At the moment, he was finishing up a bowl of chili, sopping the remainders with some cheesy kind of bread.

Apparently, dancing worked up quite an appetite. Although he wasn't sure what he'd been doing with Audrey tonight could officially be called dancing. Not yet. After watching him go back and forth across the room, rehearsing the steps by himself, Audrey had suggested they do the steps together. They weren't exactly tripping the light fantastic, just going forward in one direction, from one end of the room to the other. Then they'd turn around and go back the other way. All the while, Jim's mind was locked into gear, counting off the steps.

Audrey had laughed. "You look like you're in some terrible pain," she'd said. "But that's okay for now. Your goal eventually will be to have these steps memorized, allowing you to stare adoringly into your wife's eyes."

Jim smiled as he thought about it. He may have looked like he was in pain, but he was rather enjoying himself. And he hadn't stepped on Audrey's toes once.

"Hey, Dad."

Jim looked up into the concerned face of his eldest son. "Hey, Tom. Let me get this tray out of the way so we have some elbow room. You want to get some coffee?"

"I'm fine, just had a cup on the way over."

"I'll just refresh mine then and be right back." Jim walked his tray over to the trash can, then refilled his coffee cup. He glanced over at Tom, who was staring at him, that same concerned look on his face. It made Jim instantly forget his fond first-dancing experience. He didn't know why, but he was dreading this moment.

"So what's up?" Tom asked as Jim sat down.

"It's kind of hard to explain. Let's just say, I've been getting some marriage advice."

"Are you seeing a counselor?"

"Of a sort," he said. "Anyway, she suggested I do something, and when she did, I thought of you."

"Okay . . ."

"I just need to ask you some questions, about me. About what I'm like. And I need you to be brutally honest with me, to just tell it like it is. Even if you think what you say will hurt my feelings."

"Okay, I guess I could try." He winced a little. "I've gotta admit, this feels kind of awkward for me."

"I know, I'm sorry."

"It's not like we have conversations like this every day."

"I know."

"Really, never."

"Okay, I guess that's a clue then."

"A clue?" Tom asked.

"That we never talk like this, on this level. I suppose that means you've got a huge backlog of things you need to unload on me. I'm not sure I'm emotionally ready to hear it all at once, so why don't you just start with one thing. It can be a big thing. Maybe even the biggest thing." Jim was so nervous. He was babbling like a fool. "Okay, two or three things. If you need to go over more, we can set up another time. I just want—"

"Slow down, Dad. I'm not even sure I have one big thing."

"You're not? I mean, you can't even think of one thing?"

"What's the question again?"

"I guess I'm wanting to know if there are things about me, about the way I treat you, or have treated you in the past, that really bug you. That make it difficult for you to relate to me. Not just as a father but even as a person. But you can include things about my fatherhood."

"Oh."

Oh, Jim thought. That didn't sound good. The "oh" was followed by a long pause. Jim studied Tom's face. He figured Tom must be trying to think of how to say whatever had just come to mind.

"It's kind of hard, Dad. You've always been . . . the way you are. I haven't had a hard time with you, for the most part. You're just you. You know? For the most part, I admire you. All the success you've had, the way you manage your time and your affairs. Your people skills. Well, with most people. I know Michele struggles more with you. And Doug too, I guess."

"And your mother, of course," Jim added.

"There is that," Tom said. "Maybe you'd be better off talking with Michele and Doug."

Jim knew he'd have to eventually, but he wasn't quite ready to face that. "But seriously, Tom. You've got to struggle with me on some level."

Tom looked away. After a few moments, he blinked his eyes several times. When he looked back, Jim saw tears welling up. He wiped them away. "I guess there's one thing," he said. "It's this, doing this very thing. Talking about things like this. We never do it. We never have. I can understand why when I was a kid, but not as I grew older. Now I'm married with kids. You don't know how many times during that first year with Jean that I would lie in bed at night alone, knowing I had just wounded Jean by saying something stupid. But I didn't know how to fix it, and there was no one to call. I would have loved it if I could have heard your voice then. Even if you didn't have the magic words to make it all go away. Just to be able to talk . . . like this."

Jim didn't know what to say.

"I've always envied the way Michele and Mom talk," Tom said. "They open up about everything. You and I never do. You're like a vault. Locked up tight. All the time. And I've never been able to figure out the combination."

Jim stared at Tom, trying to comprehend, as tears filled Tom's eyes again.

34

Marilyn was so nervous. But then, she had a right to be. It was Tuesday evening. She was standing outside the Windsor Dance Studio waiting for Roberto. He must be running late. She certainly hoped he hadn't forgotten. She was glad it was summertime, and she wasn't standing there in the dark. This was supposed to be their first dance lesson together for this big contest he'd asked her about on Friday.

She had called him on Saturday with all her reasons why she had to turn him down. By the end of the phone call, he had talked her into it. Now she felt a little sneaky, showing up here like this, and she didn't like it. Like Charlotte had said, it was just dancing; she wasn't doing anything wrong. She had told Charlotte about their meeting, even about Roberto's invitation to be his partner in this dance contest. Of course, Marilyn had played everything down and didn't share any of the details.

Including that she'd be coming here tonight, alone, to practice with Roberto. As far as Charlotte knew, Marilyn was working till closing at Odds-n-Ends. Marilyn hadn't actually said that. Charlotte had just assumed it, and Marilyn hadn't corrected her.

Then there was the matter of the red dress.

It was just a dress, a dance costume, really. That's what Roberto had called it on Saturday. He'd mentioned they weren't going to be doing a waltz for the contest, but the rumba, a Latin dance. It required a flashier costume, and he wondered if she owned a bright red dress. He'd explain why later. She remembered this one, the one she was wearing right now. It was very expensive, something she'd bought a year ago for one of Jim's high-end business parties.

When she'd picked it out at the dress shop, the salesclerk seemed wowed by how she looked. The clerk said it reminded her of that romantic song "Lady in Red" by Chris De Burgh. Marilyn loved that song. It was sung by a man dancing with the love of his life who was wearing an amazing red dress. As they danced, everyone else in the room had suddenly disappeared, and the man only saw her . . . his lady in red.

Back then, Marilyn hadn't entertained any notions that Jim would actually dance with her, but she'd hoped the dress would at least turn his head, maybe stir some romantic ideas. All he'd said was, "Looks very nice, hon. Can you grab your purse? We're running late."

Right now, this lady in red felt like an idiot, standing on the sidewalk all dressed up like this. But it was a better feeling than what she'd experienced two hours ago. She'd gotten off work at four-thirty, then hurried home to sneak into the house to fetch the dress in the back of her closet. All the while hoping Jim wouldn't come home early.

What would she say if he'd caught her? Thankfully, that didn't happen.

A light turned on inside the studio office. Marilyn got closer to the glass door to see. Good, there was Roberto, coming out of the office into the studio. But he wasn't alone. Angelina, that beautiful jazz dancer who'd danced with Roberto during the first class, was right behind him. She wore a gorgeous red dress, and she looked gorgeous in it. Marilyn didn't understand. What was she doing here? Roberto saw her peeking in the door and instantly rushed over to let her in.

"I'm so sorry, my dear, to leave you standing there like that. Please forgive me." Marilyn walked in, looked at Angelina, who nodded and smiled. "I had a burst of inspiration. I had planned to just watch a video of the song I'd selected for us to use for the contest. Then I remembered Angelina. She and I had danced to this very song a year ago, worked out all the choreography for it. Of course, you and I will do a simplified version, considering the time we have left to practice. But I thought it would be much better for you to see us dancing through the song together. So I called her, and she said she'd be happy to help us."

"Maybe you should do the dance with her," Marilyn said. "If you've already done it and she knows all the steps. Really, I wouldn't mind."

"Angelina is a professional instructor. The contest requires my partner to be a novice, remember? Don't be intimidated by what you're about to see. On the way here, I discussed with Angelina some of the things we'll leave out of our routine, to make the dance something you'll be able to easily pick up with the time we have left before the contest."

Marilyn sat on the chair to put on her shoes. "How much time will we have to practice?" She was beginning to think she had made a terrible mistake.

"That's part of the contest requirements. The judges know some contestants would have a lot more time than others to prepare, so to make things fair, they insisted we're only allowed five practice sessions to perfect our routine."

"Five?"

"Don't worry," he said. "You'll have this down in three. I promise you. And to help you, there's no stipulation about you practicing on your own in between our lessons together." He was setting up a camcorder on a tripod. "This camera here will record Angelina and I. Later tonight, I'll upload it to YouTube, and then you can use it to practice as much as you'd like at home. Can you meet me here, over the next four Tuesday nights?"

"I think I can get my boss to make that work, if I give her enough notice. Will Angelina be joining us each week?"

"Oh no," Angelina said. "I can't even stay for the rest of the night."

Roberto led Angelina by the hand out to the center of the dance floor. "She'll be leaving right after we make the video. Then you and I will begin to practice. How late can you stay tonight?"

"I . . . I don't know." She didn't have to be at work tomorrow until noon. But she wasn't sure how late she wanted to stay. Especially being alone with a man. "Maybe a couple of hours," she said.

"That should give us plenty of time. We can accomplish a lot when we have no one else in the studio to distract us. Would you be a dear and push the pause button on the camera. It's all set to go. Then tap the play button on the iPod. I've already got the song ready. It will start playing in a few moments, and Angelina and I will begin our routine. Once we do, just sit back and enjoy. And imagine yourself dancing just like her a few weeks from now. I have every confidence in you."

Marilyn looked over at the big glass windows that bordered

the sidewalk. The curtains were open. She stood up. "Before I turn the music and camera on, can I close these drapes?"

"What? Why?" he said.

She knew how much he enjoyed being watched while he danced, not to mention the free advertising it provided for passersby. But she hated being watched in equal measure. "I'm not comfortable dancing like this with everyone watching."

"But Marilyn, you know everyone will be watching the night of the contest. Hundreds of eyes will be on no one else but you and me. I think it would be good practice for you to get used to . . . being watched."

"That may be so for the contest," she said. "But I'm not comfortable with people watching me here."

"Are you serious?"

"Very," she said. "In fact, if you insist we keep the drapes open, I'll have to pass on being your partner."

"If you feel that strongly, then, of course, by all means close them."

Marilyn walked over and closed them. Her real reason—or at least the deeper reason for wanting them closed—wasn't the fact that everyone who walked by would see her dancing with Roberto. There was just one pair of eyes she really cared about.

Jim's.

What would he think if he came back to spy on her? He'd already pitched a fit just watching Roberto innocently kiss her on the hand that first night. How would he react to watching her dance the rumba with this handsome Latin man? Just the two of them. Alone in the studio.

That would never do.

"Thank you, Roberto," she said as she walked over to the camera.

"Not a problem, my dear. We're ready whenever you are."

Marilyn pushed the pause button then stepped carefully around the tripod to hit the play button on the CD player. She took a seat on one of the cushioned chairs.

Oh no, she thought as the music began to play. She couldn't believe it. The song Roberto had picked for their dance was "Lady in Red" by Chris De Burgh. She sat mesmerized as Roberto and Angelina danced gently and softly to the music. It was so elegant and lovely, and so romantic. But she also realized, in places, quite sensual.

Could she really do this? Dance like this, the way Angelina was doing now?

35

Audrey Windsor stopped in at the dance studio just after lunch on Wednesday afternoon. She volunteered on most Wednesdays. She'd straighten things up on the desks, put things back in their place, and review the studio's monthly schedule. Just to avoid any train wrecks. Besides the weekly classes, the different dance instructors were allowed to schedule private lessons at the studio, but they weren't always careful to write them in the proper time slots, or to write them down at all.

She was reviewing the calendar when she saw it. Roberto had written for the next four Tuesday nights: *Private dance lessons—Roberto with Marilyn Anderson, 7–9:30 p.m.*

What in the world?

Okay, she told herself, don't react. It could be nothing. But she also knew Roberto, the additional charm he always turned on like a switch whenever he was around attractive women, and she was aware of the troubled relationship Marilyn and Jim were having now. The idea of Marilyn and Roberto meeting for private dance lessons seemed like a path headed for trouble.

Should she say something? Roberto was sitting in the office

right now doing some paperwork. It was a good time. Other than the two of them, the studio was empty. If she was going to say something, she'd better do it now. The calendar showed a girls' ballet class starting in thirty minutes.

She walked to the doorway and peeked inside. She may get into all sorts of trouble here, but she felt she had to at least say something, let him know in a discreet way that she had her eyes on him. "Excuse me, Roberto? Do you have a minute?"

"What?" He looked up from the desk. "Oh, Audrey, it's you." The Latin accent was gone. He never used it anymore when they were alone. Another reason she didn't fully trust him. "What can I do for you?"

"Nothing really. I was just going over the monthly schedule. You know, like I always do."

"And I always appreciate it."

"I know. Well, I noticed something you wrote down, I guess it was last night or this morning." His eyebrows drew close together. "I guess you're starting private dance lessons with Marilyn Anderson?"

"Yes . . . is there some problem?"

"Well, no. I don't know. Maybe. There could be."

"I don't understand," he said.

"Do you mind if I ask . . . did she request to have private lessons?"

"What? No, she didn't." His voice was becoming a little stern. "It was my idea. She's a very gifted dancer. A novice, for sure, but did you see her after that first night? You weren't here last week, but she's become quite skillful already. I've chosen her to be my partner in the teacher/pupil dance contest in September."

"Are you sure that's a good idea?" Audrey said. "I mean, you and her meeting here for private lessons . . . at night?"

"What do you mean?" His tone and expression suggested he knew exactly what she meant.

Audrey stepped farther inside the office. "Well, did you know she and her husband are separated? It just happened a few weeks ago. I've talked with him. He's desperate to win her back."

Roberto set his pen down. "Well, good for him. She's a wonderful lady. Attractive, vivacious, a genuinely kind personality. You don't often see that combination these days."

That sounded good to Audrey, to hear him talk like this. Maybe she was worried for nothing.

"I might add," Roberto said, "that she never talks about him. I've only surmised she is separated by piecing little things together. I don't know what the man's done to her, but I wouldn't, let's say, encourage him too much about winning her back. At least not anytime soon. To me, she seems like a bird let out of a cage. Free for the first time in years, and loving it."

Now they were back to things not sounding too good. "But you're not . . . pursuing her in any way, right?"

"Mrs. Windsor, I'm surprised you'd ask me such a thing. No, I have not set my sights on Mrs. Anderson. I wouldn't feel right doing such a thing—this early on, anyway. Not when she's just left her husband. She'd be too vulnerable right now. It would be pure manipulation on my part, and that's not who I am."

Audrey wasn't so sure. And the way he'd said it wouldn't be right to pursue her "this early on" certainly left the door open for him to pursue Marilyn when the time was right. Just when might such a time be? A week from now? A month? Roberto lived life on his own terms, did as he pleased.

No, this conversation did nothing to assure Audrey. She'd have to keep her eye on the situation. And somehow, she'd have to think of a way to break this news to Jim. Better for him to hear it from her than to hear darker versions of the news through the grapevine.

She thanked Roberto for his time, apologized if she had offended him by inquiring. He insisted she had not. She left the office, and as she did, she said a prayer for the Andersons. *Lord, please don't let this thing go from bad to worse. Keep Marilyn's feet from stumbling with this man. Help her see what she'd be throwing away. And please open Jim's eyes to see the things he desperately needs to see about his own heart. This is much too big for me to fix.*

Jim stopped off to buy Chinese takeout on his way home. He waited in the parking lot a moment, hoping to reach Doug to see if he should buy any food for him too.

"Hey, Dad."

"Wow, it's you. It's really you. Not your voice mail."

"Stop, it's not that bad."

It really was, but he decided to let it drop. "Listen, I'm picking up some Chinese right now and wanted to know if I should get anything for you."

"Are you paying?"

"Of course I'm paying. It's dinner."

"Well, yeah then. If you're paying. You know what I like."

Jim did. Sweet and sour chicken, fried rice, and an eggroll. "They've got a ton of other things on the menu, Doug. You've been getting the same thing since you were ten. Sure you don't want to branch out? Just a little?"

"It's what I like, Dad. Could I just get that?"

"All right. But at least try a few forkfuls of my dish."

"Fine. So when are you coming home?" Doug said.

"As soon as I pick up the food, maybe fifteen minutes. Where are you?"

"On my way home from Jason's. I'll probably beat you there."

"Great, see you in a few," Jim said. "And Doug . . . listen, tonight could we eat together? There's something I want to talk to you about." Doug would usually grab his food and head up to his room.

"Uh-oh. Am I in some kind of trouble?"

"I don't know, have you done anything wrong? You know what the Bible says, the guilty flee when no one is pursuing."

"What? No, I haven't done anything wrong. I don't even know what that means."

"I'm kidding, Doug."

"You are?"

"I really am."

"Oh. Well, let's pretend I got it and laughed."

Jim laughed. "Okay, let's pretend. I'll see you in a few."

"Wait," Doug said. "You still haven't told me if I'm in any trouble."

"No, Doug. You're not in any trouble. I just want to talk." If anything, I'm the one who's in trouble, Jim thought. "Believe it or not, I've been getting some help recently, and some good advice."

"Really? From who?"

"That doesn't matter. The point is, this person thought it would be a good idea if I did some serious listening for a change."

"Listening to who?"

"You, Michele, and Tom. I've already talked with Tom. Now I want to talk with you."

"Waiting for Michele to go last. Good idea."

Even Doug understood this. Jim sighed. "Yeah, well . . . Anyway, I don't want to go into it all now, and I certainly don't want to make you get all nervous. I just want to hear anything you have to say. Any thoughts you're sitting on."

"Really? What about?"

"About me. Any struggles you're having with me. Let's start there. Anything that's bothering you, about your mom and me, what we're going through."

"Really?"

"Yeah."

"Okay, I'll try. See you in a few minutes then."

Jim hung up, got out of the car, and headed toward the takeout window of the Chinese restaurant. That didn't go so bad. His conversation with Tom two nights ago had gone better than he'd hoped for too. It had been difficult on an emotional level. But Jim hadn't blown up at Tom or gotten defensive even once. When they had finished talking, Tom had thanked him and given him a hug. Jim had promised Tom he'd try to be more open with him in the future.

Of course, he had no idea how to pull that off. He was sailing through totally uncharted waters here.

36

For the first ten minutes, Jim and Doug sat there eating on bar stools by the kitchen counter. Doug eating his sweet and sour chicken, Jim his Mongolian beef. It had a nice kick to it. Doug had kept his promise and tried a piece—one piece. He went right back to his favorite Chinese dish. "They're just Chinese chicken nuggets," Jim said, breaking the silence. "You know that, right? It's not really even a Chinese dish."

"Really, Dad? Are you going to keep hassling me about this? I tried your spicy beef. It wasn't bad. I just like this better."

"All right." He chewed some more, looked at Doug, who dipped another nugget with the chopsticks in that sickeningly sweet red sauce. At least he knew how to use them, Jim thought. He could never get them to work right.

How was he going to break into this conversation they were supposed to be having?

"The way I see it, Dad, I've only got about five more minutes of food left. Are we going to do this, or what?"

Jim laughed. Do what, he thought. How does one "do this"? He envied Marilyn at this moment. All women, really. How did they just open up and start talking at a heart level? It seemed effortless for them. A woman could sit on a bench next to another woman, a complete stranger. Five minutes later, they're pouring out their hearts to each other, sharing things at a level men wouldn't even begin to acknowledge after six months of "male bonding." This felt like walking through thick woods without a trail.

Take responsibility for yourself, Jim thought. He was the adult here. He needed to be the one to initiate, try to make it easy for Doug to open up. "Well, guess I'll just jump in then. Would you describe me as a control freak?"

"What?"

"A control freak. You know, someone who—"

"I know what a control freak is, Dad. I can't believe you just said it. Took me off guard a little."

"So . . . is that what I am?"

"Yeah, I guess. A little."

"Just a little?"

"No." Doug grinned. "More than a little. I'm sorry, this is a little intimidating for me."

"So I intimidate you?"

"Well . . . yeah. You're my dad." He grabbed another fried chunk of chicken, dipped it in the sauce, and plopped it in his mouth.

"You mean, that's what dads do? Intimidate their kids?"

Doug finished chewing. "I guess. You do, anyway." He thought a moment. "Jason's dad isn't like that, though. He jokes around a lot with us. Kind of gets down on our level. At least he tries to. Sometimes he tries too hard. But he's a really nice guy."

Doug had just implied Jim wasn't a nice guy. "How does Jason feel about me? Do you know?"

"What? Well . . . yeah, I know."

It was clear he didn't want to say. "Well . . ."

"Basically? You scare him."

Jim couldn't believe what he was hearing. He'd never given it much thought, why Jason never came over. He was just glad it was true; the kid really bugged him. "I don't get how I scare him. We've hardly said two words to each other."

"Yeah, well . . . that's part of it. Jason's dad always talks to me when I come over, if he's there. Sometimes, he stops what he's doing and watches us on the Xbox. Or he'll ask me questions, like he's trying to connect with us. At least makes the effort."

"And I don't do that?"

"Dad . . . c'mon. You and I don't even connect. When was the last time we talked like this? Uh . . . how 'bout never? When was the last time you asked me anything about what's going on in my life?"

"We talk sometimes." Jim was sure they did.

"No, *you* talk sometimes. I listen. They call those lectures. Usually it's about something I'm screwing up on, or some way I made you mad. Some chore I forgot to do. Lately, it's about me getting a job. But I wouldn't call that talking."

Jim was starting to feel totally discouraged.

Doug set the chopsticks down on the counter. "Can you tell me even one struggle I'm having at school? Do you even know? I'm gonna be a senior this year. You have any idea what college I want to go to, or what major I might be thinking about? Or . . . if I even want to go to college at all?"

Jim didn't have a clue.

"You know who *does* know those things? Jason's dad. And you know why? Because he asked, and then he listened. Here's something . . . Tom tells me you're having some financial problems, and that's part of the reason you're bugging me about starting to pay my own way around here. Is it?"

"Am I having financial problems?"

"Yeah."

"I guess that's fair to say."

"Fair to say? Dad, can't you just say it? I'm not a kid anymore. Why didn't you tell me you were having money problems? I don't need to know all the details, but something, anything would have been nice."

"Would that have motivated you to get a job? If I told you?" Jim said.

"It would have motivated me to care about you. And by the way, since Tom told me, I've been looking a lot harder. I've probably filled out a dozen online applications."

"I'm . . . I'm glad. I appreciate that."

Doug looked down at the tile floor. That glazed look came over his face, the one he would get when he started to shut down.

"C'mon, Doug. Keep talking. I'm here now, and I want to hear what you've got to say."

He looked up. "The point is, Dad . . . we never talk, not like this. We don't relate on a personal level. I just live here, over the garage." Doug picked up the chopsticks, poked them around in the little white box. "Do you remember when we met at Starbucks? The night you told us Mom left, and I said it didn't surprise me? You never followed up with me on that. I just told you I wasn't surprised Mom left you, and you don't say anything? Don't even ask me about it? I think you don't ask us questions because you don't want to hear what we might say if you did. You'd rather just think the little happy picture you've created in your mind is what's really going on."

Tears filled Doug's eyes. "Did you know, I cried almost the whole drive home that night? Not because my parents were splitting up. I was feeling bad for Mom, for all the years she's put up with you being like this. She and I aren't even all that close anymore. But I bet you don't know about that either, do you? How would you? But I still love her." Tears rolled down his cheeks. He set the food down.

"You're the reason she's not in this house anymore, Dad. She's left all this to hang out in some dinky little apartment. But I'll bet she's happier now than she's been in years. And I'm guessing you don't have a clue what's really eating at her, what's made her so unhappy. All you seem to be able to come up with is, maybe she's seeing another man. That's crap, Dad. You know? In your happy little world, everything is fine. Everyone is fine. Everybody's doing things your way, so we're all getting along. Right? But what's really going on is, everyone's struggling with all kinds of things, but we're struggling all alone, because you're too busy and self-absorbed to care. The few times I tried to talk with you about things, all I got was cut off, and then a bunch of Bible verses strung together in a little speech."

Doug dropped his chopsticks, slid his stool away from the counter, and stood up. He wiped the tears from his eyes. "I'm sorry for saying all this. Really, I am. But . . . you asked. Look, I've gotta go. I can't do this anymore." He walked off toward the hall leading out to the garage.

"Wait, Doug. Please, come back."

"Not now, Dad. I can't."

Jim heard the back door open and close.

He sat there in stunned silence. He felt like he'd just been run over by a truck. He'd had no idea Doug felt this way . . . about anything. About him. About his mom. He had no idea what to do, what to say. How to fix this.

You can't fix this, Jim.

He heard Audrey Windsor's voice in his head. She was right. All his efforts to control everything in his life were just illusions.

His happy little world.

37

On Friday, Marilyn had the day off. Michele didn't have any classes that afternoon, so they'd scheduled to meet at 3:00 p.m. at a bridal shop in River Oaks to pick up Michele's wedding dress. She'd already picked it out months ago, but today the alterations were supposed to be done. Since the bridal shop was just two blocks from Marilyn's apartment, she'd decided to walk. It was a beautiful sunny day. The downtown area was always a little busier on Friday afternoons. But Marilyn hardly paid attention to anything or anyone as she walked through town. Her mind kept drifting back to her private dance lesson with Roberto on Tuesday night, to the events that happened after Angelina had left the studio.

For days, she had been telling herself she had no reason to feel guilty. She wasn't doing anything wrong. It was just dancing. Dancing wasn't wrong. It belonged in a separate category. Couples who had absolutely no romantic relationship, nor any intention of ever forming one, danced together all the time. The problem was, while they danced they often acted like they did, but that's all it was—acting. That's how Roberto had explained it to her after Angelina had left.

He'd turned off the music and sat her in a chair. "There's something we need to discuss, my dear, before we begin," he'd said. "Did you see how Angelina and I danced together? It is such a romantic song, don't you agree? So when we dance, we must allow the meaning of the lyrics and the beauty of the melody to infuse our movements, our facial expressions, even the way we look at each other. We are like actors on a stage, pretending to live out the roles demanded by the song. So we must dance like two lovers in love. I must see her through new eyes, like she is the love of my life, and I'm seeing her in this amazing red dress, as if for the very first time. And I am undone by her beauty. Do you understand?"

"I think so," Marilyn had replied.

"And did you see how Angelina looked at me, how she started off somewhat coy and aloof, as if I had neglected her for far too long, but then she begins to respond eagerly to my passion? She begins to feel the fire of the love we let drift away. Through the dance, it is returning. Not just for me, but for her as well. Could you see that?"

Marilyn remembered. It was incredibly romantic. She was swept away by the power of the song and the way they had interpreted it on the dance floor. And she tried not to think about how close the lyrics of the song hit home.

"So do you see, my dear, how important it is for you to not only learn the steps to the dance but to see yourself as an actress playing a role? The dance floor is your stage. The judges will not only be judging how well we dance together but how effectively we move their emotions. Can you see that? More importantly . . . can you *do* that?"

She didn't know why, but Marilyn said she would try. And so she had. For nearly an hour after that. By the end of that hour, she had almost learned all the steps Angelina had just modeled for her, and she'd completely given herself over to the role. It stirred things inside she hadn't felt for years, if ever. Roberto's presence throughout the dance—the role he was playing—was so powerful, the look on his face and in his eyes, so intense . . . He genuinely seemed to treat her—as the song said—as if she took his breath away.

But it wasn't wrong, what they were doing. It was just acting. Dancing and acting. But the feelings it had stirred in her continued to linger long after. They seemed to stir again, even now, just recalling all this to mind.

She turned the corner. There was the bridal shop up ahead. And there was Michele just getting out of her car by the sidewalk. So if it wasn't wrong—this dancing with Roberto—why didn't she share any of these things with Charlotte the next day when they'd eaten breakfast together? Charlotte had asked her how the dance lesson went. Marilyn had only shared a few general things, then quickly changed the subject. Fortunately, Charlotte didn't notice and seemed happy to go with the flow.

And now Marilyn was meeting with Michele, wrestling with the idea of even mentioning any of this to her. But that would be wrong, she decided. To *not* share it with Michele. She and Michele talked about everything. And really, she had nothing to be ashamed of. It was just dancing. That's all this was.

Dancing and acting.

"So . . . what do you think?"

Marilyn looked up at Michele in her wedding dress. "Oh Michele, it's perfect."

"Does it look too tight?"

"No, not at all. Is it comfortable? Let me see all of it." Marilyn moved around to catch every angle.

Michele stood on a pedestal with mirrors all around. "Feels a little snug, but I'm still losing weight. I hope to knock three or four more pounds off this last month. So I'd rather it be a little tight than a little loose. Can you believe it? Only a month to go?"

"No, I can't. The time is moving way too fast. But Michele, it came out so nice. Allan is going to lose it when he sees you walk down the aisle in this."

"You think?"

"Definitely. I wouldn't be surprised to see your father shed a tear or two."

"He is still walking me down the aisle, you know." Michele took one more look in the mirror. "Did I tell you?"

"No, but I didn't think he'd pull out."

"And, like you said, he told us not to worry about the money. We can still use the budget figures he gave us when we met after we got engaged."

"Your father was always good with money."

"So you think the dress is ready? I can pay the balance and take it home?"

"I'm happy with it if you are," Marilyn said.

Michele giggled. "I love it. It's just what I wanted."

"Really, Michele, it's beautiful. Now . . . why don't you go back in the dressing room and change? I'll get the girl who was helping us and send her back to meet you, so she can put it in the hanger bag. If you want, we can stop off at Starbucks before you have to head back."

"I'd love that."

"Great," Marilyn said. "It'll give me a chance to update you on my dancing classes."

"Oh, that's right," Michele said as she disappeared down the hall. "I want to hear all about it."

All about it? Marilyn thought. Did she want to tell her *all* about it?

Twenty minutes later, they were sitting at a table under an outdoor umbrella, sipping their drinks. Marilyn got an iced coffee. They had driven here in Michele's car, so she could drive back to school right after.

"So how are you and Allan doing with the wedding just one month away?" Marilyn asked. "Getting more excited or more nervous?"

"It depends what time of day you ask me," Michele said. "Well, that's me. Allan seems like he's only ever excited. I don't see him being nervous at all."

"So what kind of things make you nervous?"

"Oh, you know . . . the wedding night for one. It's been hard, but we've kept ourselves for that night. So, I'm worried what Allan will think. You know, when the time comes."

Marilyn was so proud of Michele for keeping that conviction intact all this time. "Michele, you are a beautiful girl. And Allan loves you so much. He's going to love being with you on your wedding night. Just remember all the things we talked about. Try not to put so much emphasis on *that night*. You're getting married for life. It's not like the movies. You have your whole lives to . . . well, improve things." She smiled. "What else are you nervous about?"

"Oh no you don't," Michele said. She set her cappuccino down. "You're going to use up all our time drawing me out. I want to hear about you. Tell me about your dance lessons."

Marilyn took a deep breath. "I told you about the dance contest, right?"

"Dance contest? You certainly did not. You signed up for a dance contest? I guess you're feeling pretty confident. Haven't you only had a few lessons so far?"

"Yes, two lessons. Well, three really, counting the one with just me and the dance instructor."

"What? You're taking private lessons too?"

"Let me explain. It's pretty amazing, actually. Apparently, all that dancing in the living room with you when you were little paid off. He says I'm a natural. And I didn't sign up for the contest. Roberto selected me from the class to be his partner."

"You're dancing with the dance instructor? In the contest?"

Marilyn thought Michele sounded excited about this news, not concerned. That made her feel better. "I was shocked," she said. "It's a special contest for dance instructors throughout central Florida. They have to pick a beginner and can only teach them the dance over five lessons."

"That's so exciting, Mom. I'm so proud of you. When's the contest?"

"It's the Saturday before your wedding in September."

"Oh, I hope I can come see it. Allan and I have so many things on our to-do list for that weekend, though."

Marilyn was actually glad to hear this; she didn't want anyone she knew there.

"So what song are you dancing to, do you know?"

"Yep. We already had our first practice Tuesday night. It's an older song, not sure if you've heard of it. 'Lady in Red'?"

"Oh Mom, I love that song. Heard it on an oldies station a while back. It's so romantic. But it's not a waltz, right? What kind of dance are you learning for it?"

How should Marilyn describe it? Over the next few minutes, she did her best to explain but left out all of Roberto's instructions about them acting like a couple in love. Still, Michele's reaction was a little alarming.

"Oh my, Mom. That sounds . . . interesting. How do you feel dancing that way with, you know. . . ."

"Another man?" Marilyn said.

Michele nodded. "I've seen pictures of Roberto on the studio website. He's quite a—"

"He is handsome, but he's been a total professional about this. He said couples who dance romantic songs like this in contests should see themselves as actors playing out a role." She wanted to add that she just pretended Roberto was actually Jim, but that wasn't true. Jim's total hatred of dancing made that an impossible fantasy.

"Well," Michele said, "I can see that. But still . . . seems like you better be careful on this. You know, since you and Dad are . . ."

Right, Marilyn thought. Since she and Jim were . . .

38

It was Monday evening, just after the dinner hour. Of course, for Jim that didn't mean much these days. He was sitting in his car outside Audrey Windsor's house, waiting a few more minutes for their class to start. On his way home from work, he had picked up a chicken strips salad for himself from Chick-fil-A, some nuggets and waffle fries for Doug. Doug had thanked him and headed up to his room. They hadn't talked much since Doug let him have it last Wednesday.

The next morning, Jim had made an effort to apologize, but really, what could he say? Sorry for how I've been your whole life? He didn't remember exactly what he did say. Doug had replied, "That's all right, Dad. Thanks for listening."

Listening.

That's really all Jim had done. But he realized it was something he hadn't done with Doug for years. Or Tom. Or Michele. Or Marilyn, for that matter. Especially Marilyn.

He missed her so much right now.

He missed her cooking; she was an amazing cook, night after night, for all those years. He missed the way she took care of the house: immaculate, spotless, everything in good supply. He missed her being with him at church and social events. He'd never told her this, but she'd always made him feel proud because she took such great care of herself.

Why had he never said things like this to her? Why had he never told her how grateful he was for all the things she did? The answer was a terrible cliché, but it was still true. He had taken her for granted. She was there. She would always be there.

He also realized—and this realization was painful— he didn't miss Marilyn's friendship. For the simple reason that . . . they weren't friends.

He'd never let their relationship develop that way. He had treated her more like an attractive domestic servant who also functioned as a nanny to his children, a decorator for his house, and a hostess for his parties. To have a friendship with someone, you needed to do fun things together. Have lots of conversations. Ones where you asked questions, took an interest in what your friend had to say. Shared hopes and dreams. Were each other's shoulder to cry on.

Jim just wasn't that kind of guy. Or that's what he'd always believed. He just wasn't "wired that way."

And because of it, he was alone.

Then another terrible feeling overwhelmed him. What kind of emotional pain did Marilyn feel in their sexual relationship? Always having to please someone she didn't feel loved by, or even enjoy being with . . . for years? *What kind of man have I been to her? I haven't been a real husband, let alone a good friend.*

He wished there was some way to tell her how he felt now.

These depressing thoughts came as he pondered his conversations with Tom and Doug. Natural conclusions flowed out of equally dark thoughts about what a lousy father he had been.

Sure, he'd provided for them. Sent them to the best schools. He'd never missed a single birthday. Bought them what they wanted for Christmas. If you opened the drawer in Jim's brain called "Fatherhood," these were the things you'd find on file.

But he had never related to them on a friendship level, never did fun things with them or waste time with them, even when they'd become adults.

He wasn't wired that way.

He dreaded what he might hear if he worked up the courage to listen to what Michele had to say. If Tom and Doug struggled with him this much, what would he learn from a heart-to-heart with her?

Audrey peeked out her front window again. Jim's car was still there. It was almost ten minutes past the time when their lesson was supposed to begin. She bent down a little. She could see him sitting in the driver's seat. He didn't appear to be on his cell phone. Of course, nowadays, people used those hands-free devices.

Should she wait a few minutes more? No, before it got much later she should find out what was going on. She opened the front door and stepped onto the porch. Just then his car door opened.

"I'm sorry, Audrey." He walked around the car. "Guess I was daydreaming. I actually got here on time."

She held the front door for him, and they both went inside. Instantly, she could tell something had changed in his demeanor. "Is everything okay?"

He sighed as he walked over to the couch and began putting on his shoes. "Yes and no," he said. "Physically, I'm fine. I'm just . . . well . . . it's been a rough week."

He spent the next ten minutes summarizing two conversations he'd had with his boys, Tom and Doug. She had expected those conversations would be difficult, especially for someone like Jim, who'd never put much of a premium on listening to others. But he seemed almost devastated emotionally. He then explained why he might need a little more time to connect with his daughter, Michele, whom he described as "pretty much in Marilyn's camp."

Audrey assured him that was fine. "I'm proud of you for reaching out to your boys like that," she said. "That took courage on your part." She sat beside him on the couch.

"I just hope it's not too late. I don't know what it's going to take to get my relationship with them to a better place."

"Well," she said, "what you've done is a good start. It's going to take some time." Maybe a lot of time, she thought. "But if you're serious about taking responsibility for the wrong things you're starting to see, I think they'll eventually come around."

Jim spent the next few minutes sharing things he'd been thinking about Marilyn over the last few days too. Good things. Big things. It was clear to Audrey that God was doing some major work in Jim's heart. At one point, he got all choked up. She got up to get him a tissue. "Here," she said. "Take this."

"I'm sorry. I can't believe I'm telling you all this."

"Don't apologize. That's what friends are for."

She wasn't looking forward to sharing the news about Roberto and Marilyn dancing together in that contest. She would wait until after the lesson. Jim had a right to know, but right now he needed a positive distraction. "Why don't you take a moment to pull yourself together while I go get us a couple bottles of water? Then we'll head into the studio. Tonight we're going to build on the steps you've learned and do something I think you'll enjoy."

"Like what?" he said. He took a deep breath and stood.

"Well, by the end of this lesson, you're going to feel like you might actually be a dancer. I'm going to show you the proper way to hold a lady while dancing the waltz, then how to do these same steps we've learned as we circle the room together, spinning and swirling to the music."

"You think I can do that? Tonight?"

"Yes, I think you can."

When the dance lesson was over, Jim seemed to be in an entirely different place. He really was getting it. And he was smiling. Audrey was happy to see it. Dancing had that effect on most people. Like laughter, it was good medicine.

She hated to ruin it by breaking the news to Jim about Marilyn and Roberto. But it had to be done. She'd thought of a way, though, to tie in part of the story with the dance lesson.

Jim was sitting back on the couch, changing out of his dance shoes. "That was really fun, Audrey. I mean it. By the end there, I felt like . . . well, like you said, almost like a dancer."

"You were doing great, Jim. Say, before you leave, there's something I need to tell you." She walked over and sat beside him.

"Uh-oh. This doesn't sound good."

She said a quick silent prayer. "There's no easy way to say this. And before I do, you need to know, I don't think anything bad has happened, and nothing may come of it. But I still feel you have a right to know."

His face showed immediate concern. "What is it? Just tell me."

"I've learned Roberto has asked your wife to be his partner in a dance contest."

"What? A dance contest?"

"They're meeting once a week for extra lessons to prepare. I think the contest is about a month away."

His face fell. "But I don't understand. She's only been taking lessons a few weeks. One week more than me. How could he ask her to dance with him in a contest?"

It was obvious that Jim wasn't buying this as the real reason they were spending more time together. "I've looked into it, and the contest is real. The reason he picked her is because it's a special contest for dance instructors, to showcase their ability to teach. The idea is, they all pick someone from their beginners' class, and they have five weeks to get ready."

Jim sighed. "I knew something like this would happen."

"Something like what?"

"I knew that Roberto would find a way to start drawing Marilyn into a relationship. I could see the way he looked at her."

"Jim, I don't think that's what's going on here. Marilyn really is a gifted dancer. I could see that the first night. And she was the only one in class without a dance partner."

Jim's expression didn't change. He wasn't buying it. His head dropped, and he stared at the carpet.

"Listen, Jim." She waited a moment until he looked up. "It's very important that you don't go rushing over there to confront Marilyn right now. That's the worst thing you could possibly do."

"But I'm going to lose her!"

"You might if you do that," Audrey said. "Right now, she's very vulnerable. But I don't believe anything bad has happened. Not yet. You do that, you might just push her right into his arms."

"Then what do I do? I can't do nothing."

"Well, for starters, you could use the pain you're feeling right now to get in touch with the kind of pain Marilyn's probably been feeling for years."

"What? I've never left her for someone else."

Audrey softened her tone and expression. "Remember at the beginning of this lesson, I talked about keeping a safe distance between you and your partner throughout the dance. That's part of the elegance of the waltz, and a good way to make sure you don't step on each other's toes. Well, that's a life lesson you need to grab hold of right now with Marilyn."

"Keeping a safe distance?"

"Not so much the distance but the idea of making her feel safe. Let me say it this way: how would Marilyn expect you to react to this news?"

Jim thought a moment. "Probably me blowing up and getting in her face."

"Right. And every time you've done that in the past, you've shut her down. She doesn't feel safe talking to you, opening up and sharing her struggles with you. That's why you didn't even know she was unhappy enough to walk out on you a few weeks ago."

"But she needs to know how I feel about this thing."

"No, not really. I'm sure she already knows you'd disapprove. What you need to learn is how *she* feels about things. And the best way to start is by not reacting to things she says or does that cause you pain. To create a safe environment in your relationship for her to open up to you. I don't think that's ever been a part of your relationship with her before."

"It hasn't. But what do I do? How do I . . . make her feel safe? She won't even talk to me."

"Use the pain you feel right now to help you understand her better. I think, in a way, Marilyn has been feeling this same kind of pain since the two of you were married. You're experiencing the same feelings Marilyn has about your 'other lover.' She's felt this deep hurt over your affair with your company and your financial reputation. My guess is she's never felt as important to you as your business and network associations. Right now, Jim, you're getting a glimpse into the kind of pain she's been dealing with all of these years."

"I don't want to lose her," Jim said as his eyes filled with tears.

"Then my best advice to you, Jim, is . . . don't react. Don't confront her. Don't say anything at all about this. Pray and look for ways to show her that you've changed. Concrete, tangible ways to demonstrate that you really do love her. Then trust God for a breakthrough, that he will speak to her heart and help you find a way to win her back."

39

Two days later, Jim was still not over the news about Marilyn. It was near the end of the work day. He was sitting in his office, waiting for Lynn, his secretary, to finish a few things so he could lock up for the night. Try as he might, he couldn't get the image of Marilyn dancing with this Roberto guy out of his head. Before he'd left Audrey's on Monday evening, he'd asked her if she would at least tell him what kind of song they were dancing to, hoping it was something harmless and mild like the waltz.

Audrey was hesitant to say, which made him feel even worse. Sensing that, she reluctantly agreed. She said she'd found out they were dancing a modified version of the rumba to a song called "Lady in Red."

Jim had never heard of the song, at least not by its title. And all he knew about the rumba was it sounded like some kind of Latin dance. He couldn't sleep when he'd gotten home that night, so he looked up both on the internet.

Then he really couldn't sleep.

The lyrics of the song weren't dirty or immoral, but it was a majorly romantic ballad about a guy head over heels in love with a woman he was dancing with . . . cheek to cheek. The rumba was indeed a Latin dance, but the examples he saw on YouTube were anything but harmless and mild. A woman announcer in one of the videos called the rumba "definitely the hottest and sexiest of all the Latin dances."

The thought of this man holding his wife that way made him sick. He couldn't get the image out of his head. How could she do this to him? Audrey kept insisting she had no evidence of anything "untoward" going on between them, and that Roberto had even said he wouldn't dare make advances to someone like Marilyn, whom he agreed was in a "vulnerable state."

These words hardly helped.

He remembered the advice he and Marilyn had told their kids as teenagers, before they'd go out with their friends at night. *"Don't forget who you are while you're out having fun. A lot of fun things can lead to serious trouble."* Their kids would protest that their friends weren't like that, and that Marilyn and Jim had nothing to worry about. And of course, the kids would inevitably say, "Don't you trust us?" And Marilyn would come back with, "Part of your heart I trust, but there's another part that I don't . . . and you shouldn't trust that part either."

Well, Marilyn, he thought. Looks like someone needs to say the same thing to you right now.

He wondered if he should call Michele, see if she knew about this dance contest, and suggest that very thing to her. Michele would remember this advice. Of all their kids, she'd heard those warnings the most from her mother in high school. Jim didn't even want to know the kind of trouble Michele had gotten into before she'd come back to the Lord that first year in college, before she'd met Allan.

"Mr. Anderson?" The words pierced the quiet atmosphere in his office.

He looked down at his desk phone. It was Lynn on his intercom. "I'm here, Lynn. You ready to head out?"

"I am, but that's not why I buzzed you. Michele's on line two. She said she tried calling your cell phone, but you must have it turned off."

Jim pulled his cell phone out of his pocket. He had turned it off during an appointment at three. "Thanks, Lynn. I'll get it. You can go home if you're ready. I'll lock up as soon as I'm off the phone."

"Okay. Have a nice evening."

Lynn always said that. Every night. Even since Marilyn left four weeks ago. Jim pushed the button down for line two. "Hey, Michele, what's up?" He couldn't believe she'd called. Maybe it was a sign.

"Hi, Dad. Nothing too big, just trying to check off some more items on my ever-growing to-do list for the wedding."

"That's right," Jim said, trying to sound pleasant. "It's just a month away now, isn't it?"

"Don't remind me."

"Really? I thought you'd be excited it was getting so close."

"I am. It's just I've still got so many things left to do."

"Well, how can I help?" He was somewhat surprised by Michele's tone of voice. It was soft and kind, no edge at all, almost like old times.

"This is kind of an awkward thing to ask. I don't mean to pressure you at all. And before I tell you what it is, I want you to know, I won't be offended if you can't do this. Mom already suggested I call Tom."

"Is it about walking you down the aisle?" Jim said. "You know, I already said I'd be happy to do that."

"No, this is about the reception. You know, one of the first things that happens after the bridal party arrives is they do all these special dances. The bride and groom, then the groom with his mom, and then . . . well, you know—"

"The bride dances with her dad," Jim said.

"Right. But I'm okay if you say no. I know how you—"

"I'll do it."

"What?"

"I'll do it. I'll dance with you, Michele."

"You will?"

"It would be my honor."

"Really?"

It sounded like she was getting choked up on the other end. "Don't expect much," he said. "I'm not known to be much of a dancer."

She laughed. "I can't believe you said yes."

"I'll put it in writing, if you want."

"You don't have to do that."

"But listen, Michele. Would you do me a favor? Can we keep this a secret? I . . . I don't want anyone else to—"

"Sure, Dad. I'll just make a little check here on my list and won't say another word. I'll pick a real slow song, and a short one."

"That'll help," he said.

"Before I let you go, there's something I thought I should mention to you. Something about Mom."

"Oh?"

"It's nothing, really," Michele said. "I just found out about this earlier today when we talked. She said the yellow engine light came on in her car the other day. And it comes on now, every time she starts the car. You know, she knows nothing about cars, and she's afraid to take it to the mechanic. It's a few months past the warranty, and she's worried they'll start fixing all kinds of things it doesn't need and charge her hundreds of dollars."

"I see."

"You always took care of the cars," she said.

That's right, Jim thought. He did. She still needed him for some things. He was just about to say something he'd probably regret when he got an idea. This engine light thing gave him a legitimate reason to see Marilyn. "I'll take care of it," he said.

"She asked me not to say anything," Michele said, "but Allan said you can't ignore a warning light like that."

"He's right. Don't worry. I'll see what I can do."

"Appreciate it, Dad. And thanks again for saying yes about the dance. I can't believe you're going to do it."

"You're welcome." He could tell she was just about to hang up. "Say, Michele, can I ask you something?"

"Sure."

"Do you know anything about Mom entering into some dance contest with her instructor?"

"Uh . . . yes. She told me about that. But how did you—"

"It's a small town," Jim said. "Mind if I ask what you think about it?"

"Well, kind of. You know I don't want to get in the middle of this thing between you two. But honestly, Dad, when I talked to her about it, it was crystal clear to me, there's nothing—and I mean nothing—going on with her and this guy."

"You really believe that?" he asked.

"I really do," she said.

The finality in her tone shut down Jim's idea of asking Michele to confront her mother about this.

40

Marilyn was loving this assignment. It was Thursday morning, a few minutes before noon. The truck that left Odds-n-Ends an hour ago had dropped off this adorable selection of Norman Rockwell collectibles. Harriet had walked Marilyn over to an aisle that she'd cleared four shelves from the night before. She'd handed Marilyn the price sheet and said, "I'm going to let you set up this whole collection right here. Price everything according to the sheet and arrange things any way you'd like. I've been watching you these past few weeks. You've got a real eye for décor."

Marilyn was thrilled.

For the last thirty minutes, she'd been furiously attaching price tags and loading the items on the shelves, trying to get them all priced before it was time to quit for lunch. Harriet didn't like them to leave boxes in the aisles when they went on break. Her cell phone vibrated. They were allowed to read texts on the clock, just in case a family emergency occurred, but otherwise they had to wait until they were off to reply.

Marilyn looked at her phone and saw a text from Michele. She opened it and read: *Call me ASAP. Dad knows about the dance contest.*

Her heart sunk. She instantly tensed up.

How could he know? Was he still spying on her? He had reacted so badly when he'd found out about the group lessons. What would he do about something like this? He must be fuming right now. The old fear returned; her stomach started tying up in knots. Images of their last confrontation at the dance studio a few weeks ago began replaying in her mind. But as they did, she became aware of something else. The anger she'd felt at being intimidated and manipulated by him all these years. She remembered the strength that had come over her in the parking lot when she stood up to him, told him off, and drove away.

She could do this. She could face him. He wasn't in charge of her anymore.

"Marilyn, you almost done unpacking the Rockwell merchandise?" Marilyn looked up at Harriet standing at the end of the aisle. "It's almost time for your lunch break."

"Just two more small boxes," she said. "I'll have them priced in a few minutes. But Harriet, don't look at what I've done here. I haven't even started arranging everything yet. Is it okay if I do that when I come back? I just wanted to get everything on the shelf, so I could get rid of these boxes before I leave."

"That's fine," Harriet said. "Can't wait to see what you come up with." She smiled and walked away.

Marilyn made quick work of the last few boxes, flattened them out, and walked them out to the recycle bin. She let Harriet know she was through and clocked out. Let's get this over with, she thought. She took a deep breath, sat at the break table, and called Michele back.

"Hi, Mom."

"Got your text," she said. "You got a minute?"

"You mean about Dad?" Michele said.

"That's the one."

"Before I say anything, I don't want you to freak out or anything. My phone call with Dad was actually pretty pleasant. In fact, he actually agreed to—wait a minute. I'm sorry, I can't get into that."

"Get into what?" Marilyn asked. It wasn't like Michele to keep secrets from her.

"It's not a bad thing. Just something Dad agreed to do for the wedding, but he asked me not to say anything. The point is, Dad didn't seem his normal angry self. It was actually an easy phone call."

"He didn't seem angry about me and this dance contest?" Marilyn found that hard to believe.

"Well, we didn't really talk about that too much. It was just something he mentioned at the end of our conversation. Before he could get into it, I politely shut him down."

"Did he say how he found out?"

"No. I asked but all he said was 'It's a small town.' I could tell he was getting a little tense, and I didn't want to ruin the conversation, so I let it drop. But I did tell him, Mom, that there's absolutely nothing going on between you and Roberto. It's just a dance contest." She paused a moment. "That's the truth, isn't it? I mean, there isn't anything going on between you and—"

"Michele," Marilyn snapped. "I can't believe you'd even think such a thing."

"I'm sorry. Really, I—"

"We're just dancing. That's all."

"Okay. Really, I'm sorry. I didn't mean to get you upset. I just wanted to warn you. I'm not sure if Dad's going to make a big deal about it."

Of course, he will, Marilyn thought. "That's okay," she said and stood up, walking toward the hallway. She needed to walk and talk if she hoped to get something to eat before her break was over. As she entered the hallway, she glanced to her left, toward the front door. "Oh no," she said.

"What's the matter, Mom?"

It was Jim. "Your father, he just walked through the front door."

As Jim entered the store, his eyes instantly went to the counter. Marilyn wasn't there. He knew she was working today; he had driven behind the store, saw her car in the employee parking lot. He was just about to start scanning the handful of aisles when he spotted her in the hallway at the far end. She was hanging up her cell phone, a panicked look on her face.

He'd hardly slept at all last night, finally had to take two Benadryl. Even then he'd tossed and turned until the alarm bell rang. It had taken him three cups of strong coffee to overcome the hungover feeling from the meds. All night long, he'd wrestled with images of Marilyn dirty dancing with that Latin guy, followed by Audrey's forceful appeals last Monday night, pleading with him not to say anything about it.

"Don't react. Don't confront her. Don't say anything at all about this. Pray and look for ways to show her that you've changed. Concrete, tangible ways to demonstrate that you really do love her."

Suddenly, Marilyn turned and faced the back door and all but ran toward it. Jim ran through the store after her. "Marilyn, wait."

"No, I won't wait," she said and disappeared behind the metal door.

"Excuse me, sir," a young woman with a store name tag said. "You're not allowed back there."

Jim ignored her and ran down the hallway. He burst through the door to find Marilyn hurrying toward her car. "Stop, Marilyn. Don't leave."

"I don't want to talk to you," she said, not even looking back.

"I'm not here to talk," he said, as gently as he could. "Would you please stop?"

She paused, standing next to the open car door. Finally, she looked at him. "What?" she said angrily.

Jim was trembling inside. His heart raced as he slowed to a walk. When he got closer, he stopped. "Michele said—"

"I know what Michele said."

Jim ignored her remark, tried not to react to her fierce stare. "Michele told me your engine light came on a few days ago."

"What?"

"The yellow engine light. She said it came on in your car, and it stays on all the time now. Is that still happening?"

"Yes," she said in a gentler voice.

"Well, I don't want you—I mean, it's not safe to drive the car like that. Not until we find out what's causing it." He reached in his pocket. "Here," he said.

Marilyn looked at what he held in his hands. The keys to his Audi. A confused look crossed her face. "You never let me drive your car."

"I know." It sounded so stupid, hearing her say it. But it was true. "Well, I'd like you to drive it now. At least till I can get your car looked at, find out what's going on with that light."

"Really?" she said. "That's all you came here for."

Jim swallowed hard. "That's all."

41

Over the next two weeks, Jim followed this new strategy with Marilyn. Not reacting to things she did or said. Instead, he looked for tangible ways to care and serve her. Gaining control over his emotions and fears took a mammoth effort. And it was clear, even with all the changes he had begun to make, she still didn't trust him and still wouldn't talk with him.

Things had improved a bit with Michele, however. She rarely spoke harshly to him anymore. And a few times, she actually confided in him, sharing observations about how his efforts to win her mother's heart were being perceived. Just yesterday, she'd said, "I think Mom sees the effort, but right now she's not buying it. But I noticed when you dropped her car back off, how nice it looked and that you'd filled the gas tank up."

"Besides the gas, I had it detailed at the car wash," Jim had said.

"It looked great. When I asked Mom what she thought about it, she said, 'That was nice, but it doesn't change anything. I think it's just a new tactic your father's working to try and manipulate me.' But see," Michele said, "she started off with, 'That was nice.' I see that as progress."

Jim had focused more on "it doesn't change anything" and "it's just a tactic," so he didn't quite share Michele's enthusiasm about the so-called progress. But the fact that Michele had shared these things with him—in confidence—was itself progress, and he tried to be grateful for that.

He was also grateful for the changes he was starting to see in his own heart. He'd been praying for God to change his heart every morning. The fury and boiling anger was gone. The chronic and dark imaginations he used to have about her almost every day had greatly diminished. He was sure he still had a long way to go, but even this much progress had produced in him a measure of hope.

Jim had two more dance lessons with Audrey over the past two weeks, which meant there was only one left. He was encouraged with the strides he was making there, and so was she. Except for an occasional misstep, Jim could now waltz Audrey around the room, spinning and swirling her at all the right places, keeping perfect time with the music and just the right space between them.

At the end of the last lesson, she informed him of one significant problem he still must overcome. "When you dance, your face looks like it's in pain. Or else, I see your lips moving, counting off the steps. It's time for you to start learning how to listen with your heart, not your head."

When Jim had asked what that meant, she said, "You need to hear the music, down inside. Let it permeate your being until you feel the steps. Maybe it will help if you close your eyes. Let the music take hold and allow the joy of what you're doing to take over."

It had all sounded like hogwash to Jim, but he tried to do what she'd said, and it worked. In no time at all, he was dancing with real feeling, and real joy was the result. It was as if his hands and legs now knew what to do and all he had to do was turn them loose and let them go.

"Now you're getting it," she'd said when they were done. "And now I want to share with you the marriage life lesson that goes with this fifth dance step." She spent the next fifteen minutes talking about Jim's need to listen to Marilyn's heart, not just the words she said.

Jim had admitted he wasn't good at this and admitted that when Marilyn said things he didn't agree with, he typically reacted by trying to straighten her out. "As far as communication goes," Audrey had said, "that's the equivalent of you dancing with your face all scrunched up, mouthing the steps as you go." She explained he needed to move beyond the words Marilyn spoke and learn to listen for the feelings and emotions behind her words. "Why did she really say that? What's really eating at her? Those are the kinds of questions you need to ask yourself as you listen." The fog was beginning to lift. "Instead of knee-jerk overreactions," she said, "which is what you're used to doing, do the very opposite. Don't try to fix her. Just ask her more questions. All the while listening to her heart."

"How will I know when I've made that connection?" he'd asked.

"You'll know."

As he drove home that night, he felt more encouraged than before, but mostly about how well the dancing part of the lesson had gone. He still struggled to believe that all these "life lessons" were really going to amount to much with Marilyn. How could they? She still wouldn't even talk to him.

His discouragement with his marriage situation worsened when he gave in to the temptation to drive by the dance studio the following night. He knew no good would come of it. It was Tuesday evening, a little after nine o'clock. As before, the drapes across the front windows were closed, which only made Jim more suspicious. On Thursdays, when she danced with the whole group, the curtains were pulled to the side, allowing everyone on the sidewalk and street to see the entire dance floor.

Why were they closed now? Why only when Roberto and Marilyn danced alone? Jim didn't want to look like a pervert peeking through the cracks. So he sat across the street, two cars down, and looked at his digital clock. They should be done in about ten minutes, based on things he'd found out from Michele. Maybe he should wait here till the lights went out, see where she went after.

He wanted to but then changed his mind. What if she looked across the street and saw his car. Then she'd know he was spying on her. That might set things back to square one between them. He couldn't bear that. Turning on the car, he looked both ways and headed out into the street.

Please Lord, let her go home alone tonight.

42

The following Saturday night, Jim did something different. He called Michele and asked if he could visit her church in Lakeland.

"You want to do what?"

He repeated the question. "I'd like to go to church with you and Allan tomorrow. I'll drive over to Lakeland. Then take you guys out for lunch after. What time's it start?"

"Ten, but . . . are you sure?"

"I've been wanting to visit your church for years. Now seems like a good time. This past week I resigned my membership at our old church. For the most part, you were right about the people there. It was time to move on."

"I can't believe what I'm hearing," Michele said. "But sure, I'd be happy to have you come to our church. Only Allan won't be with us." She sounded a little annoyed.

"Oh? Why not?"

"Our church has another ten-day mission trip to Africa scheduled this week. Allan had agreed not to go, since it's only two weeks till our wedding. One of the key guys got sick and had to bail out at the last minute. They asked Allan to step in, because he'd been there before and his passport was up to date. Of course, he instantly said yes . . . without talking to me."

Jim liked Allan but did find him a bit impetuous and idealistic, especially about these mission trips. He was all about saving the world for Christ. Which, for the most part, Jim considered a good thing. But Allan wasn't a single guy anymore. "So he's left you to handle all the final wedding details on your own?"

"Pretty much," she said. "But Mom's been a great help. And I'm really glad he cares about things like this. It's just not the best timing."

"Well, I'll keep you company at church and still take you out after. You pick the place."

"Great, Dad, I'd like that."

"And Michele, could you do me a favor?"

"Sure."

"Could you bring along a wedding invitation and an envelope, and one of those little reception cards?"

"I guess. Who's it for?"

"I'll explain over lunch."

Jim had a great experience at Michele's church. A younger pastor than he was used to, a younger congregation on the whole, a nice building but no frills. He hadn't been in church for several weeks, and the message was very encouraging. He especially enjoyed sitting next to Michele; that hadn't happened in a church in years. Throughout the service, she kept checking on him. He'd give her a nod and an "I'm okay" smile.

The preacher finished his message, they sang a closing song, and as Jim and Michele made their way out the door, she had introduced him to over a dozen friends. All of them seemed very nice and all had asked her about Allan, how he was doing in Africa.

Once they got to the parking lot, Michele suggested they eat at a nearby Applebee's. "If we go there now, we might beat the rush."

Jim followed her in his car so he could head home right after. During the lunch, Jim worked hard to apply some of the new communication things Audrey had taught him. He never realized how hard it was to just sit there and listen, to be the one asking questions, the one taking an interest in the other person. She'd barely get two words out, and he'd feel this almost overpowering urge to interrupt her and either adjust something she'd said or talk about himself.

But he didn't.

He also did his best to stifle every curious question he wanted to ask about Marilyn. Secretly, he hoped Michele would bring up the subject, but she never did. Instead whenever she talked about her mom it was regarding things Marilyn thought about Michele's wedding or reception, which were less than two weeks away.

Michele finished talking about the reception plans. As she did, she thanked him three different times for being willing to do the father-daughter dance. Jim saw an opportunity to ask her about something he'd spoken about on the phone last night.

"Say, Michele, did you bring the wedding invitation I asked you about?"

"I did." She reached for her purse. "And the little reception card. It's right there in the middle," she said, handing it to him.

"Thanks, I appreciate it."

"So . . . who you planning to invite?"

He wasn't sure, but her look seemed more like concern than curiosity. "Somebody I don't think you know."

"Not from the old church, right? None of the crossed-off names?"

"No one from the old church." He wasn't sure any of them would come now even if they were invited.

"Then who?"

"It's just . . . this woman I met."

"What?"

He suddenly realized how that sounded. But he didn't want to tell her who it was, or she'd know he was taking dance lessons. How else would he know someone like Audrey Windsor?

"Dad, you're not bringing some woman you're seeing to my wedding."

"No, it's nothing like that. I would never do that to you or your mother."

"Then who is she?"

A month ago, Jim would have felt compelled to say, "It's none of your business. I'm the one paying for this wedding." Instead he said, "She's this nice elderly lady I met about a month ago. She's been very kind to me, and I wanted to thank her by inviting her to the wedding. But I won't do it if you're uncomfortable with it."

"That sounds okay. Does Mom know her?"

"I think she does, but please, Michele. Don't mention this to your mom. Would you promise me that?"

A puzzled look came over her face. "All right. I guess it's no big deal."

"It's really not," Jim said.

The following night was Jim's last dance class with Audrey. He showed up on time. They small-talked as he put on his shoes, then they just danced. Audrey had lined up a number of great waltz songs, so they could just keep dancing one after the other. Jim was amazed again at her energy and stamina. By this point, it was fair to say he was thoroughly enjoying himself. A man set free from a lifelong fear. He couldn't dance as well as he played golf, but he definitely had shed all his resistance and most of his inhibitions. Secretly, he wished there was a way to keep this going after tonight.

While they danced, Audrey shared with Jim her last marriage life lesson. As with the other lessons, she used the metaphor of dance. It was a simple idea. "Marriage and good dancing both require the same thing—teamwork," she said. "This kind of dancing, anyway. The classic dances. Obviously, some people like to be out there on the floor doing their own thing, much more mindful of who's watching them than being focused on their partner. But for classic dancing like we're doing here, it takes a team."

Jim wanted to add that he was no longer part of a team, but Audrey had gently corrected him every time he'd say something like that. "Have faith," she'd say. "God hasn't given up, so don't you give up."

As he stepped to the side and spun her gently around the corner of the room, she added, "For a team to be successful, you need to adopt a 'No Losers Policy.' It's very simple. When you and Marilyn finally get back together and she starts talking to you again, you need to stop trying to get her to see your point of view all the time. Conversation is not about you winning or being right and her being wrong or vice versa. On a team, there's no such thing as that. Either you both win or you both lose. The goal is to arrive there together, to come up with a solution you both feel happy about."

This sounded nice, but Jim had some problems with it. They were at the other end of the room by now. "But Audrey, it's pretty clear in the Bible . . . the husband is the head of the house. Sounds a little bit like you're contradicting that."

Audrey smiled as they spun around the corner again. "Is Jesus the head of the church?"

"Yes."

"Did he wash his disciples' feet at the Last Supper?"

"Yes. I guess he did."

"What kind of a head does that? Here's another question. Didn't he say he came not to be served but to serve?"

"Yes."

"You know that chapter in Ephesians where Paul talks about the husband being the head of his wife?"

Jim nodded.

"In my Bible," Audrey said, "in that same passage, Paul also said a husband must love his wife like Christ loved the church . . . and gave himself up for her."

Jim didn't know what to say. Seems like she had him.

"That's the kind of head of the house I think you're supposed to be. You're supposed to love Marilyn the same way you love yourself. That's the kind of team any Christian woman wouldn't mind being a part of. I know this firsthand. After Ted learned this, he started treating me like a queen." Tears welled up in her eyes. She blinked them away as the song ended.

Fifteen minutes later, Jim was on the couch, changing out of his shoes. "I can't believe this is our last lesson."

"I've really enjoyed being your dance instructor," she said. "Honestly, it's been a pleasure."

Jim stood up. "Audrey, you've been much more than my dance instructor. I've learned things from you that, well . . . I just wish I'd learned them years ago. Maybe Marilyn would still be here."

"Don't go there, Jim. You're talking like it's hopeless. I believe God can still turn this around."

He talked like it was hopeless because that's how he felt. Marilyn wasn't an inch closer to coming home. She still refused to talk to him. "I appreciate that," he said. "Here." He took the invitation out of his pocket. "I know it's short notice, but I'd love it if you could come to my daughter Michele's wedding. It's a week from Saturday."

Audrey opened the invitation and read the front page. "I'll have to check my calendar," she said, looking up. "But if I can, I'll certainly be there."

Jim made his way to the door. She reached out her hand. Jim took it and drew her into a hug. "I think you've changed my life, Audrey. Because of you, I'm going to be dancing at a wedding for the first time in my life." As he pulled back, he started choking up. "I actually said yes when Michele asked me to do the father-daughter dance. And I wasn't afraid. In fact, I'm kind of looking forward to it."

43

When Jim arrived home from work the next day, a familiar bright yellow '68 Chevy Impala with a black vinyl top was parked in the driveway.

Uncle Henry.

Why didn't he ever call first? He always just dropped by. It wasn't like he lived in the neighborhood. As Jim pushed the garage door opener and pulled up beside him, he noticed Uncle Henry didn't react. Jim looked at him more closely; he was sound asleep, his mouth wide open, head tilted to one side.

At least, Jim hoped he was asleep.

He slid the passenger window down and was relieved to hear Uncle Henry snoring. Jim smiled as he pulled his Audi into the garage. What a character. As he walked back toward Uncle Henry's car, he became aware that he didn't resent the sight of him like he usually did. His uncle was obviously there to check up on Jim, as usual. Standing there, staring at him, Jim remembered some of the things Uncle Henry had said the last time they spoke, right here in the driveway over a month ago.

Everything Uncle Henry had said back then was either true or had come true.

Jim wondered if his newfound friendship with Audrey Windsor had anything to do with this, but he felt a warmth inside looking at his uncle just now. "Uncle Henry," he said, rubbing his shoulder.

"Huh?" His head moved slightly, and his eyes opened. "What?"

"It's me. Jim. You're in my driveway. You must've fallen asleep."

Uncle Henry sat up then looked up. "Jim, there you are."

"How long have you been here?"

"What time is it?"

"Almost five-thirty."

"Then not long at all. Guess I dozed off. Got here at five-fifteen. I was coming back from a trip to Orlando, thought, how can I drive by my favorite nephew's place and not stop by to say hello? I knew you always came home from work on time."

He began to open the car door. Jim stepped aside. Uncle Henry held out his hand. Jim didn't know why but he hugged him instead. "It's good to see you, Uncle Henry."

"Well," he replied, stepping back from the hug. "How you holding up?"

"Okay, I guess. Marilyn's still gone. It's been more than a month now."

"I'm sorry," Henry said. "You doing okay? You seem . . . better somehow."

Was he better? "Maybe it's just the shock has worn off, and I'm getting used to it."

"No, I don't think that's it. You seem calmer, on the inside."

"I guess that's possible. I took your advice, by the way."

"What advice?"

"About humbling myself, getting some help."

Uncle Henry leaned back against his car. "That so? Tell me about it."

There was no way Jim was going to tell him about the dance lessons. "It's a long story. But oddly enough, I met this elderly lady, and she's given me a lot to think about. Her husband passed away, but they were married over fifty years."

"I imagine she has lots of insight," Henry said.

"Yeah, she does. I can see a lot of things I've done wrong with Marilyn." Jim sighed. "A whole lot."

"Wow," Henry said.

"What?"

"The Jim I talked with a month ago would never have said something like that, or said it that way."

"Maybe not. But I'm not sure it matters now."

"Why?"

"Marilyn can't see any change. She still won't even talk to me."

"I'm sorry, Jim. That's gotta hurt."

"Yeah." Jim wanted to tell him about his fear that he was losing her to this dance instructor, but he didn't say anything.

"But you know, you're putting yourself in a good position to get all kinds of help from God now."

"How so?"

"Are you starting to turn to him with your troubles or are you still keeping them all bottled up inside?"

"I've started praying more often," he said. "And I'm reading my Bible again in the morning."

"That helping?"

"I guess. I'm not as depressed," Jim said. "Don't feel as angry inside about all this."

A surprised look came over Uncle Henry's face. "Jim, that's huge."

"What's huge?"

"What you just said. Do you know how unusual that is for people going through the kind of trouble you're having who are totally depressed all day and full of rage inside?"

"Yeah . . . no. Well, I guess."

"They're taking pills every day or drinking up a storm, anything to take the edge off."

"I never really thought about it."

"You're experiencing God's grace, Jim. That's what's going on here. God gives grace to the humble." A big smile came over his face.

Jim had never thought of it that way, but it kind of made sense. Uncle Henry had never made sense before. Jim would have called this kind of conversation spiritual mumbo jumbo a month ago.

"What's the matter?"

"I'm not sure how any of this progress helps me and Marilyn get back together."

Uncle Henry walked over toward him, put his hand on his shoulder, and said, "Don't be afraid, Jim. It's gonna be all right. Somehow, I just know it. Your aunt and I pray for you guys every night. Even this talk we're having now is an answer to prayer. God hasn't given up on you, so don't you give up."

"Man, that's crazy."

"What?"

"That elderly woman I told you about, she says almost the exact same thing whenever I get down about this."

"I like this lady." Then Uncle Henry got a strange look on

his face. His eyebrows drew close together. "I got an idea, and I think you should consider it."

"What?" Jim was open to almost anything at this point.

"Start practicing what you want to say to Marilyn if you got the chance. Like an act of faith. I know she's still not talking to you. But we're hoping someday that's going to change. You be ready when the time comes."

"Practice?"

"Yeah," Henry said. "Start writing it down. Ask God to help you, show you all the things you wished you could tell her, all the things you're sorry for."

"You think I should send her a letter?"

"I don't know, the idea's not that clear to me yet. But I just think you should do it. Take some time—you got plenty of that—and start practicing."

"Okay, Uncle Henry. I will. Say, do you want to come inside? Don't have anything fancy for dinner. Just some premade dish I bought at Sam's for Doug and me, but you're welcome to join us. There's plenty."

Uncle Henry took a step back; it looked like tears were forming in his eyes. "I'd love to, Jim. But I told Myra I'd be home by seven. Going to take her out to dinner. But you know something? In all the times I've stopped by over the years, this is the first time you ever invited me in."

"Really? I'm sorry, Uncle Henry. That's terrible."

"Don't worry about it. It's just one more answer to prayer. You go on in there and give Doug a hug for me. I better get home."

They hugged again, and then Jim stood there and waved as Uncle Henry drove off.

A few minutes after he got in the house and set his things on the counter, Doug came running in kitchen. "Dad, you been watching the news?"

"No, what's up?"

"Some big tropical storm has formed in the Caribbean. The track has it clipping the Keys in a couple of days then heading into the Gulf." He walked over and picked up the remote, clicked to the local station, one that constantly gave updated weather reports.

"You know those things hardly ever come here, Doug. Not to central Florida." Jim watched the TV as the anchorwoman turned things over to the weatherman. The weatherman pointed to a map of Florida and the Caribbean. The familiar hurricane symbol appeared just south of Cuba with the name "TS Harold" beside it. A half-dozen colorful lines had it tracking a half-dozen different locations. The farthest one to the right had it coming across the state.

"See that one?" Doug said, pointing to the track. "Coming right our way."

"Doug . . . that's just speculation. The last time a hurricane hit here was in 2004. I can't even remember the last one before that."

"You're probably right," Doug said. "But don't you think we ought to call Michele? Even if it misses us, look at the days they're projecting. Won't that mess up her wedding? It's outside, down at Riverfront Park."

Jim looked at the TV screen again. "It should be well past us by next week," he said. "If it goes where most of the tracks take it, we might not even get any rain."

44

Marilyn wasn't at all sure about this. The fact that she'd all but lied to Charlotte about where she was going tonight also bothered her. It was clear by Charlotte's probing questions that she'd become increasingly nervous about Marilyn's private dance classes with Roberto.

But she had no reason to be, Marilyn kept assuring her. Here it was Tuesday night, their final dance lesson, and Roberto had been the perfect gentleman all along. This was the first time he'd asked to see her outside of the studio. At first, she'd said no. But Roberto had told her it was appropriate for them to celebrate their achievement. This Saturday was the big contest, and he was amazed at how well she'd done. He was confident they would either win or place very high in the scoring. He wanted to thank her tonight, the night of their final practice, by buying her dinner.

What was wrong with that?

She saw the restaurant up ahead, an upscale bistro in the historic downtown section of Sanford, maybe twenty minutes away from River Oaks. As she got out of her car, she saw Roberto standing by the doorway. He carried a gift box under one arm.

"Ah, my dear, you've made it," he said. "I have reservations. They just called for us." He escorted her to the front, where the maître d' greeted them and led them to their table.

"This is so nice," she said.

"Have you never been here?"

"No. I'm sure I would have remembered."

He placed the gift box under his seat then came around behind her and pushed her chair in after she sat. "I hope you didn't mind the little drive," he said, taking his seat. "I know you are . . . *sensitive* about such things, not wanting to give others the wrong impression. River Oaks is such a small town, I thought—"

"I didn't mind the drive at all. I'm glad you thought of it." And because he had, she hadn't worried the whole way here about someone catching her doing something she had no reason to feel guilty about in the first place.

The waiter came up and took their drink orders. "Would you care for an appetizer," he said, "or do you want a few minutes to look over our selections?"

"Do you like calamari?" Roberto asked her.

"Yes."

"They have the best I've ever tasted here. Lightly battered, with this delicious spicy sauce to dip it in."

"Sounds wonderful."

"We'll have that," he told the waiter, who wrote it down and walked away. Looking back at her, Roberto said, "Let's look over the menus before we start to chat. Pick anything you like, my treat."

As Marilyn looked over the menu, the prices shocked her, which was a funny thing. She and Jim rarely went out to eat, but when they had, he'd always go to high-end places like this and would often spend a great deal of money. Her mind had already adapted to eating cheaply, entrees that cost less than even the appetizers here. For that matter, she had even grown to enjoy eating Lean Cuisine dishes with Charlotte around the dinette table.

"See anything you like?" Roberto asked.

"Too many things."

"Are you more in the mood for beef, chicken, or seafood? They also have some amazing pasta dishes."

"I think seafood."

"Are you allergic to anything, like shellfish?"

"No."

"Then allow me." He waved to the waiter, who was already heading in their direction. "You're going to love this."

"Are you ready, sir?"

"Yes, Albert," he said, reading his name tag. "I'll have the bronzed sea bass with lemon shallot butter. And she'll have a dozen—make that two dozen—of the broiled rock shrimp."

"I can't eat two dozen," Marilyn protested.

"Have you ever had them?" She shook her head no. "They're pretty small, actually. They taste like little lobster tails."

"Two dozen then?" the waiter said. "Would you like melted butter with that?" he asked Marilyn.

"Of course," Roberto answered for her. "For our sides, rice pilaf and Caesar salad. Is that okay, Marilyn?"

"Fine," Marilyn said.

The waiter wrote this down and walked away. Roberto turned toward her with that full, deep gaze of his, the one he clicked into whenever they danced. "You look lovely. Really, that dress is amazing on you. Heads were turning the moment you walked in the door till you sat down."

She didn't know what to say. "Thank you." Surely, he was exaggerating. And she was wearing the same red dress she'd worn at every practice, because they were going back to the studio right after. He was looking at her as if he'd never seen it before.

He took a sip of wine. "These past weeks with you have been a total joy for me. You have completely exceeded my expectations."

Again, she was taken aback by his words. He had always been complimentary during their lessons, but now he seemed different somehow.

"I'm actually dreading the thought that our time will be coming to an end," he said. "That is, after this weekend."

"Well, the other class, the group one, doesn't end until next Thursday." She remembered this because Friday, the very next day, was Michele's wedding rehearsal and rehearsal dinner.

"That's not what I'm talking about," Roberto said. "I'm talking about the times we've been alone."

There was that look in his eyes again. She didn't know how to respond, but she was starting to feel uncomfortable.

"I wish there was some way it wouldn't have to come to such an abrupt end," he said. "You've become like a habit for me. A good one. One I would rather not break."

The waiter walked up to refresh their drinks and drop off a basket of fresh bread. "The bread smells delicious," she said, trying to change the subject.

"I have something for you." He reached under his seat and pulled out the gift box. It was light brown with a dark burgundy ribbon. Handing it to her, he said, "Go ahead and open it. You won't be able to see it properly here, of course."

"What is it?" She took the package and untied the ribbon.

"Open it and see."

She lifted the lid and saw an article of clothing. At first, she thought it was a bright red scarf, but there was far too much material. Was it a blouse?

"It's a new dress," he said. "I want you to wear it this weekend at the contest. You will simply blow them away in this."

"But I already have a red dress."

"Yes, and it's lovely. You know how much I like it. That dress is fine for the studio. Or even for a fine restaurant like this. But the contest, it's . . . like a Broadway stage. You need a costume that fits the occasion. You've seen the dresses dancers wear on TV."

"Like *Dancing With the Stars*?" she said.

"Yes. Like that. Only this . . . this one is even more amazing than anything I've seen on TV. I can already picture you in it, both of us, dancing our routine before the judges. They won't be able to take their eyes off you."

Marilyn was stunned. She had watched that show before. There was no way she'd feel comfortable wearing most of the costumes the women wore. And the way Roberto was looking at her now . . . she was almost certain she didn't want to wear the red dress nestled in this box.

What she wanted to do was set the box down, get up, run out the door, and forget all about the "big contest" this weekend.

45

For the next two days, Marilyn was in torment.

She was standing in front of her dresser mirror in Charlotte's apartment, wearing the flashy, skimpy red dress Roberto had given her Tuesday night.

Her bedroom door was shut. And locked.

The dress did make her feel beautiful, and she had to admit . . . it did look good on her. It made her feel at least twenty years younger. Roberto's comments on Tuesday—first at the restaurant then later throughout their last practice—not only flattered her but stirred feelings inside she hadn't felt for a long time. But she didn't want to feel those feelings. At least not with Roberto.

Why couldn't Jim treat me like this? she thought.

She spun slowly around in the mirror. It was Thursday evening, group dance class night. She would see Roberto again; he was certain to ask her what she thought of the dress. The big dance contest was this Saturday, just two nights away. "You can't wear this," she said aloud.

At the restaurant on Tuesday, he had continued to imply he

wanted to keep seeing her after the contest. Every time he said something, she quickly changed the subject, hoping he'd get the hint. He was a handsome, incredibly charming man, at least ten years younger than her. Dancing in his arms these past several weeks had thrilled her; she couldn't recall doing anything else in her life that had made her feel so alive.

But she knew what she really meant to him. She was nothing more than a conquest. He looked at that young dancer, Angelina, the same way he looked at her. And every attractive woman in the restaurant on Tuesday night. Roberto was a ladies' man to his core. And she was sure he'd had plenty of ladies willing to play his game, if only for the pleasure of enjoying his undivided attention while it lasted. Until he grew bored and moved on to the next conquest.

She regretted ever saying yes to being his partner in this contest. She'd have to face him tonight, tell him at the very least that she was not about to wear this dress. If he still wanted her to dance with him, he'd have to be content with the red dress she wore at the restaurant and during practice.

But she needed some help. She walked to the bedroom door and unlocked it. Opening it slightly, she called out to Charlotte, who was putting the finishing touches on their dinner. "Charlotte, can you come in here a minute? There's something I need to show you."

"Sure, hon," she said. "I'm just trying to get this thing finished. Don't want to make you late for your class."

"That's all right," Marilyn said. "It won't take a minute."

"Be right there," she said.

Marilyn closed the door but didn't allow it to latch, then stood in the center of the bedroom. Just for effect, she struck the pose she was supposed to use at the opening of the dance.

Charlotte walked in. "Oh my goodness," she said. "Oh . . . my . . . goodness."

Marilyn couldn't read the look on her face. Was she horrified? Was she—

"So does this mean you and Jim are getting back together?" Charlotte said.

"What? No . . . why would you say that?"

"It's lingerie, right? It's gorgeous. I mean, you look gorgeous. I just figured . . ."

Marilyn stopped posing. She felt like grabbing a blanket and covering up. Lingerie? It was worse than she thought.

"It's not lingerie, is it?" Charlotte said. "I'm sorry. I thought it was some slinky little outfit you got for . . . well, never mind. So, what is it? It's a dress?"

Marilyn nodded.

"No, don't tell me. This isn't your dress for the contest Saturday night?"

"It's supposed to be," Marilyn said. "It's what Roberto wants me to wear. But I'm not going to."

"Thank you," Charlotte said. "I'm so relieved. Because I was gonna say—"

"Your reaction is just what I needed." Marilyn sat on the edge of the bed.

Charlotte sat on the small upholstered chair in the corner. "I mean, it makes you look really beautiful, but—"

"I know. It's totally inappropriate."

"You gonna tell him tonight?" Charlotte asked.

Marilyn sighed.

"He's going to be upset, I take it."

"I think so. But I don't care. I wish I'd never agreed to do this."

"What's happening, hon? You were so excited before. I was

the one getting concerned about it. He starting to pressure you? Putting on the moves?"

"He wasn't before. Not until Tuesday. I didn't tell you, but we met at a restaurant before class."

"Oh."

Yes, *oh*, Marilyn thought. "He said it was just to celebrate our last class and the upcoming contest. Then he sprung this dress on me, said he wanted me to wear it Saturday. Of course, I didn't know then what it looked like, but I had an idea by the way he was talking."

"What'd he say?" Charlotte asked.

"The kinds of things a guy says when he's 'putting on the moves' as you said."

"What'd you do?"

"I kept changing the subject. But I can't keep putting him off."

"No, you can't. A guy like that needs a two-by-four right in the forehead. That's the only kind of hint he'll pick up."

Marilyn smiled. "Well, I'm putting an end to it tonight, after practice."

"You're not going through with the contest?"

"I might go through with it," Marilyn said. "If he agrees I can wear the red dress I've been wearing. If not, then I'm backing out."

"Good for you." Charlotte sniffed the air. "I smell something burning. I better get back to the kitchen."

"And I better get changed. Thanks so much, Charlotte. You've been a great friend."

"No big deal," Charlotte said. "And you be strong when you get to class. Stick to your guns."

"I will."

Just as Charlotte left the room, Marilyn's phone rang. She picked it up. It was Michele.

"Mom, have you been watching the news?" She sounded almost frantic.

"No, I haven't. Why? What's the matter?"

"Tropical Storm Harold has just been upgraded to a hurricane!"

"What tropical storm? I didn't even know one had formed. Is it supposed to come here?" She instantly began to tense up, remembering 2004. Charley, Frances, and Jean. Three hurricanes that bombarded central Florida in the span of six weeks.

"Some of the tracks say it might," Michele said. "Some say it will hit the Panhandle, maybe Pensacola or Mobile. A few take it west, out into the Gulf toward Louisiana."

"Well, Michele, you know hurricanes almost never come here."

"I know, but they can. And two days ago, none of the tracks had it coming across the state. Now three or four of them do. They're saying everyone should keep watching the news for updates. They might be putting us on a hurricane warning by midnight or morning."

"Oh my," Marilyn said. "Is it that close?"

"They said there's a chance it could be here by the weekend."

"This weekend?"

"Yes! By Saturday or Sunday."

"That quick?"

"It depends which way it turns. If it turns east in the next day or two, it could be here by then. Oh, Mom, this could ruin my wedding."

Marilyn tried to get hold of her fears. They were piling up inside and felt like they were about to run free any moment.

She took a deep breath. "We might be fine, Michele. There's still a chance it won't hit here, right? And even if it does, your wedding's not till next weekend. It will be here and gone way before then."

"But Mom, you remember what Charley and Frances did? All the trees they destroyed? The damage to all the buildings? Riverfront Park will be a mess. The power could still be out. Out of town guests might not be allowed in because of the damage." She was starting to cry.

"It's okay, Michele. Let's don't go there yet. None of this may happen." But inside the same thoughts were right there, staring at her. "We have to trust the Lord," she said. "God will take care of us. We made it through the last time just fine." She wanted to ask her a question but was afraid it might stir up more fears in Michele. But she had to ask. "If it does come, where will you go?"

"I'm not worried about that," Michele said. "The college has a bunch of strong buildings. Several of them are approved shelters for the Red Cross. It's the wedding I'm worried about. Mom, what if we have to postpone it?"

46

Marilyn decided to wait until after the group dance lesson before breaking the news to Roberto about the dress. During class he treated her pretty much the way he always had, except she did catch him several times staring at her *that* way. He'd always smile and look away. Now she wondered if he'd been doing this all along or if it had increased since their dinner on Tuesday. Either way, it made her feel uncomfortable. She was almost certain this extra attention would stop once she told him no about the skimpy dress.

The class had ended about ten minutes ago. Most of the people had already left. She stayed around chatting with different ones, finished up a conversation, then said good-bye to Gordon and Faye. She looked at Roberto. He was talking with one of the other couples. Other than the three of them, the studio looked empty. She walked over to the office and peeked inside. Audrey Windsor was working at the desk. Marilyn had seen her come in during the class, but then she disappeared. Obviously, she hadn't gone home.

Audrey looked up. "Hello, Marilyn. How are you? Can I help you with anything?"

"No, I'm fine. Nice to see you."

"I'm just checking over the schedule, but I'll be glad to help you."

"No, really, I'm fine. Have a good night." She pulled away before Audrey could draw her into more conversation.

Guess we won't be talking in the office, she thought. After backing away from the door, she noticed Roberto waving goodbye to the couple he'd been talking with. She grabbed her purse from the chair and walked toward him. "Roberto, I need to leave, but I wonder if I can speak with you before I go. It's kind of important."

"Of course, my dear." A big smile on his face. His eyes lit up. "Only two more days. Aren't you excited? I can't wait to show you off. Have you tried on the dress? What did you think?"

"That's what I want to talk to you about, but not here." She spoke just above a whisper.

"What's wrong? You seem a little upset."

"Let's talk outside, in the breezeway." Now she was whispering. "Audrey is working in the office."

"Very well."

Marilyn headed out the front door. She heard Roberto's footsteps behind her. As she rounded the corner into the breezeway, she was relieved to find it empty. The couple Roberto had last talked with must have parked out front. She watched as Gordon and Faye's car pulled out of the rear parking lot. Stopping when she reached the midpoint, she turned and faced him. *You be strong . . . stick to your guns.* Charlotte's words replayed in her head. "I can't do it," she announced. "I'm sorry to have to tell you on such short notice, but you really haven't given me a choice."

He put both arms on her shoulders, as if to comfort her. "Come now, what are you talking about?" The Latin accent set on full. "Can it be that bad? Tell me, what's the problem?"

"I can't wear that dress, the one you gave me Tuesday night."

"Why? It's perfect. I'm sure you look amazing in it."

"It's not . . . it's just not right for me."

"How can you say that, Marilyn? You are a beautiful woman, you—"

"That's not what I—" She sighed. How could she say this? "I'm not *that* kind of woman."

"What kind?"

"The kind that wears dresses like that," she said. "Out in public."

He laughed. "My, my, look how upset you are. Don't be. I've seen the dress on other women. It's beautiful, yes. Stylish, yes. Provocative, maybe a little. But everything is covered."

She felt he was treating her like a child. "It's not covering up enough for me. I'm sorry. I just can't wear it. If you insist, I'll have to back out of the contest."

"Back out? But the contest is two days away."

"I know, but you only gave me the dress two days ago. I thought I was wearing the red one I've been wearing all this time."

He took his hands off her shoulders and walked a few steps away, looking down at the pavement. "I don't know what to say."

"There's nothing to say, Roberto. My mind's made up. If you want me to dance with you, you have to be okay with the other red dress." Secretly, she was hoping it would not be okay with him and that she'd be able to end everything right here.

He walked back. She leaned against the wall. He leaned toward her, putting his right arm just above her shoulder, his palm flat against the wall, like a teenage boy hovering over his girl in the school hallway.

What is he doing? she thought. He's not getting the message. She remembered what Charlotte had said about guys like Roberto needing to be hit by a two-by-four.

Jim was driving down Oakland Avenue, taking the long way home from his warehouse. For some reason, he was missing Marilyn even more than usual. Maybe it had to do with how much time he'd been "practicing" the last few nights, putting Uncle Henry's advice to work. He'd written out all the things he'd wished he could say to her if she ever gave him the chance. He knew she'd be finishing up her dance class about now, and he decided to drive by the studio, take a chance he might see her in the window.

It had been an exhausting day. The weathermen had not declared a hurricane watch yet, but if Hurricane Harold changed course as some tracks showed, the storm could be here in two days, three at the most. It was already a Category 3 and growing.

Jim's properties had suffered extensive damage in 2004 with Charley, Frances, and Jean. The insurance had covered the worst of it, but his out-of-pocket expenses were huge. In the aftermath, he'd decided to have custom plywood covers made for every window of every property, and had been storing them in rented warehouse space ever since. Years went by with no more storms. Anderson Development, Inc. had purchased four more properties. Those properties didn't have custom plywood coverings.

He'd spent the day moving heavy piles all around, making sure the plywood at the warehouse was present and accounted for, and figuring out how much more he'd need for the new properties. Then he'd spent hours in line waiting for a new shipment of plywood to come in at Lowe's. Listening to the conversations, he figured everyone in line had lived through the other hurricanes. No one was taking a chance with Harold. One good thing had come out of the wait: he'd found an out-of-work guy in line who owned a pickup truck. They'd haggled over a price for him to pick up Jim's plywood, deliver it to his properties, and make it all fit in the right places.

Hopefully, the cost of all this would be a fraction of the expense of possible damage from the storm. Then again, the stupid thing could just keep barreling north or turn west and miss central Florida altogether.

There was the studio up ahead. He slowed as he drove by. The lights were on, but he didn't see anyone inside. Darn, he'd missed her. He had no plans of stopping to talk, of course, but he really wished he could have seen her.

Wait. There in the breezeway. Two silhouettes. His car slowed to a crawl. He saw two people talking, a man and a woman. They were in the shadows, but he could swear it was Marilyn and Roberto.

She was leaning against the back wall. He had his arm straight out, just over her, standing very close.

Too close.

His heart sank. He sighed audibly and drove off. So that was it, then. He really was losing her to this guy. Within half a block, he started imagining holding Marilyn in his own arms. When was the last time he'd held her like that and kissed her tenderly?

No, please, God. I've lost the most beautiful, precious woman on earth, and there's nothing I can do now.

"Marilyn, if you feel that strongly about it, of course you can wear the old dress."

"Old dress? Roberto, that dress cost a lot of money, and it's less than two years old."

"That's not what I meant. I only meant—"

She pushed his arm down. "And there's something else I need to say. Right now." She backed several steps away from him. "I don't know if I gave you the impression that I'm interested in a relationship with you, but if I have, I—"

"Marilyn, no, I'm sorry. I know you are a married woman. I was only being playful."

"Well, you've been getting a little too playful the last couple of times we've been together."

He stood up straight, all the swagger out of his step. "Really, I'm sorry. I meant no harm. I'll behave, I promise." He was smiling again. "Can we still be friends?" He held out his hand.

"Just friends?" she asked.

"Just friends," he repeated.

"Okay." She shook his hand but kept her distance.

"And you'll still dance with me on Saturday?"

"In my *old* red dress?" she said.

"Yes, it's a lovely dress," he said. "I'm sorry I said that. So what time shall I pick you up? Five o'clock?"

"How about I meet you there?" she said as she turned and headed for the parking lot. "You stand right there. I'll be right back."

"Where are you going?"

"To give you back the red dress you gave me. It's in the car."

47

When Jim awoke on Friday morning, his mind not even fully anchored in the day, he flipped on the television to the local news station. A familiar weatherman stood in his blue suit right next to a satellite image showing Hurricane Harold inching ever closer to the lower west coast near Naples, Florida. He clicked off the mute button.

"Here he is, folks. As you can see, Harold seems to be coming our way. It's really time to start taking this storm seriously. I don't think we're going to dodge the bullet this time. Most of the tracks now show it making landfall somewhere between Naples and Fort Myers later this afternoon. Folks down there are already under a hurricane warning and have been since about 3:00 a.m. There are already reports of tropical storm winds picking up along the coast nearby. Let's switch to the screen showing the new forecast tracks." The man stood in place as the actual hurricane image became a red symbol, with multicolored tracks spewing out of its head.

"Uh-oh," Jim said as he sat back on the bed. Not good. All but two of the tracks had it coming in around Naples then heading diagonally across the state, exiting somewhere south of Jacksonville. Three of the tracks went right through central Florida. "Looks just like the path Charley followed in '04," Jim muttered. A moment later, the weatherman said almost the same thing. Jim listened some more.

"Harold may be following Charley's track, but it's actually a little bigger than Charley was and moving a little slower. Which means there's a likelihood of it causing more damage than Charley." Charley had caused a great deal of damage. More than the other two storms put together, at least around their area. Jim listened now for the timing. After a few moments, that information came.

"It's hard to say exactly when the storm will hit the Orlando-Sanford area. There's a chance it will slow down even a little more once it makes landfall. There's also a chance it will weaken significantly by the time it reaches us. It's expected to reach Category 4 by this afternoon. But those of you who were around in 2004 might remember Charley was a Category 4 when it pummeled Punta Gorda, then a strong Cat 1 by the time it got here."

The weatherman faced the camera; a serious look came over his face. "Now, don't hear the wrong thing, folks. Even if it does weaken to a Cat 1 or 2, this is still going to be a major storm event. Expect severe tree damage, even some big ones coming down altogether. We'll see roof damage and flooding in low-lying areas. Those of you in mobile home or trailer parks, you should already be making plans to pack up and stay with friends, or move to an approved Red Cross shelter. Let's go ahead and put up that list of storm shelters in our area now."

Jim clicked off the TV and stood up. He walked over to his desk to make a list of things he had to take care of right away.

At the top of the list, he wrote: *Call that guy, make sure he can get all the plywood on the windows done TODAY. Hire others, if necessary.* He wrote down to call Doug, make sure he was aware of the latest weather update and confirm where he planned to ride out the storm. Then he scratched through that one. Better just walk over to the garage and talk to Doug in person. *Call Tom and Jean*, he wrote. Both of them were responsible; he didn't have to worry if they'd do all the right things. Michele would probably stay in one of the main university buildings. They were built solid, so no worries there. But still he wrote *Call Michele* down, to make sure she would buy all the necessary supplies for the storm's aftermath.

But what about Marilyn?

He had to call her. Surely she'd be willing to talk to him with this storm on the way. Where would she stay? Those apartments built over the stores downtown were strong enough to stay intact with a Category 1 or 2 storm. But what about the windows? Did her landlady even have boards to cover them? What if the downtown area got flooded? That could happen if they got enough rain. The river could overflow its banks and move right into downtown.

He had to call her. He wrote that at the top of his list.

Charlotte and Marilyn sat at the dinette table in her kitchen watching the weather report. "This is terrible," Charlotte said. "It's really coming. Most of those tracks got it coming this way."

"Looks like it," Marilyn said.

"When I came here a couple of years ago, I asked the real estate guy about hurricanes. 'They never come here,' he said. But look, here it comes."

"It's not as bad as it seems," Marilyn said, only half believing it. "I mean, it's not going to be anything like Katrina or Sandy."

"They were talking about this storm at work last night," Charlotte said. "I didn't know anything about it. Seems like it came out of nowhere."

"It kinda did. That's the thing about storms that move into the Gulf. There's so many ways they can turn. If they go north toward the panhandle or west toward Texas, people there get lots of warning. Several days while it moves over the water. But when it turns east, toward—"

"Towards us," Charlotte interrupted.

"Right, well, when that happens, it's just right there at the doorway."

"What are you going to do?" Charlotte asked.

Marilyn wondered why she didn't say "we." "What do you mean?"

"If it comes, where you gonna go?"

"Can't we stay here?"

"What? No. I mean, I'd like to. I guess it's safe enough. But my supervisor was telling us last night that if the storm comes, she wants those of us without families to ride it out at Urgent Care. The building's solid as a rock. That way, we can look after any patients who come in."

Marilyn began looking around the apartment, trying to imagine how she'd feel sitting through a hurricane in here, all by herself. She'd barely held it together in 2004 in her big house on Elderberry Lane. "Can we put masking tape on the windows?" she asked.

"We could," Charlotte said, "but I read somewhere it doesn't do any good. Think about it. A big oak branch comes sailing through that window at a hundred miles an hour, and masking tape's not gonna matter much. Oh . . . I'm sorry. That was a stupid thing to say. Listen, there's gotta be a place you—"

Marilyn's cell phone began ringing. She lifted it up and saw it was Jim.

Charlotte saw it too and stopped talking. "Maybe you should get that, you know?"

"Maybe I should."

As Jim dialed Marilyn's number, he said a prayer, then tried to remember Audrey's admonition about not reacting to things Marilyn did or said. *"Create a safe place for her to share what she's feeling. If you react harshly, she'll shut down."*

"Hello . . . Jim?"

He couldn't believe it. She'd picked up.

"Hi, Marilyn. Thanks for taking my call."

"Are you calling about the storm?"

"Yeah, have you seen the news?" he said. "I think this one's really going to hit us."

She sighed. "I think so too."

"Have you . . . have you thought about where you're going to stay?"

"We were just talking about it. Charlotte's a nurse, so she has to be at Urgent Care if it comes."

"You can't stay in that apartment alone." He instantly regretted saying it that way, like he was telling her what to do. "I mean, you're not going to be there by yourself, right?"

"I don't want to be. I don't know where else to go."

A pause. *Just say it*. "You could come here."

"I don't know, Jim. I don't think—"

"Wait, hear me out," he said as gently as he could. "I know

it'd be awkward for you with what's going on between us. But you know this house is safe as can be. We rode out all three hurricanes here in 2004. I don't feel right with you holed up in that little apartment by yourself. Do you even have boards for the windows?"

"No, we don't."

"Here we have first-class electric storm shutters. I just push a few buttons." Another long pause. "How about . . . you come here, and I'll go stay in a shelter."

"I don't want to do that . . . to you, I mean."

"I insist. I won't be able to rest unless I know you're safe. So you stay here, and I'll leave. Maybe I'll stay with Tom and Jean." Another pause, longer this time. "Are you still there?"

"Yes."

"So you'll come? You really should get here this evening before the wind starts to pick up. Right now it's gorgeous outside, but that's going to change pretty quick once it starts heading this way. So, you'll come?"

"Yes. I think I will. Thanks for doing this."

"I'll be here all evening getting the house and yard ready," Jim said. "You can come anytime. I'll leave shortly after, when I know you're settled."

48

After getting off the phone with Jim, Marilyn had spent the morning helping Charlotte get the apartment ready for the storm. Charlotte worried about the windows being blown out and high winds and rains pouring inside. She had renter's insurance, so she wasn't too concerned about the big things getting damaged. They boxed up all her little personal things and stacked the boxes in the bathtub.

Just after carrying the last box into the bathroom, Harriet had called, asking Marilyn to come in to Odds-n-Ends a few hours early and help her prepare the store. Her husband and son-in-law were boarding up the windows, but there was a ton of little things that still needed doing. Marilyn hadn't been scheduled to come in until noon, but Harriet promised if she came in now she'd let her go home early. "As soon as the store is as safe as we can make it." She had already put a sign on the front door, telling customers they were closed today.

Marilyn knew she didn't have to worry about their house on Elderberry Lane. That was one thing she could always count on about Jim—he was thorough. And he loved that house. He probably felt pretty good about those hurricane shutters he had "invested in" back in 2005. She thought they detracted from the house's appearance. But she had to admit, she was glad they were there now.

Marilyn stepped out into the employee parking lot at 6:00 p.m. and was startled by the condition of the sky. A few hours ago on her break, it had been pleasant and calm, a sunny September day. Now it was completely overcast. Dark wispy clouds moved much too fast across the sky in odd directions. Strong winds out of the south were already causing trees to bend and sway. A brown palm frond broke loose overhead, startling her. The wind picked it up and carried it across the parking lot, slamming it into a dumpster. *It's really coming. Harold is really going to hit us.* Fears she'd suppressed all day through busyness began to surface. She hurried to her car and closed herself in, as if to escape the fear.

As she pulled onto Main Street, it was clear everyone was taking this storm seriously. Hardly any cars were on the street. Every storefront was either already covered in plywood or being worked on by store owners and employees. Someone had dumped a large mound of sand at one end of the street, and dozens of people were shoveling sand into sandbags.

She drove through the familiar streets from the downtown area to her neighborhood and saw the same thing. Big beautiful houses with windows boarded up. Many had spray-painted signs like "Leave Us Alone Harry!" or "Harry Go Home!"

As she pulled down the service lane that ran behind their house, a strong gust blew against her car, almost forcing her off the road into a fence. She swung it back just in time. Up ahead, she saw that Jim's car had just pulled into the garage. Doug's little red Mazda was parked beside it. She was going to pull into the third spot, but Doug had come in wide, taking up half her space. She parked behind Jim's car in the driveway instead. Maybe Jim hadn't told Doug she was coming. It was sad to think Doug had already formed a parking habit that counted on her absence. More evidence of the gap in their relationship and the need to mend that fence.

Jim got out of his car, saw her, and waved. She waved back through the windshield. He looked tired and his hair was sticking out in odd directions. Too much gel, she thought. That and all this wind.

Jim noticed the problem with Doug's car. "Sorry about that," he said. "Let's get your things in the house, then you and I can switch places."

"Can't we just get Doug to move his over?"

"He's not here, and I don't have his keys. He rode his bike over to Jason's a few hours ago. I told him he needed to leave his car here in the garage. He's gotten sloppy about pulling in since you . . . well, let me help you with your things."

As Jim walked up to her car, she said, "You look like you've had a rough day. Been getting the properties boarded up?"

"No, I hired a guy to do that. A couple of guys, actually. They've already finished. I'm just getting back from helping—" He caught himself. He was just about to say he'd gotten back from helping Audrey Windsor's nephew board up her place. But he didn't want Marilyn to know he knew Audrey. "I was just helping this elderly woman get her house ready. Your stuff in the trunk?"

"I can get it, there's just two suitcases," she said.

"That's all right. Why don't you go on inside? I'll get them. I just put a fresh pot of coffee on."

"You're making coffee now?" She popped the trunk.

"It's not as good as yours, but I think I'm getting close."

"Well, I could use a cup about now."

"Here, give me your keys. After I put your things inside, I want to bring some of the lawn furniture in here before the wind tosses them in the pool. Then I'll switch our cars around."

"Want me to fix you a cup?" she said.

He smiled. "I'd like that. I won't stay long." She made a face he couldn't interpret, but he didn't want to ask. She went through the garage and disappeared into the laundry room, heading for the main house. A few moments later he followed behind her. He brought the suitcases through the house into the master bedroom. He figured she'd want to stay there, but he wasn't sure. He couldn't ask her at the moment; she was in the bathroom.

Glancing out the back windows, he watched two lawn chairs lift off the ground and fly against the back fence. "I'm going back out," he yelled through the door. He was running outside to get the chairs when a fierce gust of wind blew through, knocking over the table with the umbrella.

A moment later, another burst of wind came through, stronger than the last. A loud cracking sound filled the backyard. Jim dove to the ground, certain a tree was about to fall and crush him.

49

Marilyn stepped out of the bathroom. "Jim?" She thought she heard him saying something a moment ago but couldn't hear it over the bathroom fan. She walked through the master bath suite into their bedroom, but he was gone.

The wind howled outside, vibrating the windows. A table in the pool area suddenly fell over. She stopped and gripped her dresser, gasping at a new terrifying noise, a cracking sound loud as thunder. Something moved by the back fence. Was that Jim falling in the backyard? "Jim!" she yelled and ran toward the patio door. Had he been struck by lightning?

As she opened the door, the wind ripped it from her grasp and slammed it against the back wall. "Jim!" she yelled again. He was still lying on the ground in the grass by the fence. She came around the pool, relieved to see him move. In a moment, he was on his hands and knees. "Are you hurt? What happened?"

He stood up, shaking his head. "I'm all right. Scared me half to death." He looked over toward the area behind the garage. "Oh no, look." He walked toward the white privacy fence.

"What is it?"

"Oh my gosh, I can't believe it. The storm's not even here yet, and look."

She walked around the deep end of the pool. "What? What is it?"

"Maybe you don't want to see this." He turned to look at her. "It's your car."

"What's wrong with my—" The next moment, she cleared the freestanding garage and had her answer. She could see her car over the fence. "It's crushed." A huge branch from an aging oak tree, whose limbs had watched over the freestanding garage ever since they'd moved in, had broken off and fallen right on top of her car. The roof, the windshield, and half the front end of her car were totally smashed.

"I'm sorry, hon." Jim turned toward her and put his arms out to comfort her.

She almost let him. An awkward moment followed as she pulled back and looked over the fence again. Her poor car. It was destroyed. "I can't believe it."

"We need to get inside quick," Jim said. "If a tree limb can do that to a car . . ."

"Now we can't switch cars," she said. "You're stuck here."

Jim looked back at the damage. "You're right." The biggest part of the limb stretched across the driveway, blocking in Doug's car too. "It looks way too heavy to move. Well, let's not worry about it now. You go on inside and I'll finish putting the patio furniture in the garage."

"How about I stay out here and help you, then we both go in?"

"I'm sorry, I'm doing it again."

"What?"

"Telling you what to do," he said. "All right, let's both get this stuff inside." For the next ten minutes, they worked together, wrestling the wind for each piece of furniture. A few gusts seemed strong enough to rip off more tree limbs, if not topple the trees themselves. "I hate this," she shouted over the noise.

"I should've gotten this done this morning. I thought we had more time."

When the last chair had been tucked safely in the garage and the garage sealed up tight, they ran across the grass then through the pool area and came in the house through the veranda. The next moment a torrential rain began. "Must be one of the outer rain bands," Jim said. "Either this storm has gotten bigger or it's speeding up. The last update made it sound like we weren't going to be seeing any serious storm effects until after dark."

"Maybe they don't consider this serious."

He smiled then walked into the living room. She followed him, watched him grab the remote and turn the TV on. "Yeah, see that," he said, pointing to the topmost part of the revolving cloud base that was Hurricane Harold. It covered all of south and part of central Florida. "See that band there? That's the one. That's out there right now." She was surprised to see him so animated, almost like a little boy.

They watched the meteorologist explain things she didn't understand, about why Harold was moving faster now. She thought back to the way things had been in 2004, and about one of her other "little boys," Tom. He hadn't been so little then. He was in high school, and he'd watched the storm updates like he watched the Super Bowl. The worse it got, the more fun he had. Three hurricanes in the span of six weeks, and Tom was in his glory the whole while. When Charley struck, he'd wanted to be out there during the worst of it. Trees were falling, branches flying down the road. The rain whipped so hard against the windows, Marilyn was sure they were all going to shatter.

Tom stared at the whole scene with wild-eyed wonder. He

must have said "Isn't this amazing?" fifty times. Michele was just as scared as she was. And Doug, he wouldn't even get near a window or a door. He spent the whole time surrounded by pillows in the walk-in closet of their master bedroom. Surprisingly, they only lost electricity for a few hours. Jim said it was because all the wires were underground. That helped everyone, especially Doug. He was even more afraid of the dark than the storms.

Where was Doug now? At some friend's house eight blocks away. Doug was the age Tom had been back then, almost a senior in high school. Hard to believe. They had been so close, she and Doug. What had happened to them? She loved him so much, but somehow over the past few years they had drifted almost as far apart as she and Jim had. She had called him several times after she left Jim but always got his voicemail. He rarely returned her calls. When he did, she was always at work, and he never left a message.

A sigh escaped her. "You said Doug was at Jason's? Are you sure he got there all right?"

"Yeah," Jim said. "Made him call me as soon as he arrived. Jason had invited three or four guys over, said they're going to have a hurricane party."

"You don't think they'd do anything stupid," she said. "Like high-school-boy-stupid."

"You mean like dare each other to run out in the middle of the street? See who could stay out there the longest? Remember when Tom dared me to do that with him during Charley?"

She nodded, so glad Jim hadn't given in.

"Even if they want to do something crazy, I can't see Doug joining in. He spent all his time hiding out in our closet in '04."

"He won't do that this time, not over there," she said.

"No, but I don't see him acting like a crazy man. He'll be all right."

She decided to take a chance and ask. "Jim, do you know if Doug is mad at me?"

"What? I don't know. I don't think so."

"He hasn't said anything about how he feels about me . . . leaving home?"

Jim paused a moment. "Not to me. But you know how he is. At least, how he's been the last few years. He's totally wrapped up in his own life and plans. I'm sure he misses you. He's grumbled a few times about meals and the way I keep house."

"I thought you'd get someone to do that," she said.

"It didn't work out. Anyway, I can't think of anything he said that makes me think he's mad at you." He looked down at the carpet. "Doesn't seem real happy with me right now." When he looked up he said, "Have you tried calling him?"

She didn't really want to get into any more details with Jim about this. "We keep missing each other." She changed the subject. "Maybe I'll call Tom and Michele before the storm gets too bad, make sure they're okay."

He muted the TV. "It sounds like we've got maybe two or three hours before the main bands start coming our way." He looked out the big picture window in the living room. "I put all the hurricane shutters down upstairs. Would you be okay if I waited a bit before shutting them down here? I'd love to watch the storm a little while."

She couldn't believe it. Jim never asked her things like this. He just did whatever he wanted. "I'm okay with leaving the ones under the porch and veranda up a little while," she said. "Since they're covered by the roof. But could you close the others?"

He agreed. She walked over to get her phone out of her purse on the counter.

"I'm really sorry about your car," he said.

"What?" She turned around.

"I know how much you loved that car. It's probably totaled. But we'll find another one just like it." He stumbled over the next few words. "Well . . . I mean, the insurance will give us enough money, so you can buy another one."

She knew he was stumbling over the phrase "we'll find another one." This was the first time they'd been together in almost two months, other than a few moments here and there. Would *they* be buying another car? What did the future hold for them? In some ways, being here with him felt entirely normal, like slipping into an old pair of jeans. But it also felt strained and awkward. She didn't know about the future, and right now she didn't want to think about it. But it didn't escape her notice that Jim seemed genuinely sorry for her loss. The Jim she knew would never have picked up on her feelings. He'd mostly be steaming about the money he'd have to spend meeting the insurance deductible and the hassle of dealing with the agents and adjustors.

She looked at him again, still standing in front of the picture window, staring out to the street. Being at this house was not a good thing; she could feel it weakening her resolve. It wasn't the house itself, the décor, the furnishings. It was the memories of the kids, when they were all together at a happier time. But that time was not now. And Jim hadn't made her happy then; only the kids did. This kindler, gentler Jim was just a ploy.

Don't be fooled by it. He hasn't changed, not that *much.*

Jim was actually enjoying the storm outside, which wasn't like him at all. What he really wanted to do was walk out on the front porch and get the full dose. It was amazing seeing the power of God up close this way. He looked back at Marilyn standing by the kitchen counter with her phone in hand. Better not try it, he thought. He knew how much she hated hurricanes. She'd be worried sick if he went outside.

He wasn't too sure how the two of them would get along over the next day or so. This development was totally unexpected. He tensed up thinking about it. What if he screwed up, said the wrong thing, and made everything worse? An idea suddenly popped into his head, something Uncle Henry had said when he'd visited on Tuesday. *"Start practicing what you want to say to Marilyn if you got the chance. Like an act of faith. I know she's still not talking to you. But we're hoping someday that's going to change. You be ready when the time comes."*

Jim had done this, written everything down and rewritten it a dozen times. He had no idea a chance would come so soon. He imagined it would be weeks or even months from now. Was this the time? Had God set this up? Maybe God had Doug park his car the wrong way, blocking Marilyn from parking inside the garage; maybe he had an angel break that big limb so it would fall on Marilyn's car, forcing them to ride out the storm together.

No, this was crazy. He was thinking like Uncle Henry now.

That made him smile.

He hurried into the bedroom, pulled the last version of the things he'd written out of his dresser drawer, then stood there staring at it. Was he ready for this? Should he even try? What if he left the most important thing out or said something that hurt her even more?

What if this wasn't God's plan and the whole thing blew up in his face?

50

"Mom, this is terrible. My wedding is going to be ruined."

For the past few minutes, Marilyn had been trying to make sure Michele was safe, but all Michele wanted to talk about was her wedding plans. "It'll be fine, Michele. Trust me, next Saturday you and Allan will get married just like we planned." She watched Jim walk around the downstairs closing most of the hurricane shutters.

"But what if Harold knocks down all the trees or destroys the gazebo? What if the whole riverfront area gets flooded?"

"Okay, what if that happens? Do you love Allan?"

"Yes."

"Does he love you?"

Michele laughed. "Yes. He's right here beside me, nodding his head."

She was relieved to know Michele was with him. "Is Allan worried about any of this?"

"No."

"Then it's two against one. I say just relax and don't worry about next week. A few trees might get knocked down, but remember the last time? Most of them were fine. The gazebo might get damaged, but it can be repaired."

"Not before the wedding," she said. "They'll probably cover it with a blue tarp and all the pictures will be ruined. What? Hold on, Allan's saying something." Marilyn waited. Michele laughed. "Allan says we can photoshop out the blue tarp if we have to."

"See? It's all going to work out. And even if the park does flood, things will be back to normal in time for the wedding. Back in 2004, the flooding receded after three or four days. We're going to have your wedding right where we've planned."

"Are you sure?"

"Yes, I'm sure." But she wasn't sure. Sounding sure at a time like this was part of a mom's job. "Now where are the two of you staying?" she asked. "Are you both safe?"

"Totally," Michele said.

"Where are you staying?"

"We're with a bunch of friends in an interior lobby of the dorm. It's one of the approved shelter areas in the school."

"Do you have food and water, some batteries? What about blankets? Are you—"

"Mom, we're fine."

"Okay. Well, you call me if anything happens."

"I will. So . . . where are *you* staying? Are you safe?"

Marilyn took a deep breath. She almost didn't want to say. "I'm here at the house."

"With Dad?"

Marilyn's phone beeped. She looked at the screen; it was Roberto calling. She decided he could leave a message. "It's a long story, but yes, I'm here with your father."

"How's that working out?"

"So far, we're fine. It's a little awkward, but . . . we'll be fine." Did she really believe that?

"You guys really haven't spent any time together since you left, have you?"

"No, not really."

"I didn't think so."

"Pray for us." Marilyn wasn't sure what to tell Michele if she asked what to pray for.

"Oh, believe me, I will."

They hung up as Jim walked past her. "I'll just get the windows on this side of the house. Was that Michele? Is she all right?"

"She's fine. She's with Allan and a bunch of friends at a school shelter."

"That's good."

"Excuse me, I've got to call someone back." Now, why did she say that? She wasn't going to call Roberto back. She'd already checked; he'd left a voice mail. Jim said okay and walked away. Then she realized that was why she'd said it, to get him to keep moving. She was avoiding him. Avoiding the awkward feelings that surfaced whenever he came near. But she couldn't keep doing that, not for the next day or so. They'd be shut in this house together for at least that long.

She went to her voice mail and listened to Roberto's message: "Marilyn? This is Roberto. As you can imagine, this hurricane has totally ruined our plans. I've just been informed that the dance contest has been canceled, postponed indefinitely. I'm so disappointed. I'm sure they'll reschedule it as soon as the weather clears up, if the damage is not too extensive. Well, so sorry. Stay safe."

Deleting the message felt so nice. She determined right then to also delete the contest from her life for good. She didn't need the stress. She still loved dancing, more than ever. But she didn't want to dance with Roberto anymore. Not alone anyway. Perhaps she could sign up for lessons in a few weeks with one of the other instructors.

One of the women instructors.

She found Tom's cell number on her contact list and called him. Jean answered and said they were doing fine. Tom was outside putting up the last piece of plywood on the last bedroom window. "In this wind?" Marilyn said. "Tell him to be careful." Then she told Jean about the limb that had crushed her car.

"Tom's almost done," Jean said. "Just one more window. Were you in the car when it happened?"

"No," she said, which led to her having to admit she was stuck at home with Jim, at least for the next day or so. Which led to another strained piece of communication: Jean trying to gently probe for more details, and Marilyn trying to remain as vague as possible. At about that time, Jim walked up, so Marilyn made an excuse for getting off the phone. Michele and Allan were safe. Tom and Jean and the kids were safe. Doug was safe. Now she could relax. Then she looked at Jim standing there staring at her.

There was no way she could relax.

"Say," he said. "I have an idea. You weren't expecting me to be here. And I don't want to make things worse by having to deal with me being here. So how about we share the house? You can have the whole downstairs. I'll go upstairs in the loft. That way you can sleep in your own bed, hang out in the living room or great room. I'll stay up there for the most part, except when I need to come down to get something to eat. The food and pantry are full, by the way. When I was out I bought some things I knew you liked."

He started to walk away. "I'll close the rest of the shutters down here, get a few things from the bedroom, then the downstairs is all yours."

"Hey, Jim." He turned around. "Thanks," she said. She thought she should say something more but changed her mind.

51

Did the floor creak enough to hear it downstairs? No, Marilyn didn't look up. She'd have looked up if she'd heard it creak. This house was solid, the best money could buy. Jim peeked down at her, getting as close to the wooden railing as he dared. She was sitting in her favorite corner of the couch, legs tucked up, like she always did, pretending to read a book.

He knew she was pretending because she hadn't turned a page in over ten minutes, and she was a fast reader. Jim knew why. She was terrified of the storm. Didn't matter that the house had made it fine through the last set of hurricanes and that, since then, he'd added these top-of-the-line shutters. Every time a branch banged against the roof or the side of the house, Marilyn jumped. She'd close the book, look around the room, then slowly open the book up again.

He wished he could go down and comfort her, at least provide some kind of distraction. What he really wanted was to talk to her. Not small talk—things that mattered. The kinds of things on his list. When he'd gone upstairs a few hours ago, he'd prayed about it. He got a strong impression he wasn't supposed to initiate this conversation. It was too big a thing, and too delicate to force.

He felt God wanted him to be patient, to wait for her to make the first move. If she asked him to come down there and be with her, he had a green light from God to have *that* talk. But not until then.

It had been hours since that prayer, and she hadn't glanced up at the loft. Not even once. He would have known.

He hadn't taken his eyes off her.

How many times had he seen her reading a book in that very spot over the years? A hundred? A thousand? He'd walk right by, sometimes not even stopping to answer her when she'd ask him a question. Too preoccupied with whatever was on his mind to even show her common courtesy, let alone the desperate love he longed to pour out on her now.

You stupid fool!

No, don't keep doing that. Self-loathing had become an almost constant companion since he'd started . . . *practicing.* Writing down how wrong he'd been, how sorry he was, and how much he longed to make things right was certainly necessary, and he saw the value in it. But, it was so painful. Reading the words, rereading them. Writing, rewriting them. Over and over until he'd gotten it just right.

But was it just right? Would it do a thing to soften her bitterness toward him? He didn't fault her for it. She had a right to all of her feelings. But still, no matter what happened, if he got that green light, he had to try. He looked down at her again. *Please look up here. Please, Marilyn.*

She was so beautiful.

He knew why that dance instructor was pursuing her. The guy only saw what a lot of men did: an extremely attractive woman who looked at least a decade younger than her age. Jim had caught countless men at his business parties staring at her, some doing their best to flirt with her. She never seemed to notice. If she had, she never let on.

In some sick way, he'd treated her beauty like a matter of pride, as though evidence of the kind of man he was—someone who could catch a beauty like this and keep her all to himself. Then show her off when it suited him, to enhance his own image.

It was always about him. Always.

He never told her how beautiful she was anymore, as though giving her compliments would somehow ruin her. Perhaps lessen her vulnerability, her complete dependence on him. He'd acted like she was his possession, not his cherished partner.

But he hadn't kept her, had he? There she was, not thirty steps away, but the distance might as well be thirty miles.

You stupid fool!

An incredibly strong gust hit. It felt for a moment as if the house would lift off its foundations. Marilyn gasped. Then a loud bang thumped against the side of the house, the loudest one so far. Marilyn screamed and jumped to her feet. "Jim!" she yelled.

She looked up, terror on her face.

"It's okay, hon!" he yelled back, calling her hon from instinct. He leaned over the railing. "I'm right here. It was just another limb. A big one, but we're okay."

"I hate this!"

"I know. But we'll be all right."

"How much longer is it going to be like this?"

He had to tell her the truth. "Quite a while. The worst of it is still an hour away. After the eye passes, it'll take just as long on its way out."

"I don't think I can take it much longer. It feels like the house is falling apart. And we've got those huge oak trees all around us. Any one of them could come down right on top of us."

"That could happen," he said gently. "But I don't think so. It's been downgraded to a Cat 1, and the more Harold stays over land, the weaker it gets. I paid those tree guys over twelve hundred dollars back in June, remember? To check the trees out and prune any branches they thought might cause trouble."

"I remember. But do you remember the huge limb that crushed my car?"

"Well, yeah. I know. Let's just keep praying. I think we'll be okay."

She sat back in her spot on the couch. He backed away from the railing.

"Jim," she yelled.

"Yeah?"

"Could you come down here? I don't want to be alone anymore."

52

It was all Jim could do not to run down the stairs like the kids used to on Christmas morning. He grabbed his "practice" sheets, folded them, and put them in his pocket. He uttered a number of silent "Thank you, Lords" as he walked as calmly as he could down the stairs. He went into the kitchen, poured her a Diet Coke, and brought a bag of her favorite snack, Cheetos, to the living room.

"Thank you," she said, trying to restrain a smile. "This'll help."

"How about I turn the TV on?" he said. "We can watch the weather, just for a few minutes. I've had it on upstairs. I think it will help you calm down."

"How can that help, seeing the storm climb its way across the state right at us?"

"Because I think your imagination is making it worse." He clicked the TV on. "After a few minutes of weather, we'll watch an old movie. That'll take your mind off things while the worst of the storm passes."

"Really?"

"Sure."

"But you hate old—"

"Doesn't matter." He wanted to say "It's not all about me anymore," but that would sound fake, even though he meant it. "It'll probably do me some good too. Keep my mind off all the cleanup work I'm going to have to do tomorrow." He sat in his spot, in the recliner closest to her corner of the couch.

Over the next two hours, they watched the weather then almost all of *Casablanca*. Mostly in silence. A major gust smacked against the house. The lights went out, just as Bogey and Bergman were about to do their famous good-bye scene at the airport. It startled them, but Marilyn didn't scream this time. Instead, she calmly lit the candles she had placed on the coffee table.

Jim got up to turn on a few oil lanterns and grab the big flashlight on the kitchen counter. "They'll probably only be off a little while," he said, hoping that was true. As he picked up the flashlight, he got a strong impression the lights had gone out just now for a reason.

It was time. Time for the talk.

Instantly he tensed up, wrestling with the idea. What if it was a mistake? What if she shut him down before he finished? They'd sit around in an awkward—no, worse than awkward—silence till sunrise.

But the impression wouldn't leave. Another strong gust blew, making the house vibrate.

"Jim, could you come back here?"

He hurried back to his chair, pulled out his practice sheets as he walked. "It's okay," he said. The eye of the storm had passed sometime during the movie. The winds had now shifted and were blowing against the house in the opposite direction. That usually meant more tree damage, as limbs that had weakened during the first half of the hurricane would now snap off in round two.

"How much longer, do you think?"

"Not too much," he said. "Maybe a couple of hours, then the winds will start to drop as the storm gets farther away."

"I hope the electricity comes back on soon," she said. "Watching the movie helped."

"It helped me too." He brought the papers out so he could see them but kept them out of the light. "Say, Marilyn. I was thinking, maybe with this interruption, you know, with the lights . . . maybe you and I could talk."

"I don't know, Jim."

"Well, actually, you wouldn't have to talk, just listen." She made a face. He realized what he'd said. "No, wait, I didn't mean that like it sounded. You can say anything you want." He took a deep breath, then exhaled. "What I'm trying to say is . . ." He turned the flashlight on his practice sheets. "I've been wanting to do this for a while, to say some things to you. Things I need to say, to—"

"Jim, I don't want to get into an argument."

"No, it's not anything we should argue over. Really. It's mostly an apology. I wrote it down because . . . well, I'm no good at this. I just want you to know how sorry I am about some things. Some important things. You don't have to apologize back, or say anything at all if you don't want to. This is about me saying some things to you that I've already talked to God about. But that's not enough. I need to say them to you."

She looked toward the kitchen. He heard her sigh.

"Would that be okay?" he said. "After, if you feel like I've made things too awkward for us, I can go back upstairs." She turned and looked back at him. He couldn't read her face. "Is that okay?" He looked down at his sheets. "It's not very long. I wrote it down so I wouldn't ramble on, but mostly so I wouldn't forget anything that mattered." He looked back at her. "Can I say this? Can I read this to you?"

She nodded. Her face seemed hard as a rock. He tried not to let that get to him. As he held the sheets of paper, he set his hands firmly against his lap so he wouldn't tremble. "Here it is."

Marilyn,

I think I get now why you left. I'm not upset anymore, and I want to apologize first for getting so upset. I acted as if you had no right to leave me or had any reason to be unhappy. Like you said, I didn't have a clue. Obviously, you wouldn't leave me or this house you love, or our life together, to move into a little apartment if I hadn't made you profoundly unhappy for a long—

He took a deep breath, fighting a wave of emotion.

—long time. I have been so stubborn and selfish. Really, I think for our entire marriage. I tried but I couldn't recall any clear examples of when I did things around here or made decisions for us that weren't—

He started to choke up again. He had to get himself under control.

—that weren't mostly about me and what I wanted. Even the church I made us go to, and all those business parties. I never thought about you, your needs, or the kids.

I didn't pay near enough attention to you or things you cared about. Not just lately.

He looked up, tears welling in his eyes. She was looking away but still listening.

I've been demanding and legalistic. I hardly ever encouraged you or the kids. But I was always quick to point out someone's mistakes or something I didn't think was done right.

I've been talking with our kids lately. Actually, listening to them.

Tears poured down his face.

I've got a long way to go to start trying to make it up to them, and to you, but I'm going to try if you'll let me. I'm sure I'm only seeing a fraction of the pain I've caused you, but even the part I am seeing . . . well, it's killing me inside.

But that's okay. The part it's killing needs to die. It's the part that's made you so unhappy you felt you had to leave, to try and escape it.

He wiped the tears off his face.

But I want you to know . . . I do love you, Marilyn. You are the best thing that's happened to me. Ever. I didn't treat you like you were. I'll regret that for the rest of my life. But now I know what I've lost. And I almost can't bear it.

The only hope I may ever have with you is to earn your respect again by proving my love for you. If it takes the rest of my life, I'll do it.

He could hardly continue; his body was shivering with regret.

You are such a wonderful, beautiful person and I don't deserve you. But I have the rest of my life to help you find happiness again, and whatever that takes, I'll try to help you find it. I'm just asking that you don't quit on us yet. Please give it some more time. See if God will change your heart back to where it was before I crushed it.

He looked up and said the rest from memory. "I'll be here, Marilyn, as long as it takes. Begging God to keep changing my heart to where it needs to be. Waiting for you to come home. Hoping I can become the man you've always wanted me to be. Please forgive me, Marilyn. For all of it. I love you and always will."

Tears dropped down onto the page. He wiped his eyes again and looked at her. *Please look at me, Marilyn.* She was still looking out toward the kitchen, but he saw a single tear roll down her cheek. "I've been thinking, after this storm is over, I'm going to move out, find a place to live till you make up your mind about what you're going to do. This is your house too. You should stay here. I know that'll make Doug happy too."

Nothing was said for the next few minutes. Felt like an hour. "Well . . . thanks for letting me say all that. I really am so sorry. So very, very sorry." Just then, the power came back on and all the lights. The TV too. "That didn't last too long," he said, trying to break the ice. He wished she would look at him, say something.

Finally, she spoke, eyes fixed on the TV. "Could we finish watching the movie?"

53

Later that night after they'd finished watching *Casablanca*, and sometime during a second movie, *Sabrina*, Hurricane Harold finally left the area. The torrential rains stopped. The winds dropped from hurricane force to tropical storm force, then to intermittent gusts.

Marilyn had missed Harold's grand exit. When Harrison Ford's character flew off to Paris trying to win Sabrina back, Jim looked over; Marilyn had fallen asleep on the couch. It was her favorite part of the movie, but he didn't want to wake her. He brought out a pillow and blanket. Half asleep, she'd added their presence into whatever dream she was having, rolled over, and went back to sleep.

The next morning she walked around downstairs as if Jim had never read that letter to her. They went outside together and surveyed the damage, first in front on Elderberry Lane. Trees and limbs were down everywhere, up and down the street. But none of their oaks had fallen. Some big limbs were gone. There were some scuff marks here and there where branches had smacked against the side of the house. Jim couldn't see a single shingle missing from the roof.

The biggest damage, of course, was the limb that had crushed Marilyn's car. By lunchtime some neighbors with chain saws had made quick work of it. Putting her car in neutral, they were able to move it just enough so they could get to Jim's and Doug's cars. Doug had come home from Jason's right around then to check in. He was in awe of the damage done to his mother's car, less in awe of the news that he'd be riding his bike for the next few days. His mom needed to borrow his car until they could get her a rental while the insurance adjustors added everything up.

His joy returned when he'd learned his mom would be moving back in, at least for a while, and his dad would be moving out. It did Marilyn good to see Doug's reaction. "See," Jim had whispered to her. "If he was mad at you, he got over it."

By day's end, the River Oaks' city workers and countless volunteers had the streets pretty well cleared of debris, at least enough for cars to pass by carefully in between piles of tree limbs and branches stacked head high on either side.

The electricity never did go out again. That fact had given Jim some hope that perhaps God really had set up that moment, just so he could tell Marilyn the things he needed to say. When it got dark, Jim took his final shower at the house, hoping he might be back before too long. He packed a few bags and told Marilyn he was going.

She was cleaning one of the many messes in the house that Jim had apparently made. "Did you hear me, Marilyn? I said I'm going." She still didn't answer. Was she ignoring him on purpose? Jim stood there a full minute, watching her. *Well I guess that's it,* he thought, and he turned and headed toward the back door.

"Wait!" she yelled down the hallway, just as he opened the door. "I'll walk you to the car."

It was at least something. She followed him through the laundry room into the garage. Neither said a word. He turned to face her before getting into the car. She gave him a look he couldn't read, so he got in and pushed the garage door button. He waved as he backed out. She hesitated, then waved back.

Just as he pulled onto the service road, she started saying something. He rolled his window down. "I'm glad you said what you said last night," she said. "Really. I'm . . . I'm not ready to do anything about it just yet. But I will pray."

It wasn't what he had hoped to hear, but it was better than the awkward silence. "That's okay, Marilyn. Just know I meant every word. Take as much time as you need. I'm not going anywhere."

Of course, he was going somewhere, for now. He had decided not to rent a place, figuring their cash flow would take a big hit with the storm repairs. During the day he'd remembered that one of his properties—the one he'd been trying to get that doctor to lease—had a full bathroom in the biggest office. And a small kitchen area for employees. Jim had decided to sleep on a blow-up air mattress in that office for the next several days, and hoped that it wouldn't turn into the next several weeks.

That, of course, wasn't entirely up to him.

54

Over the next six days, Marilyn was able to shift her full attention from hurricane matters to Michele's wedding. Tomorrow was the big day. In two hours, she and Michele would be leaving their house on Elderberry Lane and returning to Riverfront Park for the wedding rehearsal.

The park had sustained some damage in the storm. A few trees had fallen; quite a lot more sun now came in through openings created by fallen limbs. But there had been minimal flooding, and all of it had receded by Tuesday. City workers had the park all cleaned up and ready to go by this morning. The only setback was the gazebo. Half the shingles on one side of the roof had blown off. As of this morning, to Michele's horror, a blue tarp had been placed over the damaged area to keep future rain from making things worse.

Marilyn had persuaded the park supervisor to let them take the tarp off until after the wedding. The weather was predicted to be clear and sunny all through the weekend. She'd promised they'd replace the tarp before they left the park tomorrow and headed to the reception hall.

She and Michele had just left the park after spending the afternoon putting up decorations. They were driving back to Elderberry Lane to get ready for the rehearsal and the dinner after. "It doesn't look bad," Marilyn said. "The gazebo roof, I mean. Really, you can hardly tell there's any damage."

"From the front," Michele said.

"That's the view that matters most, Michele. It could have been so much worse."

"I know. I'm okay with it. It was just so perfect before. Now half the crowd is going to be sitting in the sun." One side of the park had suffered far more tree damage than the other.

"But it'll be fine," Marilyn said. "It won't be in their faces that time of day, and the temperature isn't supposed to get higher than the low eighties tomorrow."

"You're right," Michele said as they pulled into the driveway and waited for the garage door to open. "It's just . . . there's still so much left to do."

Marilyn put the car in park. "Michele, it's time to let everything go. You've been working on this wedding for weeks and weeks. It's all coming together wonderfully. Everyone's doing what they're supposed to do. Everything will happen the way it's supposed to happen. And if it doesn't, we'll make some memories we can all laugh about down the road. It's time for you to shut the Michele-machine down and start enjoying yourself. Just be the bride."

Michele smiled. "You're right." They got out of the car. "Allan said almost the exact same thing."

"See? God knew I wouldn't be around to keep you on track once you left home, so he picked Allan." They walked through the garage and then through the laundry room as the door rumbled and closed behind them. After they stepped into the house and set their things on the counter, Michele asked, "How does it feel to be home? Are you used to it yet?"

"Almost, but I really liked that little apartment I shared with Charlotte."

"It's a shame she couldn't come to the wedding," Michele said. "She seems like a nice lady."

"She is," Marilyn said. "We're going to stay friends, even if I don't move back in with her." The hurricane had left most of Charlotte's furniture alone, but one of the side windows had broken, and the rain had destroyed the carpet. Charlotte had decided not to stay in a motel while she waited for the repairs. Instead she took a two-week vacation to Boston to visit her son.

Michele's expression changed. "Does that mean you might be getting back with Dad soon?"

"I don't know where we're at, to be honest. I'm just taking it one day at a time." They walked through the living area into the master bedroom suite.

"I've seen some changes in Dad. Since you left, I mean. Not at first, but in the last several weeks. I'm not sure what it is exactly, but he seems . . . nicer. Less tense."

Marilyn had noticed that last weekend during the hurricane. Earlier, Michele had asked about how their time had gone. Marilyn had told her most of what happened but for some reason left out the part about Jim's big apology moment. She was still trying to come to terms with it herself, unsure of whether Jim was sincere. He'd said some nice things, but did he really mean them or was he just saying all that to get her back? What if the changes he'd made were only superficial? What if she did come back, let things go back to the way they were, only to find herself getting stepped on all over again?

"What are you thinking?" Michele sat on the bed. "Are you

worried about tonight? How you and Dad will do at the rehearsal dinner?"

"Not really," she said. "I'm sure your dad will behave. He'll be the perfect gentleman. We'll keep a polite distance, do what's expected. He won't make a scene."

"I wasn't thinking about that. Do you plan on having any fun? Are you going to be able to enjoy yourself tonight, with him right there?"

Marilyn thought a moment. "Yes. I'll be fine. You've got us at separate tables, right?"

Michele made a face. "Yeah."

"What?"

"I don't know, it's just so . . . strange. I never imagined this, the wedding finally being here, and you and Dad not being together. But I'm a big girl. It's not a big deal."

"You want me to sit at the same table with your father? Is it going to embarrass you if we don't sit together?"

"No. Half my friends come from divorced parents."

"Well, your father and I are not divorced."

"I know, I'm just wondering what . . ." She didn't seem to know how to say what she wanted to say.

"Wondering what?"

"What's going to happen with you two? I kind of find it hard to believe that the two of you spent all that time together during Hurricane Harold and you didn't talk."

"We talked."

"You said you watched some movies. Then the next day you both were just busy cleaning up the mess. Didn't you guys talk at all about *you*? Where you're at? Where your future's headed? Nothing at all like that?"

Marilyn sighed. All week long, different things Jim had said in his apology moment kept trying to find their way into her conscious mind, but she'd kept blocking them. Some of them were trying to surface now.

"What's the matter, Mom? What aren't you telling me?"

Marilyn breathed deeply, sat on the edge of the bed, and said, "Yes, we talked. Or rather, he talked and I listened. He tried to apologize, as best he could, I guess." She began sharing things she remembered. "He told me how sorry he was for being too bossy and controlling. How he knew his actions must have hurt me a lot, but that he had never noticed my pain. He said he was sorry for that too. But I don't know, it—" She started crying. So many memories over the years began to surface, things she didn't want to remember. This was ridiculous. Why couldn't she stop crying?

Michele grabbed a Kleenex box off the dresser and joined her on the bed. "I remember the way he used to talk to you, Mom. Like you were a child. And other times like you didn't have a brain in your head. It made me so mad. I always wondered how you put up with it."

Hearing this made Marilyn realize how wimpy she had been all those years. She wished she had been a better example to Michele. But it was also oddly comforting, hearing Michele talk this way. She had been able to see how wrong it was all on her own.

"Why didn't you tell me all this before, when I asked you how your time with Dad went?" Michele asked gently.

"I don't know," she said. "I've been trying to stay strong all week and not let the things he said get to me."

"What's that mean, 'get to you'?"

"To make me weak, so that I'll come running back to him. What if he didn't mean it? What if he just said all that because he's tired of living alone? I don't want to go back to the way it was with your dad. Not now. Not when I'm finally free of it. It was horrible before, Michele. Just horrible." Jim's face appeared in her mind. That look he got. The one that accompanied a hundred lectures, a thousand cold stares. She started crying all over again.

Michele just let her. It went on for several minutes. Marilyn wasn't sure how long she cried. When she regained her composure, Michele looked at her with tender eyes. "Mom, I don't know why I'm saying this. You know I've been totally on your side the entire time, but . . ."

"What?"

"I'm thinking God may have really done something with Dad during this time. Something at a heart level. And I'm worried that you've become so bitter, you might not be able to see it. Don't get me wrong, I really understand how you must be feeling because of Dad's actions all these years. I don't understand how you survived it. But . . ." She started tearing up herself and reached for a tissue. "I haven't told you this. He asked me not to tell you."

"Tell me what?"

"Remember when you suggested I ask Tom to stand in for Dad at the reception tomorrow, when it came time for the father-daughter dance? Because Dad would never be open to such a thing?" Marilyn nodded. "Well, you were wrong. Dad said yes." Tears rolled down Michele's cheeks. "Dad said he'd be honored to dance with me tomorrow, no matter how bad a dancer he is. He wants to do this for me. He called me his little girl."

Marilyn could hardly believe it. Jim was going to dance?

Could it be possible? Could Jim really have changed?

55

Everything was set. The big moment had come. His daughter's wedding.

She should be here any minute.

Jim was all dressed in his tux, standing in the shade by the front of the park, waiting for the cars carrying Michele and the bridesmaids to arrive. The ladies had all changed at the house; the park didn't have any special room set aside for this, and public restrooms were out of the question.

He was so nervous, but he didn't know why. The rehearsal last evening went smooth as silk. And his part was so easy. Walk slow, don't trip, and say "Her mother and I do" when the pastor asks who gives this woman to be married to this man. What could be simpler? Then his job was done, until the reception.

Was that it? Was he nervous about dancing for the first time at the reception? He didn't think so. By the sound of it, most of the steps he'd learned wouldn't be called into action. At the rehearsal dinner last night, Michele had whispered to him, "Don't worry about the dance. I picked a very slow song. And a short one."

Was he nervous about Michele getting married, now that the moment had come? The idea of losing his little girl? His emotions were certainly stirring about this. Several times he fought back tears at the dinner, seeing her across the room with Allan. Scenes of her as a baby kept popping into view, then as a little girl, then as a teen. Like some Hallmark commercial. But it was real now. The little girl in the scenes was Michele. Even now, tears rushed to his eyes, and he blinked them back.

He looked down the aisle. The crowd was all here. There was the pastor and Allan. Standing next to him was his best man. Next to them stood Tom and Doug. The ushers were seating a handful of stragglers. He looked down the road in the direction the cars should be coming from. Still no sign of them.

He looked back at Allan. No, he wasn't nervous about giving his little girl's hand to this young man. Jim had more life experience than Allan, more knowledge about business and economics, but he didn't have half the character and kindness he saw in Allan. Allan had made Michele extremely happy so far, and Jim was certain Allan would keep his vows and keep on trying to make her happy for the rest of their lives.

Jim looked back toward the street. There they were, the cars were coming. They pulled up to the curb. Out of the first car, the two bridesmaids popped out, laughing and talking. Jim looked to the second car. Marilyn got out first, from the passenger side. She looked at Jim, then at the backseat toward Michele and her maid of honor.

Jim tensed up. Instantly. He suddenly knew why he was so nervous.

It was Marilyn.

He'd talked to Uncle Henry about this nervousness yesterday morning. Uncle Henry said he thought it was Jim's expectations.

They were all fired up, and they had no reason to be. Not yet anyway. Jim had said his apology last weekend during the hurricane. He'd meant every word. But Uncle Henry had told him almost exactly the same thing Audrey Windsor had.

"She needs time, Jim. Time for the Lord to work on her heart, and time to see you really mean the things you said. It's not like there's some kind of switch Marilyn can flip, and everything's all better. Words don't do it for a woman whose heart's grown cold. Even nice words like you said. You've gotta be strong. If you meant all those things, then live 'em. Day after day. Trusting God to get through to her in his own way and time. Never give up doing what is right no matter how difficult things get."

Michele's car door opened. Jim walked over and spoke softly to Marilyn standing beside the car door. "May I?" he said. Marilyn looked at him, smiled briefly, then stepped to the side. Jim reached out his hand and helped Michele out of the car. Her maid of honor hurried around the back of the car and smoothed out her train on the grass.

As they began to walk, the music changed. "Mom, hurry," Michele said. "You need to get over to the aisle for the seating of the moms."

"Okay, I will." She gave Michele one more quick hug and a peck on the cheek. "You look wonderful." Tears filled her eyes. "My little girl. It's finally here."

"Go on," Michele said, "or you're going to get me started again."

Jim looked at Marilyn. "You look amazing."

"Thank you," she said, forcing a smile.

Jim took a deep breath and followed Marilyn with his eyes as she walked away. *Patience. Give her space*. He turned and looked at his daughter standing before him. The bridesmaids hurried over to their positions. A wave of emotion hit him like a gust of wind. His eyes filled with tears. "I've never seen a lovelier sight than what I'm seeing right now." He reached down and gave her a strong hug.

"Don't say another word," she replied as they pulled away. "Or I'll lose it completely."

"All right, but—"

"Not another word, Dad. It took a long time to get this makeup right."

Jim looked away toward the gathered crowd. Held out his arm for Michele to take and said, "Shall we?"

Marilyn stood by her seat in the front row. Everyone was standing now. The bride was coming down the aisle. She glanced over at Allan standing next to the pastor. His face was beaming. She looked at Michele, so beautiful. Michele's eyes were fixed on one spot—Allan's face.

Marilyn remembered that moment in her wedding. Everything else, every other person, had faded into the background. There was only Jim looking at her. The love in his eyes, the joy in his face, the anticipation of their life together about to begin.

She glanced at Jim now. His eyes were still looking at her, and her alone. But something different was in his eyes now. There was love there but also something else. What was it? Weakness, fear, longing?

She quickly looked away.

This wasn't their time, it was Michele and Allan's. She wasn't going to let anything spoil this moment. Today, she was a mom, first and foremost. The mother of the bride. And a proud mom at that. How could she not be? Her daughter was beautiful. They were the best of friends, and she was marrying a man who Marilyn was certain would treasure her long after this day.

Her eyes filled with tears—happy tears. Her baby was getting married.

56

The wedding had gone beautifully. Michele and Allan were so happy. There was hardly a dry eye in the park as they'd read the vows they had written for each other. The pastor had done a great job mixing in bits of humor along with the prayers and solemn, sacred words.

They had decided to use one of Jim's larger, unrented properties to hold the reception. It worked out well. It was just the right size, almost cozy, after Michele had reduced the invitations to include only family and close friends. With the money they had saved, Jim had hired a small four-piece band, one Michele had chosen, so they could have live music: a piano player, stand-up bass, jazz guitar, and drums. The piano player's voice sounded a little like Michael Bublé.

Jim and Marilyn were seated, as planned, at separate tables. But the tables were right next to each other. At Marilyn's table were Tom and Jean, their kids, and Doug and his friend Jason, who had actually put on a suit and combed his hair. There was an empty seat next to Marilyn. When Jim first saw it, he'd thought Marilyn must have changed her mind and wanted him to sit with her. He'd sidestepped over to take a look and saw Charlotte's name on the card in front of a fancy napkin. His heart sank. Apparently, no one had told the caterers she wasn't coming anymore.

So Jim had sat at his table. But that was okay. He needed to be patient, love her with deeds. Besides, Audrey Windsor had come, and Uncle Henry and Aunt Myra were also at his table, so he wasn't really alone. As the band played and the crowd mingled, Jim would occasionally glance Marilyn's way. Several times when he had, she was looking right at him. Then she'd instantly look away.

But he was encouraged. He was probably making more out of it than he should, but it seemed he was seeing something different in her eyes. They looked softer somehow.

He had to stop this. He was only setting himself up for deep disappointment.

Ten minutes had gone by. The band had stopped playing so the emcee could introduce the bridal party as they walked through the doors. Then before the meal was served, they went straight to the special dances. First, the bride and groom.

It was great, seeing the look in Michele's eyes as Allan led her across the dance floor to the song "When I Fall in Love." Sheer happiness, total satisfaction. But Jim also felt an ache in his heart; he now understood the joy he had denied Marilyn at this same moment so many years ago, the terrible humiliation she must have felt. Jim looked around the room; all eyes were on the bridal couple, including Marilyn's. Jim swallowed hard as he saw tears welling up in her eyes.

"Your new son-in-law is not a bad dancer," Audrey leaned over and said to him. "Are you ready for your big moment?"

"I think so," Jim whispered. "Thanks again for all your help, Audrey. I wouldn't have been able to say yes without you."

"It was my pleasure. I can't wait to see you up there myself."

The song ended, then Allan escorted Michele to her seat and led his mother to the dance floor. They had decided to let Allan go first, thinking it might help Jim somehow if they did. The band played, they danced. Allan smiled, his mom smiled and cried, as did half the women watching them. Jim looked across the table at Uncle Henry. He mouthed the words "praying for you" and smiled.

When the song ended, everyone clapped, and Allan and his mother took their seats. The emcee said, "And now the bride will dance with her father, Jim Anderson."

Everyone applauded as Jim stood up. He heard especially strong clapping from Marilyn's table. It was Tom and Jean. Marilyn wasn't clapping, though. But she was looking right at him.

This time, she didn't turn away.

He smiled. She smiled briefly back, then looked away. She reached for her napkin. He turned his gaze to Michele, who was walking his way. Tears were falling down her cheeks. "Be happy, my beautiful daughter," Jim said. "It's your wedding day."

"I am happy, Dad. *So* happy."

He took her in his arms, as Audrey had taught him. The band began to play. The song was much slower than Jim had expected, but he quickly adjusted. He reminded himself not to count the steps, though he'd already decided to play it safe and use only the most basic ones.

"Look at you," Michele said. "Dad, you're dancing."

"I am," he said, smiling. "Look at me."

They danced some more, and Jim drew Michele a little closer.

Enough to whisper, "I am so proud of you, Michele. And so happy for you. I could not have picked out a better man. Allan is so . . ." Jim began to choke up. "So *not* like me."

"Oh Dad, stop. I love you. Thank you so much for this. For this dance, this reception, the wedding. For all of it."

"You are very welcome." As Jim gently spun Michele around, he glanced at Marilyn again. She was shaking her head, as if in amazement. Again, she didn't turn away. He thought for a moment she must be looking at Michele, but he realized that wasn't true. She was looking at him.

Jim could tell the song was about to end. He looked at Audrey, who was doing a silent clap and smiling at him. His teacher approved. Then he looked at Uncle Henry, who had a peculiar look on his face. Uncle Henry turned his gaze to Marilyn, then back at Jim. Then he nodded, as if conveying some kind of preplanned signal.

Uncle Henry repeated this same thing again: looked at Marilyn then at him. What was he trying to say?

The song ended. Jim hugged Michele, then let go of her hand. Allan came out to meet her and they walked back to the main table. As the crowd applauded, Jim looked at Uncle Henry again and suddenly understood what he was suggesting.

And it scared him half to death.

57

No one said a word as Jim stood there at the edge of the dance floor. Every eye was on him, puzzled looks all around.

He looked back at Uncle Henry and nodded. An odd thought came to him then. Something Audrey had said that helped Jim take that first dance step at her home several weeks ago. What he was feeling must be something like what the apostle Peter must have felt the moment he stepped out of that boat to join Jesus on the water. With that thought came a surprising boldness welling up inside him.

He must go through with this, no matter the consequences.

With everyone watching, Jim walked over to the emcee and asked him to wait a few moments. There was something he needed to do. He walked to the piano player next and made a request. The band leader nodded and said, "We can do that." Jim walked toward Marilyn's table.

An unplanned song began to play throughout the reception hall.

Jim looked at Marilyn and could tell she instantly recognized the tune. It was the song they were supposed to dance to at their wedding . . . "Unforgettable."

Tears began to fall down her cheeks. Michele and Allan looked at Jim and Marilyn. Tom, Jean, and Doug were all looking at them with stunned, uncertain expressions. The wedding guests seemed to sense something significant was happening but didn't understand what.

Only Uncle Henry knew. He was wearing the biggest smile.

Jim said a quick prayer for strength. He held out his hand and said, "Marilyn, I believe I owe you something I should never have taken away. Could I honor you with this dance?"

Marilyn nodded, wiped her tears with a linen napkin, and took his hand. Jim led her to the center of the dance floor. When they arrived, the piano player brought the song back around to the beginning. Marilyn seemed stunned as Jim began to lead her gracefully across the floor, dancing with almost expert skill. He decided to let everything go, every fear, every inhibition. He had never danced to this song before, but it felt as if it was the only song he had ever danced to. As Audrey had taught him, he didn't count a single step. It was as if he knew just where every footstep should fall next.

Instead, he looked deep into Marilyn's eyes. She was an amazing dance partner, responding perfectly to every move he made.

What was happening? Marilyn felt so strange inside, but it was a wonderfully safe and pleasant feeling. She was dancing to her wedding song. With Jim.

And he was amazing.

She quickly stopped thinking about everyone staring at them, the stunned looks on their faces, and just let go. They were dancing the way she had always dreamed they would one day. But it wasn't a dream. It was really happening.

Suddenly Michele and Allan stood. Then the wedding party, along with Tom and Jean and Doug. They were all smiling. Soon the whole crowd stood, watching Jim and Marilyn dance.

How was this happening, Marilyn thought. When did he—how did he—learn how to dance like this? As they came around to the front of the dance floor again, her eyes fell upon Audrey Windsor. She was glowing and smiling, wiping tears from her face. Marilyn had wondered why Michele had invited her, since they weren't all that close. Now she understood.

Jim had invited her.

As they spun around the dance floor one last time, Marilyn looked in Jim's eyes. They were filled with love and longing, and she saw something else.

Hope.

She remembered Michele's words to her yesterday: *"I'm thinking God may have really done something with Dad during this time. Something at a heart level. And I'm worried that you've become so bitter, you might not be able to see it."*

But she could see it now. And as they danced, she could feel her bitterness melting away. This was the way she wanted to feel about Jim. What she was feeling in her heart right here, right now.

As the song drew to a close, Jim pulled her close and whispered, "I love you, Marilyn. More than words can say. And I always will."

When the song ended, Jim allowed the moment to linger, then stepped back, holding her hand. She didn't say anything, but tears escaped from both eyes.

The whole room suddenly erupted into applause. For the first time since they had begun to dance, Jim was aware there were other people in the room. He was embarrassed by all the attention. He and Marilyn turned and smiled, first at Michele and Allan, then at their other children, then at the crowd. Everyone returned to their seats.

He didn't want to let go of Marilyn's hand but knew he must. She needed time. What had just happened was more than he dared hope for. So, he let it go as they walked back toward their separate tables. To his great surprise, Marilyn quickly grasped his hand again and led him to her table. She picked up Charlotte's name tag and turned it over.

It was an invitation. Jim sat down beside her. Every eye was still on them.

Michele began to tap her champagne glass. Soon Allan did the same, then their other children joined in. Then all the gathered friends and family. All of them looking at Jim and Marilyn.

Jim looked at her, unsure of her response. Marilyn leaned forward and kissed him, and the kiss lingered, to where it was clear . . . something real was happening between them. In that kiss, he felt all the joy and excitement of their first kiss in their junior year of college. It was too amazing to be true. After the kiss, he said, "Are you sure you're okay with me staying here for the rest of the reception?"

She leaned over and kissed him again. "Not just for the rest of the reception," she whispered. "Why don't you come back home?"

"When?"

"How about tonight, as soon as Michele and Allan are off for their honeymoon."

Jim couldn't believe it.

But he didn't want them to remain the center of attention. It was Allan and Michele's big day. He looked over at Michele and Allan at the table of honor and began to tap his glass. Soon Marilyn and the others followed. Allan leaned forward to kiss his new bride.

Two couples began new lives that day. One family had just begun.

Another had just begun again.

Acknowledgments

I'd like to start off by thanking my co-author, Dr. Gary Smalley, for picking me to work with him on the Restoration series. Thanks also to Sue Parks, for getting my books into Gary's hands. When I got the call saying he'd read them and was excited to work with me, it didn't take me long to say yes. Gary is a legend in the area of marriage, family life, and personal relationships. He's helped millions of people gain a better understanding of God's will and purposes for these critical areas. I know this firsthand; I'm one of them. Gary's first book, *If Only He Knew*, saved my marriage more than thirty years ago.

After working closely with him over this past year, it was a wonderful surprise to discover he's such a warm, generous, and encouraging man. And now, a good friend. I can't wait to see what God has in store for us in the days ahead.

Next, I want to thank my *best* friend, my wife Cindi. I'm thanking her for more than just the time she sacrificed, freeing me up to write this book. She's been totally involved from day one. I cherish her input, which is reflected throughout these pages. After her, I must thank my editor and friend, Andrea Doering. This is our seventh book together. My respect for her wisdom and insight has grown with each one.

I'm grateful for the entire staff at Revell. What a joy it is to work with them: Twila Bennett, Michele Misiak, Robin Barnett, Claudia Marsh, and so many others, including Kristin Kornoelje, who never misses a thing.

Thanks also to my Word Weavers critique group in Port Orange, Florida, for their input on many of these chapters. And lastly, to my fabulous agent and friend, Karen Solem. I'm so glad for the way you look out for me. Because you're there, doing what you do best, I get to write these books. I can't imagine doing all this without you.

Gary and I would also like to thank Roger Gibson, Gary's son-in-law, who brought us together in the first place.

Author's Note from Dan Walsh

Thanks so much for reading *The Dance*, the first book in an exciting new series Gary Smalley and I are writing together. This first book has mostly been about the unraveling of Jim and Marilyn Anderson's twenty-seven-year "Christian" marriage. But by the time we reached the climactic wedding scene, we began to see the beginnings of its restoration.

That will be the theme for all four of our books about the Anderson family—restoration. The God we serve is all about healing broken lives and restoring shattered dreams. Gary and I have experienced this firsthand in our personal lives and have seen it in the lives of the people we've ministered to for many years. We hope these stories about the Anderson family will touch your life in a deep way.

Today, our culture seems to have almost given up on the family. When they speak of things like passion, love, and romance—either in songs or film—those things are rarely located *inside* a family relationship. The family is always portrayed as broken beyond repair, filled with discouragement and despair. Love and romance are only seen as possible in a brand-new relationship or in some forbidden affair that takes place outside of marriage.

We believe God's plans for love and romance are meant to be experienced and enjoyed by real people in real relationships that really work. And God's design locates these greater joys *inside* the family relationship. But if that's true, why do so many Christian families fail to experience these greater joys? Why do people who love God, believe in the Bible, go to church regularly, and try to raise their kids to do the same miss the mark?

The Bible says, "We all, like sheep, have gone astray, each of us has turned to our own way" (Isa. 53:6). That's what happens. We go astray. Over time, our hearts can shift in subtle ways from loving God and others the way we're supposed to.

But we serve a Good Shepherd who is committed to restoring lost sheep. When we stray, God sets in motion a plan to redeem our lives and restore our hearts much like we see with Jim and Marilyn in *The Dance*. As this mending begins, we get a taste of what God has always intended: real love, real joy, and real passion happening right there . . . *inside* the home.

What will happen to Jim and Marilyn's relationship from here? Will they be able to fully rekindle their love on a second honeymoon in Italy or will the problems of their past return? What about their adult children, Tom, Michele, and Doug? They've been raised in a Christian home filled with legalism and harshness, by parents who have drifted apart. How will this affect their own family relationships in the future?

How will it affect Tom and Jean's marriage (didn't we learn that Tom is just like his dad)? How about the newlyweds, Michele and Allan? Will Doug continue to follow the Lord as he transitions from high school to college? Will he pursue the values he's grown up with or abandon them altogether?

Join us for books 2–4 as a number of new storms come, revealing the "sand foundation" the Andersons' lives have been built upon. They will face some of the same problems you and I face every day. Through the lives of this fascinating family we'll see how God restores and mends broken lives, bringing hope and healing in place of heartache and pain.

As with *The Dance*, I'll be drawing from the rich resource of Gary's wonderful books on marriage and family relationships. Gary has spent the last thirty years helping millions of people understand the beauty and wisdom of God's Word regarding these critical issues. His insights, wisdom, and humor are legendary. My own marriage has benefited greatly from reading Gary's books, and I was thrilled when he asked me to consider writing this series together.

While writing *The Dance*, I drew heavily from Gary's bestselling book *The DNA of Relationships*. I served as a pastor for twenty-five years. Putting it simply, I've never read a better book on marriage and family relationships than this one. You've got to get it!

I invite you to take a few minutes to read a follow-up interview I did with Gary, talking about *The DNA of Relationships* as well as *The Dance*. I wanted to give him a chance to elaborate on some of the things Audrey Windsor and Uncle Henry shared with Jim. I'm sure it will bless you.

I can't wait to get back to work on the rest of the Restoration series. Be on the lookout for *The Promise* due out in the fall of 2013. Between now and then, feel free to visit me at www.danwalshbooks.com. From there you can send me emails (I'd love to hear from you), read my blog, connect with me on Facebook, or follow me on Twitter.

Dan's Interview with Gary about *The Dance*

Dan: Of all the characters in this book, which one do you relate to the most and why?

Gary: With the husband, Jim. As we were working on this book, I remembered so many things that I had said and done to my wife Norma, things like Marilyn had to put up with. Norma could have left me after five years, because I didn't have a clue of how to value her above fishing, the church where I worked, and the youth department where I also ministered as the youth pastor. I took better care of other church kids, wives, and husbands than I did my own children and wife. When she admitted to me, after five years, that she was "dead" inside when it came to love from and to me, I woke up and started changing. She told me that she was never going to divorce me because she had committed herself to God and had given me the promise that she would remain forever until death. But the death came earlier than she had imagined.

I began to listen to her more, to interview older wives in my church on how to love Norma, and to read everything that I could get my hands on to improve as a husband. I started teaching a college Bible study on marriage, and the students helped me refine my message to couples. My new knowledge actually began the roots of my present ministry to couples.

The main thing that I began to learn was that no one can love a person until they first learn what it means to honor them. Honor is to consider someone highly valuable. One way to honor someone is to list everything about them that is praised, valued, important. That is, valuable memories with them, things about them that are beautiful, character qualities that reflect the high value of God. A person can find unlimited reasons to value someone, and as Christ said, "Whatever a man treasures, that is where their heart will be also." (Matt. 6:21) Affection, desire, caring—all spring from honoring someone.

The second thing I learned was the awesome importance of keeping my anger as low as possible toward Norma, my kids, and all others. Anger destroys love and connection between people. First John 2 indicates that when a person harbors anger or hatred toward another, they cannot live in God's love or light. If you say that you know God but you hate your brother, the truth is not in you and you don't love God or others. It is impossible to continue hating someone while God's love is flowing within you.

Dan: I drew much of my inspiration for our story from your bestselling book *The DNA of Relationships*. In that first dance lesson in chapters 26–27, Audrey introduces Jim to a word picture she calls the "Fear Dance." Is there anything more you'd like to say about this Fear Dance?

Gary: The Fear Dance has been one of the best metaphors that Norma and I use to remain in harmony and love. There's an entire chapter about this in the *DNA of Relationships* book. When my son, Greg, taught us how our "core fears" affect us, we began to understand why we argued in anger at times. For instance, my core fears are of being belittled and of being controlled. One of Norma's core fears is the fear of failure or not doing things right.

When Norma believes that some of my actions toward her or others are not up to the highest standards of God, she may try to suggest certain changes in my behavior. But for most of our married life, I would perceive her suggestions as her way of trying to control and belittle me. I would react by requesting that she not point out my flaws, and she would hear me telling her that she was not "doing the wife job correctly." She would then react by trying to change me, and I would again perceive her as trying to control or belittle me. When we figured this "dance" out, our new understanding allowed us to take full responsibility for our own core fears and start working with God and his words to become more mature in him.

Dan: Can you share an example of what it looks like to break free from a "core fear"?

Gary: One time, Norma was inside our house getting the final touches of a big Fourth of July party ready. My daughter Kari yelled across the creek that she didn't have anything for dinner. So I invited her and her two kids to join us for dinner just as Norma was walking out the back door. She immediately knew that two grandkids can destroy an entire house in seconds and that the meal I was offering to Kari was actually being readied for the next day.

It seemed to me that she was belittling me and controlling me as she uninvited Kari. I wanted to say, "Wait a minute, I live here too." But instead, I kept my mouth closed and took full responsibility for my emotions and thoughts. I began praying and immediately remembered two very important things I had been needing and praying for in my own life.

I'd been asking God to show me how to establish him as the controller of my life and how I could become more like his Son in humility. So, in that moment, I thanked him for taking me under his wings and showing me how to lay down my life for my wife and daughter.

Once I saw this, I suggested quickly that we all go out for dinner, my treat.

Dan: In my experience as a pastor, I often found that the wives seemed more concerned about the quality of the marriage relationship than the husbands did. Has that been your experience? If so, why do you think that's the case?

Gary: God said that it is not good for man to be alone. So, he gave us a "completer." I have found that most wives have a built-in relationship manual. They use this natural gift from God to help their husbands become a better lover and a better parent. I have never found an exception to this amazing gift given to women of all ages. I can interview women from any country on earth, and they all know what a good relationship should look like.

Most tell me three things that make a marriage or friendship a better relationship. Better communication, better loving (with a gentle touch), and better ability at honoring each other. Communication, they tell me, is listening in order to understand, which places a high value on who the other person really is. The result is the number one cure for divorce. That is, a husband listens until he deeply understands his wife and vice versa. Then, they value each other's opinions and ideas and try to help their mate "win" arguments because of the high esteem they have for each other. When they both like a suggested solution to a disagreement, they both feel like a winner, and deep harmony and love remain between them.

Dan: In chapter 32, during the lesson where Audrey and Jim actually danced for the first time, she explained to him a concept called the Power of One, which is right out of *The DNA of Relationships*. What was it about this truth that caused you to decide it should be the first "dance step"?

Gary: The Power of One is when a husband or wife decides that their mate is neither the cause nor the answer to a higher quality of life. God and his words are the source of the highest and best life possible. When the husband or the wife expect their mate to "fulfill them" somehow, those expectations result in stress, frustration, or anger. It is amazing what happens to a person when they "fire" their mate as the one responsible for their ultimate happiness. Christ is the source of life as Colossians 3:4 states. The enemy of God is the ruler of this world, and he is a liar and tries to steal, kill, and destroy all that is good in people's lives. Whereas Christ came to give us a more abundant life! So, when a mate finds the secret to the abundant life is in Jesus, and makes it their responsibility to see him as their source, the happiness they get in their relationship with their spouse becomes more of an additional blessing, not their only hope.

Dan: At the end of another dance lesson in chapter 38, Audrey talks with Jim about the importance of safety in a marriage relationship, particularly in the way couples communicate. Could you share a little more about that? Why is that so important?

Gary: Marriage researchers have discovered that when a husband or wife feels safe with their mate, an amazing thing happens. When a person feels like they will no longer be condemned, criticized, or judged, the safer they feel. The safer they feel, the more they begin to open their heart, and the best type of friendship happens naturally. The single greatest goal a married couple should set for themselves is developing a lovingly safe environment for each other.

Dan: To keep the story moving in *The Dance*, we sort of skimmed over the third and fourth dance steps mentioned in the *DNA* book. Could you tell us what they are and a little about them?

Gary: All four of the actions taken in the Fear Dance are: (1) When someone pushes my *fear* buttons, I start hurting and feel very uncomfortable. For instance, if I believe someone is trying to control me, it hurts and I want to make the pain stop. (2) I *want* something. I mainly want a solution to stop this person from pushing my buttons. I may believe that when a friend or my mate realizes their actions are hurting me, they'll say, "Oh, sorry, I won't keep doing that" or "I'll never do it again." Wrong. People are not like that, and, if anything, just by the way that I explain my hurt, I might be pushing one of their fear buttons. Then, the dance gets moving faster for both of us. (3) Now, I really do *fear* that my relationship with this person may be damaged, and I really don't want that to happen. My fear increases, and the dance may become worse. (4) I tend to *react* then by using my best skills to get the other person to change their ways toward me. But, more often, the fear dance just turns ugly instead.

It's always best to stop the dance at any point and begin to address your own core fears and seek God and his words to find your own healing and maturity. Stop blaming your mate or others for your own immaturity. It's your journey that you get to go on, to discover the cure to your own problems. This is one reason why life is so much fun and so exciting. I get to cry out to God, or search Google, or get advice from an older mature follower of Christ, or pursue any number of other ways that will help me grow up and take responsibility for my own life. (Note: These steps are all found on the GarySmalley.com website or on pages 25–29 in *The DNA of Relationships* book, paperback version.)

Dan: In chapter 42, Audrey talks to Jim about the fifth and final dance step in the *DNA* book—teamwork. She shares something you wrote about called a No Losers Policy. I loved that. Is there anything more you'd like to add to this?

Gary: The No Losers Policy is when a couple agrees that both have ideas that are important and worthy of honor, both have opinions that are equally valuable, and it is unacceptable for either of them to feel like they are losing an argument or a disagreement. My wife and I can spend five minutes or as much as a day discussing a disagreement. But only after both of us have listened and tried to understand the deep feelings and needs of each other, then and only then will we start offering various creative ideas to solve our disagreement. After that, we can offer any suggestions whatsoever, no matter how wild they may seem (because often it's a weird suggestion that sparks a solution that we both love). I no longer lose any arguments, nor does Norma. We help each other win no matter how small the conflict. This is wonderful and highly valuable for each of us.

Dan: Finally, I wanted to mention something that both Audrey and Uncle Henry discuss with Jim—humility. What does humility look like in our relationships with God and others and why is it so vital?

Gary: Humility is simply an attitude of deep awareness of how helpless we are in developing a loving heart and having the energy or power to live a life that truly reflects God. As a human, I am not able to become like Jesus. No amount of effort on my part could earn me a place in heaven or a high spiritual position on earth. God's Word tells us that "it is by grace you have been saved, through faith—and this is not from yourselves, it is the gift of God—not by works, so that no one can boast" (Eph. 2:8). So, as it states in James 4:6, "God opposes the proud but shows favor to the humble."

Humankind cannot do any of Christ's commands unless they are filled up with God's love and power. And God gives his power and love (his grace) only to the humble; he resists anyone who is proud or puffed up with their own importance or self-sufficiency. A proud person leans toward self-centeredness, being "cocky," selfish, boasting, and crediting all their accomplishments to their own abilities and skills. They tend to see themselves as better than others, and are therefore judgmental and arrogant toward others. They are usually not aware of or grateful for all the other men and women who have helped them become what they are today. The proud tend to avoid crediting their Creator for their existence and the gifts he's given them but live as if they had created themselves and are single-handedly responsible for all of their personal successes.

The humble, however, tend to be very aware of their Creator and realize that their accomplishments are only possible because of how they were created. Their brain, body, and senses are all a part of how God created them. They happily give God the credit for everything about themselves. They acknowledge that God's commands are far superior to their human plans of finding and living the highest quality of life. If God's Word tells them that loving him with all of their heart, soul, mind, and strength and loving others as Jesus loved people are the greatest commands, then the humble person believes it, and they live that way by the power invested in them from God Almighty. As Proverbs 22:4 puts it, "True humility and fear of the Lord [standing in God's presence with awe and trembling] leads to riches, honor and long life" (New Living translation).

The humble are very aware of their helplessness and powerlessness in trying to create God's kind of love and power by themselves, with their own human abilities. They simply "cry out as beggars" to God and wait patiently for his grace to empower them to follow Christ and live in a way that pleases him.

Discussion Questions

1. Which of the characters in this book could you most easily relate to and why?
2. What do you think made Jim so dull that he didn't have a clue Marilyn was about to leave him?
3. What do you think of the way Marilyn handled her unhappiness? What might you have done differently?
4. What kind of problems could you foresee their adult children facing in the future, due to being brought up in "this kind" of Christian home?
5. What kinds of weaknesses and problems did Jim and Marilyn's "old church" have that made the members unable or unwilling to offer them any useful help?
6. What were some of the life lessons about marriage and relationships you learned (along with Jim) as he listened to Audrey Windsor? And to Uncle Henry?
7. How would you evaluate Charlotte's friendship toward Marilyn? Was she just right in terms of her ratio of acceptance vs. advice? Did she say too much, or not enough, in your opinion?

8. How do you account for Jim's change of heart toward Marilyn? What caused it? What lessons do you think he learned through this ordeal?
9. What were some of your favorite moments in the book and why?
10. What are some of the challenges you think Jim and Marilyn will face in the months ahead, now that their restoration has begun?

If you have any thoughts, comments, or questions about *The Dance*, we'd love to hear from you. Email dwalsh@danwalshbooks.com and mention *The Dance* in the subject line.

Dan Walsh is the award-winning author of *The Unfinished Gift*, *The Homecoming*, *The Deepest Waters*, *Remembering Christmas*, *The Discovery*, and *The Reunion*. A member of American Christian Fiction Writers, Dan served as a pastor for twenty-five years. He lives with his family in the Daytona Beach area, where he's busy researching and writing his next novel.

Gary Smalley is one of the country's best known authors and speakers on family relationships. He is the author or coauthor of sixteen bestselling, award-winning books, along with several popular films and videos. He has spent over thirty years learning, teaching, and counseling, speaking to over two million people in live conferences. Gary has appeared on national television programs such as *Oprah*, *Larry King Live*, *Extra*, the *Today* show, and *Sally Jessy Raphael*, as well as numerous national radio programs. Gary and his wife, Norma, have been married for forty years and live in Branson, Missouri. They have three children and six grandchildren.

CONNECT WITH THE AUTHORS

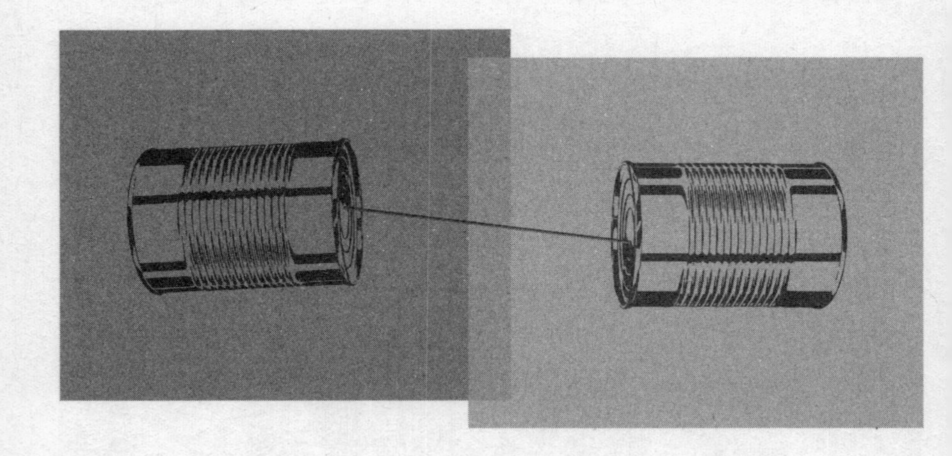

DAN WALSH

www.DanWalsh.com

CONNECT WITH DAN ON

 *Dan Walsh* •  *DanWalshAuthor*

GARY SMALLEY

Smalley.cc

CONNECT WITH GARY ON

 *Gary Smalley*